Family Secrets...

Hidden in the Shadows of Time

A novel by Virginia Rafferty

ISBN-13: 978-1518645495
ISBN-10: 1518645496

This book is dedicated to my ancestors: Maria, Maria Magdolina, Aranka, and Erzsi. They left their homes and crossed an ocean to give themselves and their descendants a better life.

This is a work of fiction. Names, characters, places, and incidents are either the product of the author's imagination or are used fictitiously.

Contents

Prologue

Reiste, Hungary
1866

The one room house was quiet. Moonlight filtered through the windows, illuminating the sleeping occupants. An owl hooted in the night.

Ten-year-old Erzsi reached for her sister's hand. "The rosebush," she whispered, "the rosebush is coming tomorrow."

The family had been visiting relatives in Kosice when their mother had stopped to admire a yellow rosebush being sold by a vendor at the market. "Isn't it lovely," their mother had said while cupping a perfectly shaped bloom gently in her hands. "It is too extravagant, too expensive," she had protested when her husband offered to buy it for her. But later, their father had returned to the vendor and, unknown to his wife, arranged for the rosebush to be delivered to their home.

"Won't Mother be surprised?" Clara, Erzsi's younger sister, said while snuggling closer to her. "It will be the most beautiful rosebush ever."

"Go back to sleep now," Erzsi said, putting her arms around Clara.

Before the sun came over the horizon, Iren, the oldest of the children, was already bringing wood for the stove into the house. Their mother and father had quietly left long before dawn to work in the fields. It was Iren's responsibility to care for the younger children while they were gone. "Is the rosebush here yet?" Clara asked, her tone anxious, excited, as she sat up in the bed.

"Not yet," Iren answered.

"Come on, Erzsi. Get up!" Clara pulled the blanket off her sister.

"Is the rosebush here yet?" Erzsi said, her voice groggy, her hands rubbing her eyes.

"Not yet," Clara declared, disappointment in her voice.

"When is it coming?" Erzsi was now fully awake.

"It will be here before Mother and Father return." Iren's voice reflected her annoyance with the repeated questions. She had other concerns, other responsibilities. She was too busy to notice the thoughtful look on Erzsi's face.

"I'll groom Pista now, before we eat," Erzsi said matter-of-factly as she reached for her shoes. She would not wait for the wagon. She had a plan.

Pista was the family's plow horse, he was only a workhorse, but to Erzsi he was a special friend. Every morning she helped her father groom him, sneaking him carrots or other treats, stroking his neck as he nuzzled her cheek. Without her father it would have been a difficult task for a ten-year-old, but grooming Pista this morning was not her intent.

"Come on, Clara, you can help." The sisters rarely went anywhere or did anything without the other.

The little girls left the house heading for the barn. "Why are we going to groom Pista? Can't we wait for Father? I'm hungry!" Clara complained.

"Because we are going to ride him," Erzsi said, her tone indicating there was no room for discussion. "I want to meet the wagon with the rosebush. I want to be sure the driver knows where to go."

Clara's eyes opened wide. She wanted to meet the wagon, but surely they would be in trouble for riding Pista without her mother's approval. "Wait!" Clara hesitated. "What about Iren? We should tell her where we are going. What about our breakfast?" While Clara usually went along with Erzsi's schemes, riding Pista without permission seemed too extreme, too extraordinary. She was not sure she wanted to do this. Anyway, she was hungry and wanted her breakfast.

"Iren won't miss us," Erzsi said, breathless as she put the bridle on Pista. Standing on a bucket, she jumped on the horse. "Are you coming, Clara?" The little girl nodded reluctantly. With Erzsi's help, Clara mounted the horse and sat behind Erzsi, holding tightly to her sister's waist.

The girls trotted the gaunt plow horse down the dirt road, in too much of a hurry to notice the fragrant flowers on the apple trees or the hawks that circled overhead. Erzsi kicked her bare heels into Pista's sides so he'd plod a little faster. She ignored the scarf that had covered her hair and now lay precariously around her shoulders.

"You are going too fast," Clara protested.

"Hold on tighter then!" Erzsi was impatient. "Come on, Pista!" She gave the horse another kick, but he continued the gentle trot. Pista was a workhorse, but he instinctively took care of his young riders.

Clara, resigned, tucked her head into her sister's back and wrapped her arms around Erzsi's waist. She held on tightly, closed her eyes, and brought her body into rhythm with the horse's movements.

Erzsi spotted their older cousin Peter striding towards them. "Did you see the wagon?" Erzsi called to him.

"What wagon?" Peter answered, laughing.

"Why, the one bringing Mama's rosebush, of course," Clara said while sliding off the horse and falling into Peter's arms.

"Oh! That wagon!" Peter said, gently lowering Clara to the ground. "Well, let me see," he said, pausing, seemingly deep in thought.

"Peter, stop teasing, you are upsetting Clara," Erzsi said, as always protective of her little sister. "Is Papa coming home soon? Will he be here when the rosebush arrives?" Erzsi asked, knowing that Peter would have seen her father in the fields.

"No, he sent me to wait for the delivery," Peter answered. Erzsi nodded, satisfied.

"Clara, do you want to ride with me to meet the wagon?" Erzsi asked.

"No, I want to stay with Peter." Clara lifted her arms up to Peter signaling that she wanted to ride on his shoulders. "I want to go home. I'm hungry."

"We should all wait at the house," Peter said, lifting the little girl. "Erzsi, you should not ride alone, you must return home with us. I'm sure Iren is worried about you." Slowly, reluctantly, Erzsi gave Pista a gentle kick and followed Peter and Clara back down the dirt road toward home.

Peter adored his cousins, bringing treats whenever he came to visit, taking them to play on Sunday afternoons, and much to the dismay of their mother, teaching them to ride Pista.

"Little girls should not be wasting time riding horses," their mother had scolded Peter when Erzsi came home with her dress covered in mud and scratches on her arm. "They could get hurt. Peter, you should know better."

Although he loved Clara, it was Erzsi who had a special place in his heart. When she was a toddler, and he just a boy of seven, he admired her persistence as she chased the chickens in the yard, never catching them but never giving up. She was strong-willed and open for adventure. At the age of five she insisted on joining Peter and his friends in fighting knights and dragons. She wielded a stick as ferociously as the boys, but most of all she made him smile when he felt discouraged, she laughed at his stories, and always openly gave her love.

Now, reaching the house, Peter gently placed Clara on the ground and was about to help Erzsi off the horse when they saw a wagon, pulled by a broad-shouldered ox, coming toward them. A young boy, not from their village, was guiding the ox with a long stick. The cousins waited at the side of the dirt road for the wagon to come closer.

"My name is Mihaly. I have a delivery for the Viarka farm," the young boy said as he cued the ox to halt. "A rosebush ordered by Mr. Viarka," he said pointing to the back of his wagon.

"This is it," said Peter pointing toward the small house. "You can pull the wagon over there."

As Mihaly pulled the wagon to a stop he noticed the girl who sat erect and proud on the horse. He was captivated by the slightly flushed face and the bright blue eyes that were sparkling with mischief. Erzsi saw him watching her. It was the first time a boy had looked at her that way. She turned aside embarrassed.

Mihaly, totally distracted, tripped as he got out of the wagon. Erzsi giggled. The boy quickly rallied and moved to the back of the wagon to get the rosebush.

"Have you been paid for the bush?" Peter asked, taking charge.

"Yes."

"Thank you then, Mr. Viarka will be pleased. It appears to be a very healthy rosebush."

Mihaly got back in the wagon and began the long trip home, wondering if he would ever see the girl on the horse again.

Book 1

Leaving Home

1 Maria

Buzica, Hungary
May, 1882

The young woman stood in the doorway of the old farmhouse. Weeds competed with the vegetables in the garden, chickens clucked and scratched as they roamed freely in the yard. A pig grunted and a rooster crowed. The sky was still dark; a faint glow on the horizon signaled the start of a new day. The air was crisp, causing her to pull her shawl tighter around her shoulders. It should have been an uneventful day filled with routine chores, but this day would change her life forever.

Maria quietly waited. She stepped over the threshold into the yard, her focus on the barn. There was the familiar smell of freshly cut hay mixed with the warm, sweet smell of the horses. The voices of the men she loved mingled with jingles and clanks as they lifted the heavy harness.

Her throat tightened as she heard the creaking of the wagon as the men led the horse out of the barn. She stood still, she could not breathe. She felt the warmth of her mother's hand as it gently rested on her shoulder and was comforted by the presence of her little sister standing next to her. It was time.

Josef, her husband of just three months, was leaving. "One year," he had promised. "I will be in America for just one year." He had gently wiped away the tears that came unbidden to her eyes. "We will have a home of our own, and children, lots of children." It was a dream they shared.

She could see the wagon now. Maria's brother Anton, strong and in command, was holding the reins as he guided the horse. Josef walked beside the wagon. They were laughing but she could see in their eyes the sorrow they were trying to hide. She was not the only person who would miss Josef.

Her father walked behind the wagon. Despite his age he was still strong and still master of the house. She smiled. Her father, though stern, was always fair with his children and it was obvious he loved his wife. "Will my marriage endure like theirs? Will our love survive? Will Josef return to me?" She pushed the unwelcome questions away.

Her body felt numb, she reached for her mother's hand.

Anna squeezed her daughter's shoulder, offering her support. She understood Maria's sorrow. Two of her sons were in the army. When they left she had collapsed into her husband's arms unable to be consoled. She had gone to the church to offer Novenas to the Blessed Virgin, asking, pleading, with the Blessed Mother to keep her sons safe. Another son, just a few years younger than Maria, had recently left for the seminary in SpisskaKapitula. "At least he is safe," she had comforted herself. "Safe in the service of the Lord."

Now Anna whispered a silent prayer for Maria and Josef. Many young men had left for America and returned to their families. Some found a life in America and sent for their wives. But some left and never returned. "Please Blessed Mother, bless this couple, and bring Josef safely home to his wife who loves him."

Maria watched her husband. She would always remember how he looked this morning, on the morning he left for America. Every detail would be held in her heart, his mustache, his strong arms, his cap that did little to hide his thick black hair. His dark eyes had a playful quality that contrasted with her serious nature. "Josef, you bring joy to my life." The sadness on her face was momentarily replaced by a faint smile that reflected her love for this man.

Their courtship had started when Maria was twenty-one. He had been visiting their village looking for work. Maria's father had invited him to stay for dinner.

He had watched Maria as she helped her mother serve the dinner. Her manner was efficient, but it was the sway of her skirts and the fullness of her bosom that caught his attention. He watched as Maria attended to her younger sister, gently reprimanding her when necessary and guiding her through her assigned tasks as the meal was served. "Maria will make a good mother," he thought approvingly.

When he joined the family for Sunday Mass he was enthralled by Maria's clear alto voice as she harmonized while singing the familiar hymns. Listening to Maria, Josef was reminded of his mother who had died when he was six years old. His mother's voice had been, soft, soothing, comforting for the little boy when he was harassed by the older boys or frightened in the night. Josef had loved his mother and now he was falling in love with Maria.

Josef, now at an age where he was looking for a wife, saw in Maria the qualities he sought. He found work in the village and odd jobs on local farms so that he could court Maria. He would look for her on market day, offering to walk her home after she had made her purchases, he sat near her in church so he could catch her eye, and when the weather was nice he walked with her along the country road near her home. And then, on a cold February day that would live forever in her memory, he had spoken with her father asking for permission to marry his daughter. They were married a month later. For three months they lived with Maria's parents.

Josef and Maria had wanted a home of their own, a place to raise their children. Above all, Josef wanted sons, lots of sons. Everyone in the village was struggling to survive. Opportunities for steady work even in the city of Kosice were hard to find. He needed to look elsewhere.

Shortly after they were married, recruiters from America had visited their village. They met the farmers in the market, passed out brochures, promised that there was work in America. The mines and factories in places called New York, New Jersey, Pennsylvania and Connecticut needed workers and would pay unbelievable wages. Some companies even offered to provide passage to America on one of the great transatlantic steamships that were making the ocean crossing easier and faster. A man could work for one year and then return home to buy a farm of his own. Josef saw the opportunity he needed to provide for his family.

When Maria saw the brochures in Josef's hand she did not need to be told what he was thinking.

"Josef, I cannot go to America. I cannot leave my family." She thought of her dear mother who needed her help. "Please don't ask this of me."

"I must go," he said while pacing back and forth. "I will go for one year."

"For our children," she lowered her eyes and in an unconscious gesture rested her hands on her body, just below her waist.

She felt the beginnings of the heartache and loneliness that would be hers while he was gone. "This is an opportunity given to us by God," she said while reaching for her husband. "But how will I find the strength to let you go?" She had lowered her head on his shoulder while quiet tears slowly rolled down her cheeks. "I love you, Josef. Come back to me."

Now Anton led the horse to the front of the house, holding him steady while Josef climbed into the wagon. He would drive Josef to the train station in Kosice. Josef walked toward Maria. He saw her sadness, but he was confident that he was doing what needed to be done. There was no future for them if he stayed in their little village. America was the answer, the only answer.

Josef stood before his wife, holding her hands. He wanted to comfort her but the words were not there. The wagon was ready, the horse was restless. They had made love and said their good-byes last night. It was time to go. Josef was already thinking about the adventure ahead. Maria would be safe and content with her family.

"Maria, it is time to say good-bye," her mother said quietly, gently, encouraging her daughter. "Josef, we will miss you and will pray for your safe return." Maria felt her knees go weak and she leaned into her mother for support.

"Come home to me, Josef," Maria whispered as she let go of his hand. He kissed her one more time and turned to walk to the wagon where Anton was waiting to drive him to the train station.

2 Erzsi

Reste, Hungary
May, 1882

The room was still dark; it would be hours before the first glimmer of light would filter through the small square windows. The woman lay still in the bed, her body tense, her mind unsettled. She listened to the sounds made by the sleeping occupants in the room, her sister's gentle breathing, a groan from her sister's husband as he turned in his sleep. One of the boys sleeping on the floor was talking in his sleep, another coughed, the baby whimpered. She closed her eyes, imagining she could see the holy pictures and colorful plates that adorned the white walls, the clothing draped on a rod above her bed. Four children, an infant, and three adults lived in the sparsely furnished room. This room had been her home since the death of her parents. In the morning she would leave this place forever.

Terrifying visions of a ship tossing in a storm prevented sleep. She was sure she would be seasick, maybe she would drown. Her stomach responded at the thought, adding to her misery.

Her name was Erzsi, Erzsébet. She was named after Elizabeth, wife of Emperor Franz Joseph I, Empress of Austria, and Queen of Hungary. It was a proud name for a peasant woman who at the age of twenty-five was without a husband, or a home of her own.

She listened to the familiar night sounds, the creaking of the cradle rocking, a mother's soothing voice. The only abrasive sound was the occasional snort from Viktor, the one man who shared the room with them. It was Viktor who wanted her to leave; the one person she would not miss.

It was difficult to breathe. The air was stagnant, filled with the stale smell of too many bodies sleeping in a small space. Smoke from the stove mingled with the sweet smell of kielbasa hanging in the attic.

Tiny feet poked Erzsi's back. Her sister's little girls had shared the bed with Erzsi most of their young lives. One liked to snuggle in Erzsi's arms while the other would sprawl out, demanding more than her share of the limited space in the bed. Erzsi loved the little girls who shared her bed. She was comforted by the presence of the children so close to her. "It is breaking my heart to leave you, my angels, but I have no choice."

The little girl, who was snuggled next to her, began to cough. Her tiny form convulsed with the effort to breathe. Her aunt lifted her, gently rubbing the child's back while whispering encouragement. The child had a sickness in her lungs; everyone worried about her. Erzsi had spent many hours comforting the frightened child as she struggled to breathe. But tonight, accepting Erzsi's tender embrace, she quickly settled back to sleep.

"Who will comfort her when I am gone?" Erszi thought looking down at the child in her arms. "Who will I comfort when I am alone?" Again anxiety coursed through her body as she anticipated the loneliness that awaited her. Burning tears filled her eyes as she gently kissed the little head resting on the pillow next to her. "Who will comfort me?"

The sleeping child snuggled closer, her warm breath gently wafting over Erzsi's arm. "I will miss you," she whispered, feeling the rhythmic beat of the child's heart next to her own.

While Erzsi and the girls shared one of the two beds in the room, the twin boys slept on the long, narrow rugs that covered the wood floor. Each night their mother Iren placed large pillows on the floor for them, in the winter, covering the boys with quilts stuffed with feathers. During the day the pillows and quilts were piled high on the two beds in the room.

Her mind wandered. "I have never been alone in the dark. Will I be afraid?" Her sister Clara had shared a bed with her when they were children. She smiled thinking of Clara. They had slept in each other's arms on cold winter nights whispering secrets, planning for the day when they would be married with a home of their own.

"Clara, my dear Clara, like Iren, you are now married too." She thought of Clara's wedding. How beautiful her sister had looked, how happy she was with her husband Elmer. "Perhaps in America I will find a husband."

She reached for the prayer book she kept under her pillow, pressing it against her chest. Inhaling deeply, she drew comfort from the tiny book.

"Give me courage. Holy God, Virgin Mary, guide me, protect me," she prayed. Without opening her eyes, she opened the book, her hand gently touched the dried yellow rosebud pressed between its pages. "That was a happy day," she thought, "the day the rosebush was delivered to our home."

On the day of her mother's funeral Erzsi had picked a small, perfect rose bud, carefully placing it between the pages of her mother's prayer book. Now the book and the rose would travel with her, a reminder of home, of family, of the love they shared. She closed the book and kissed the cover.

"I am never truly alone," she consoled herself. "God will protect me. I will always be able to talk to Mama, in my heart I know she is listening." Silently, so as not to wake the children, she pushed back the covers, placed her feet on the floor, and took a deep breath. "I am ready now."

After putting on her dress and adjusting the skirt, she placed the prayer book deep in her pocket. She reached for the small box she kept under the bed. It contained the little money she had been able to save.

On cold, dark, winter nights she had made paper flowers, large colorful creations, which she sold in the market in Kosice. Viktor, her sister's husband, had tried to take the money from her. "For the family, we need it for food," he had said reaching to grab the money from her hand. Iren had intervened reminding her husband that Erszi would need the money for a dowry. "She owes us. She eats our bread. She lives in our house. The leech needs to go," Viktor had said as he stormed out of the house.

Now, lifting the money from the box, Erzsi hesitated. She thought of the wedding she had planned, the young man, boy really, whom she had loved. "Robert, why did you need to go? If you had only stayed here with me things might have been different." With a sigh of resignation she placed the money in a handkerchief and tied it with a piece of yarn. The money, needed for her new life, was placed in her pocket next to the prayer book. The reassuring weight pulled on her skirt. She patted the pocket. "I will be safe," she reassured herself, putting on a brave face to hide her inner turmoil.

The blue and white quilted bag made by Clara was waiting next to her bed. "It matches your eyes," Clara had said when she gave the bag to Erzsi. Now, as Erzsi placed her nightgown and cap into the bag, she thought of her younger sister. It was so like Clara to pick just the right color. Extra soap, her comb, a small towel, and a few mementoes were stuffed in the corners. Warm clothing she would need for the ocean voyage, wrapped in a blanket, waited next to the front door. Everything she needed, everything she owned, was in the blue bag or wrapped in the blanket.

She lifted her feather pillow from the bed and for a moment nestled her face in its softness. It would be awkward to carry but she would not leave it behind. She placed it next to the blue bag.

Reluctantly, ignoring the inevitable cramping of her toes, she put on her worn shoes. They were poorly made and always hurt her feet. "In America I will buy a pair of decent shoes," she resolved. "It will be a good use of the money I will earn." She smiled, her fear and apprehension momentarily replaced with thoughts of a new life where there would be enough money for extravagances like a new pair of shoes. "Perhaps a hat," she thought. She had seen pictures of the hats worn by American women. For now, she would be content to wear her scarf.

Muffled voices could be heard in the bed on the other side of the room. Viktor's voice, harsh and angry, could be heard in the darkness. The baby started to cry. Viktor did not care that his rough words had awakened the child. Erzsi turned away, busying herself adjusting her apron. Privacy was not possible in the confines of the small room.

Iren's voice was soft as she tried to mollify her husband and calm her baby.

"Hopefully when I am gone Viktor won't be so angry and Iren will have some peace."

Now, with the glimmer of predawn light filtering through the window, Erzsi watched her sister as she lifted the infant from her cradle. Tiny features were just visible beneath the white bonnet with the traditional bright red embroidery. The red embroidery on the bonnet and a red string around the wrist were there to ward off evil spirits. "Hopefully that will be enough to keep the little one safe," thought Erzsi.

Erzsi walked to her older sister and took the infant from her arms. "She is perfect," whispered Erzsi, her heart heavy as she touched the infant's cheek.

The sisters stood close together, the infant between them. Their eyes met. The moment was here, the pain of the impending separation filled their hearts. Iren stepped back a little and gently tucked an unruly curl back under Erzsi's scarf.

"Just like Mama would do," Erzsi smiled at her sister. "She was always trying to manage my curls but they would not behave."

"You were as pretty as an angel with your blue eyes and blond hair," Iren gazed into her sister's eyes.

"I was too thin and far too pale," Erzsi countered.

Viktor, annoyed as usual, grumbled, pulling on pants under his nightshirt. Grabbing his shirt from the pole above the bed, he moved toward the door, ignoring the women and the child. With relief obvious on their faces, the sisters watched Viktor leave the house.

"I am going to miss you, Erzsi."

"I wish Mama was still here."

It was 1872 when diphtheria devastated the tiny village. Erzsi's parents, her brother, and Iren's young son all succumbed to the illness. Sixteen-year-old Erzsi and fourteen-year-old Clara were left without a home. For Iren there was no question but that her sisters would live with her and Viktor until they were old enough to marry.

"Viktor, they have nowhere else to go," she had pleaded.

"They could go to their cousin Peter in Budapest." Peter had moved to Budapest to become a typesetter when he was eighteen. Peter was ambitious, smart, and amiable. His talents served him well; he was now a supervisor in a large publishing house and, in Viktor's opinion, could have afforded to take care of Erzsi and Clara.

"This is their home," Iren had protested. "They can help me in the house and work with you in the fields. They have some money, and the horse." She knew that her husband could be persuaded if reminded of what the girls would bring with them.

"Money, the horse, maybe we can arrange ..." his voice had trailed off. "We will see."

At first the arrangement had pleased Viktor. He took over management of the small amount of money the parents had left to their daughters. The horse, Pista, now belonged to him. "At least they did not come empty-handed," he had shrugged.

But now the money was gone, the horse old and tired. Clara was married and Erzsi had no prospects.

"Worthless animal," Viktor declared. "Useless girl."

His family was growing. The landlord, who lived in distant Humenne, had no interest in the well-being of the tenant farmer. Each year the landlord demanded more and more. Viktor worked in the fields twelve hours a day, six days a week and still his family was close to starvation. They lived on potatoes, bread on Sundays, vegetables from Iren's garden, and meat from the pig they slaughtered once a year. A new baby seemed to appear in the already cramped household almost every other year. Iren was always tired. Viktor was always angry.

Erzsi did her best to help. When Iren was heavy with child, Erzsi ran the house so her sister could rest. She cared for the children, washed clothes in the stream, and helped with the harvest. It was never enough for Viktor.

"When will she leave?" Viktor would bellow, pointing to Erzsi with an accusing finger. Erzsi would cringe, fearing that one day he would completely lose control and strike her.

"Soon she will find a husband, soon," Iren would respond, her voice strong but sadness in her eyes.

Viktor would storm out of the house as he often did. He would find support in the tavern away from the women, children, and the constant troubles that befell the household.

"I am the victim here," Viktor would tell his companions. "I took in Iren's sisters when she asked. How much can a man do? Clara was clever and found a husband. Erzsi is lazy and getting old. She will never leave."

There had been someone, a love, a dream of a future, but choices had been made and an opportunity for happiness had been lost.

3 Lost Love

It was 1867 when Robert left home. He was thirteen years old. He didn't run away, he simply walked. When it was dark he fell asleep on the side of the road. No one looked for him, no one missed him.

He hadn't planned to leave, not yet anyway. There was no particular destination. He had often fantasized about another life, one without beatings, with enough food to quench the hunger in his gut. A life where there was laughter. He could not imagine what it felt like to love, or be loved. He had never experienced love.

Robert was one of eleven siblings. He was lost in the middle. The older boys, like their father, spent their time in the tavern. The little ones, neglected and hungry, scavenged food wherever they could find it. Their mother, the dreams of her youth vanquished, was too exhausted, too overwhelmed, and too frightened of her husband to care.

In school, it was the maps of the world hanging on the classroom walls that inspired him. He imagined that one day he would travel to the great capitals of Europe: Budapest, Vienna, Paris, and London. While Mr. Dolman, their teacher, lectured on the complexities of algebra and geometry, Robert sketched pictures of old-fashioned sailing ships in full sail. Images of explorers conquering primitive tribes, hunting exotic animals in Africa, or climbing the

Himalayas transported him from the harsh realities of the life he knew.

His dark curls, laughing green eyes, and broad grin captivated the girls. On more than one occasion Mr. Dolman confiscated a note in which Robert professed undying love for one of the girls in the classroom. The intended recipient would look away as Robert once again fell victim to Mr. Dolman's rod.

After school with his friends he would brag about his current conquest, predicting that there would be many more. He would tell tales of beautiful Indian princesses, shy English maidens, and French women of questionable repute who would fall madly in love with him. He was happy, good-natured, liked by his friends. Everything was perfect, until it was time to go home.

His father would spend the day in the tavern complaining. "There is no work for an honest man. What do they want from me?" He was filled with self-pity for his circumstances and loathing for the aristocracy that had stolen his money and his land.

The night Robert left it was almost dark when he slowly walked home. His mother was there in her dingy dress holding the baby as she stirred the pot of cabbage soup on the stove. She gave her son a weak smile as he entered the room.

"Piroshka! Piroshka! Damn woman, where are you?" Robert's body stiffened when he heard his father's shouts. He clenched his fists, his knuckles were white as his nails dug into the palm of his hand.

There was venom in Dominik's drunken voice as he shouted for his wife. Robert's anger and disgust grew as he pictured his father, retched in his drunkenness, staggering to the door. He turned to his mother. Her face was frozen in a mixture of defiance, strength, and dread.

The door crashed open, hitting the wall. The house seemed to shake on its foundation as the large man entered the room. The smell of whiskey, heavy, familiar, caused fear in the children who cowered in the corner of the room. The baby began to cry. Robert's mother, her face pale but calm, stood ready to face her husband. Sometimes she could soothe him by offering food or helping him into bed. She had placed the baby in the cradle. She was ready.

But this night there would be no peace. The belt was off. Robert placed his body in front of his mother, he ducked, the strap landed on his shoulder.

"Coward," his father shouted lifting the belt again. Swaying, his aim compromised by his inebriation, the force of the strap hit the arm of a chair. Robert lunged toward his father, knocking him to the floor. His blows brought blood from his father's nose and mouth.

"No, Robert, don't," he heard his mother's voice, distant, pleading, but the blows didn't stop until his father lay unconscious on the floor.

Without looking at his mother, Robert bolted through the door. It slammed behind him. He paused, looking back, picturing his mother. She would be helping her husband into bed and wiping the blood from his face. He put his hands in his pocket and walked away from his home.

He wandered from village to village, sleeping in barns or fields, stealing food. He was lonely and frightened, but always hopeful. Somewhere, somehow, his life would be better, of that he was sure.

It was the fall of 1868 when he entered the city of Kosice. He meandered through the narrow streets of the city, past a nail factory, a railroad, and crowded tenement buildings. The children playing in the streets reminded him of his own younger siblings. "Perhaps, it is the same everywhere," he thought. He continued walking as he entered the center of the city. Here he saw palaces displaying the coat of arms of the owners, not so different from the manor homes near his native village. Sturdy homes of craftsmen and merchants showed what was possible for those with initiative, willing to work. "I will have a home like that," he told himself. His stride was confident, his life was about to begin, of that he was sure.

There was a beer and ale delivery wagon in front of a loading dock. The driver, a corpulent man with stringy, shoulder-length black hair, sat with the reins resting idly in his lap. His mouth, with its large, moist, pink lips and cracked yellow teeth was biting into a sausage, unconcerned that the grease dripped onto his long beard.

As he approached the wagon, Robert recognized the sweet, pungent smell of beer brewing. Fresh hops, herbal, spicy, like evergreen needles mingled with the smell of yeast. His mouth watered, his stomach growled with memories of fresh baked bread washed down with a mug of beer. He paused next to the wagon, hungrily eyeing the sausage that was disappearing in the cavernous mouth of the driver. Robert had not eaten since yesterday, he needed work.

"What do you want?" the driver's voice was almost a growl, his mouth filled with sausage. "Nothing here for you." He pushed the last piece of sausage into his mouth.

"Pardon, sir."

"Go! I don't have anything for beggars."

"I thought you might like some help with those barrels," Robert's voice was confident, polite, his hands on his hips challenging the man to accept his offer.

The man eyed the boy while wiping his mouth with the sleeve of his shirt. Warily, he looked around to see if anyone was watching. Voices could be heard inside but the loading dock was empty. "Everyone will be at lunch," he thought, belching, his fist pounding his chest.

"I'll have it done before you finish eating." Robert tilted his head slightly, raising his eyebrow just a little.

"Hum!" With another loud belch the man settled back in his seat, his arms comfortably resting on his ample belly. "Why not?" he thought to himself, his eyes growing heavy. "A short nap wouldn't hurt."

"The barrels go over there," he said pointing to the loading dock.

"Careful now," he yawned as Robert dropped the barrel he had just removed from the wagon. It was heavier than he had anticipated.

"Yes, Sir. Sorry, Sir," Robert lifted the barrel to his shoulder and carried it to the dock. He returned quickly to the wagon, retrieving the second barrel.

"Stack them against the wall." The man yawned, his voice sleepy.

"Yes, Sir." The man was asleep before Robert retrieved the second barrel. When the twenty-nine barrels were neatly stacked, Robert sat on the loading dock and waited.

The rough voices of men inside the brewery grew louder, the large wooden door began to creak, slowly opening. Robert stood, jumped off the loading dock, at the same time the driver with a sudden burst of energy lowered his rotund body out of the wagon. Without looking at Robert, he passed him a coin. "Go," he said, waving him to be gone. Men from inside the brewery were now on the dock and Robert quietly slipped away.

He returned before dawn the next day and waited for a wagon to appear. As the sun rose, slowly turning the sky into a soft red glow, another wagon filled with empty barrels made its way down the street stopping at the brewery.

"Good morning, Sir. I can help you with those," he said pointing to the barrels in the wagon. Without waiting for a response he started to remove the barrels from the wagon, stacking them neatly on the dock.

The driver just watched, assuming the boy worked for the brewery.

"Who's the boy?" The master brewer had been observing him from a window on the second floor.

"Don't know, saw him yesterday unloading barrels."

"He has initiative, he's strong, bring him to me."

The brewer stood tall, a long apron over his clothes, and a notebook in his hand. He was busy, important work needed to be done.

"Want a job, boy?" he asked without looking up from his notebook.

"Yes, Sir."

"Good, be here at six am. You get paid on Saturday. Elmer, show him where to find the mops." The brewer left abruptly without ever looking up from his notebook.

Robert began to mop the floors that were continually wet from the water and beer overflowing the tanks. When he was finished, Elmer showed him how to clean the large copper vats and the lined wooden containers used for fermentation.

"Where are you from?" Elmer asked, stopping to rest for a moment.

"Ujak, a village to the north," Robert answered as he continued to scrub the large barrel he was cleaning.

"You're far from home then."

"Yup, and never going back." The look on Robert's face told Elmer that this was not a topic he should pursue.

With the past not open for discussion, the boys talked about their future. Robert had grand goals. He would travel the world, make his fortune in distant lands. Elmer wanted to be a master brewer, get married, and have a large family.

Erzsi was eating a large piece of strudel when she noticed the handsome young man leaning against a tree. He was watching her. They were outside of the church, celebrating the marriage of her sister Clara to Elmer.

"The strudel looks good," he said, walking up to her and reaching for a slice of the sugary confection. "May I?" he reached for her lips and gently wiped away a small crumb just below her lower lip. Her eyes widened at his presumptuous gesture.

"Sit with me," he said, his mouth filled with strudel. "Over there." He nodded towards the decorated wagon that had brought the bride and groom to the church. "I haven't tasted strudel this good since, well, since forever," he said while picking up another piece. Erzsi, despite herself, was drawn to his confident, forward behavior. He was asking her to sit with him and she didn't even know his name. The laughter in his eyes, the gentleness of his gesture, not to mention his audacious good looks, enticed her.

"Does the horse have a name?" Robert asked, as he absent-mindedly stroked the horse's nose.

"Pista," Erzsi replied as she affectionately scratched him under the harness. Pista gratefully leaned into her hand, bringing his head around to nuzzle her in appreciation.

"He likes you."

"I have ridden him and cared for him since I was a little girl."

"You like to ride then?"

"Yes, do you?"

"Never had the opportunity to learn. My name's Robert, by the way," he said while effortlessly lifting her onto the back of the wagon.

"Erzsi," she answered, enjoying the sensation as his hands rested on her waist a little longer than necessary.

They sat close together, perched on the back of the wagon. She told him how her father had purchased Pista when she was three years old. He was meant to be a workhorse but her cousin Peter had taught her to ride. Sometimes her sister Clara would sit behind her clutching her skirts and they would ride together through the fields. He pictured her with her family, happy together, so different from his own troubled childhood.

Robert did not tell her about his childhood, but he did talk about Elmer. "We have worked together for a long time. He will make a good husband for your sister."

"May I see you again?" Robert said, helping her down from the wagon. The music had stopped, the festivities were ending.

"I would like that," she had smiled.

The courtship lasted a year. Her warmth and tenderness softened his defenses. Over time he confided in her the sad events of his youth that he had buried deep in the recesses of his heart. Erzsi would nestle her head on his shoulder, stroking his arm gently, reassuring, and offering her love. She yielded passionately to his kisses without the coquettish teasing of other girls he had known. He was falling in love.

When he told stories of distant places, she would smile at him while running her fingers through his curls. "I will go with you, Robert. We will travel together."

"Yes, together," he would smile taking her hand. But in his heart he knew this was not possible. Frightened of commitment, unsure that he was capable of an enduring love, he grew restless. "I am not ready to take a wife," he sadly acknowledged to himself.

Erzsi waited for a proposal of marriage. She was sure that Robert loved her, that they were destined to be together forever. He had never said he loved her but she could see it in his eyes, feel it in his kiss. She knew he was restless, that he wanted to see the world, but she always thought she would go with him.

A year after they met, Erzsi received a letter.

Kosice, Hungary
March 1, 1876

Dear Erzsi,

I have news, exciting news. Tomorrow I am leaving for America. A friend knows of a company that will pay passage to anyone who will work for them for one year. The ship sails from Hamburg in three weeks so we must be on the morning train.

The year will go quickly. I can only hope that you will wait for me. This is the opportunity I have been waiting for. Our future will be more wonderful than we could ever have imagined if I stayed in Kosice.

> *Yours Forever,*
> *Robert*

At first his letters arrived with regularity. He described the trains that took him to Hamburg. The night he spent in Vienna, a beautiful city that surpassed his expectations. "So much of the world I have to see and experience," he had written. "Someday I will show it all to you." He described in detail the congestion and excitement that permeated the Port of Hamburg, the storms on the North Sea that caused great misery among the steerage passengers, and then America and the great city of New York.

He spent a year in New York City and another in Philadelphia. Two years after he left Hungary he wrote to her as he waited for a train. He was leaving Philadelphia and heading for California.

Philadelphia, Pennsylvania USA
June 15, 1878

Dear Erzsi,

I am leaving Philadelphia and going to the city of San Francisco. I am traveling with a friend. Arnold has heard about a beer they are developing in San Francisco. They call it "steam beer" for reasons I will not bore you with. It will be inexpensive and will appeal to the laboring classes. We plan to open a brewery of our own making this beer. I must take advantage of this opportunity.

The train is approaching. Give my regards to your family. I will write when I am settled.

Yours Forever,
Robert

It was the last letter she ever received from him. She waited. She cried. "Oh, Robert, where are you?" she would lament when she was alone. She thought of the stories she had heard about life in the western United States. "Indians? Is there a danger from Indians in a city like San Francisco? Has he fallen ill with no one to care for him?" That he might have rejected her for another woman was a thought that sent her to her bed with inconsolable tears.

Seven months later she received a letter postmarked San Francisco, California, USA. It was not Robert's handwriting. Holding the letter, unopened, she walked out the door. She walked for a long time, worried at what the letter would contain. Finally, after passing the last house in the village, she sat, her back against a large old oak tree. Tears filled her eyes; her hands trembled as she read the letter.

San Francisco, California USA
January 29, 1879

Dear Miss Viarka,

Robert may have told you about me. My name is Arnold Adler. Robert and I traveled together to San Francisco with plans to open a brewery.

I regret to inform you that shortly after we arrived in San Francisco Robert developed a fever of unknown origins. He was well cared for, the owners of the boarding house where we were staying were attentive and thoughtful. A doctor was summoned but the medicines did not lower the fever. In the end he left this world peacefully.

He spoke of you often, telling everyone how he would bring you to America when he was established. Realizing he was desperately ill he asked me to write to you expressing his enduring love.

In the end your name was the last word he spoke.

Respectfully and with sadness,
Yours in grief,
Arnold

Erzsi, distraught, filled her time caring for Iren's growing brood of children. She was becoming more and more isolated from other young people. Her friends did not have time for her; they were getting married, having babies. The young men of the village were either married or had left for America. Iren watched with sadness as the glow left the cheeks of her precocious little sister.

Now Erzsi was twenty-five years old and unmarried, her opportunities had slowly slipped away. She needed to leave. There was no question; she could no longer stay with Iren and Viktor.

She thought of Robert, his plans for a new life in America. There were others who had left. Recruiters often visited the villages talking of America, a promise of work, of a better life. They explained that the voyage was easier now that the great steamships crossed the ocean in less than two weeks. America offered hope, a way to escape the endless cycle of poverty. Many were tempted. There were stories of whole villages leaving. They walked, rode wagons, eventually reaching Poland where trains took them to the German ports of Hamburg and Bremen.

"Why not me?" she thought. "It cannot be worse than here." There would be work, perhaps a chance to find a husband, start a family. Leaving her home, possibly never to return, was frightening to a woman who had never lived anywhere but her small village. She would be traveling alone. "Am I strong enough, capable enough, brave enough?" she worried. She prayed for guidance, but none came.

She wrote to her cousin Peter and was encouraged by his reply.

Budapest, Hungary
December 1, 1881

Dear Erzsi,

For some time now I have been concerned about you, the life you are leading. Your sister Iren has written to me of your sorrow at the loss of Robert, and your increasing isolation from your friends.

Iren is kind, and I know you love the children, but it cannot be easy for you living in a home with one room, especially with a man of Viktor's temperament. You are right when you say there is no future for you in Reiste. Your spirit will wither if you stay locked away in your sister's house.

There was sorrow in my heart as I read your letter. The little girl who rode her horse with such joy, who dared to climb trees, braving the consequences if she returned home with a bruised knee or torn dress, seemed to have vanished. And then you spoke of your plans to go to America. In your words I heard the manifestation of the strength you have buried in your heart for so long.

My sweet little cousin, you need not cross an ocean, you are always welcome to come to Budapest to live with us. But then, perhaps you need something more.

You write that many of our countrymen are going to America. In America, you feel there is hope for a better life. I do not want to take this hope away from you.

If you are sure that you want to go to America, I can help make it possible. My wife, Yolanda, has a friend in

*America who owns a boarding house. Yolanda has written
to her and she is willing to give you a job.*

*When you are ready I can facilitate your travel,
arranging passage on a steamship from Hamburg.*

Your loving cousin and friend,
Peter

Plans were made. She would take a train to
Budapest where she would spend time with her
cousin Peter and his family. He would help her
make arrangements to travel to Hamburg where she
would get on one of the steamships taking emigrants
to America. "I will be all right," Erzsi had told her
worried sister. "I will write often."

Now it was her last morning in her sister's home.
Viktor came into the house, slamming the door,
saying nothing. He sat at the tiny table. The noise
created by the boys as they wrestled caused him to
frown. The little girls got out of the bed, their cheeks
still flushed with sleep, their hair a mass of tangles.

"Sit down," Iren ordered the boys, pointing to
their place on the benches that lined the wall of the
room. There were only three chairs at the table, the
children sat on the benches, their food in their laps.
When everyone was seated Viktor lead them in prayer.
The family ate in silence. The boys, controlled with
a firm look from Iren, the little ones assisted by their
aunt. Viktor just sat and ate. He required silence at
the table. "There is enough noise around here. I

demand silence while I eat," he would pound on the table to be sure his command was clearly understood. Everyone obeyed, the consequences, especially for the boys, could be physically painful if they did not. The strap was hung near the door.

Eventually Viktor put down his spoon and walked to the door. It was time to go. There was work to be done and driving Erzsi to the train in Kosice was just another inconvenience. "What are you taking?" he said, suspicion in his voice, while looking at the large heavy bundle waiting near the door.

"The coat and wool dress I will need for the ocean crossing are packed inside. I will carry it on my back."

Viktor swung the bundle onto his shoulder and moved toward the door. Iren handed her sister a lidded woven basket. "For the trip, you will be hungry." Later, inside a linen napkin, Erzsi would find cheese, kielbasa, and potatoes that had been baked on the stove.

Erzsi tucked her feather pillow under her arm. "You will never part from that pillow," Iren tried to smile, picturing her sister as a little girl. When Erzsi was two years old her mother had given her that pillow, even then she had clutched it tightly, finding comfort in its softness.

"Iren, you mustn't worry about me. Cousin Peter will meet me in Budapest. I will write you when I get there."

"Enough, Erzsi, come! Now!" Viktor shouted, he was already in the wagon.

Erzsi stopped to slip Pista a handful of sliced carrots. The old horse was only a shadow of the young fat black gelding she remembered riding as a child. Pista chewed the treats gratefully, shaking his head up and down to work the bits of carrot around the metal bit in his mouth.

Viktor gestured for Erzsi to hurry while he picked up the reins. The wagon moved forward down the main street of the village, seeming to find every bump and hole along the way. Iren stood at the door with the baby in her arms, the girls holding her skirts, the boys kicking at stones in the dirt. They watched until they could no longer see the wagon.

Viktor, sullenly driving the wagon, spoke only to the tired, old horse. He had no interest in talking with Erzsi. She had been a burden. He needed food for his children. He was glad she was going. Perhaps she would find success in America and would send money home. God knew she owed him.

4 An Omen

Erszi shivered, pulling her shawl tighter around her shoulders; the early morning sun had not yet had a chance to warm the cool, moist air. Her expression was stoic, her sadness and apprehension hidden in her heart. The wagon bounced and creaked as it made its way down the dirt road, slowly, steadily taking her away from her home, her family.

Her beloved horse Pista obediently pulled the wagon, not knowing that his mistress would be leaving, never to return. Head lowered, backbone sagging, Pista could barely pick up his feet. Erzsi could see his ribs, his breathing heavy, as he struggled to obey Viktor's commands.

A large white stork erupted from its nest perched on the chimney of a local farmhouse. It soared overhead. Its massive black and white wings beat with a slow, regular rhythm. The neck and beak pointed straight ahead as the bird flew with determination to its destination. "Perhaps it is a good omen," Erzsi thought, her spirits lifted.

"Viktor, look, isn't he beautiful?" she said pointing to the massive bird. "Maybe he is showing the way, encouraging me."

"Foolishness," Viktor replied his expression showing his annoyance.

"Sometimes it makes life easier to imagine," Erzsi said, sadness in her voice.

Viktor, bent forward in his seat, just shrugged.

"He has become an old man," she thought, looking at his large, calloused hands covered with cuts and bruises. A thick mustache that was once neatly trimmed was now unkempt and stained with tobacco. His cap, in his youth carefully adjusted for maximum effect, was now pulled over his bushy eyebrows, shielding sad, angry eyes.

This was not the confident, slightly arrogant young man who stood tall when he had asked her father for permission to marry Iren. Erzsi smiled, remembering how she had hidden with Clara behind the door giggling while the men discussed the proposal. Iren's father had been reluctant; he needed his oldest daughter at home to care for the younger children. In his heart he was not sure Viktor was a suitable spouse for his oldest daughter. But Iren was in love and persuaded her father to accept the proposal. Viktor rented a small house; Iren embroidered linens for her new home.

For the first two years they were happy. Iren had glowed with her first pregnancy. Viktor and Iren were prepared, they thought, for all the trials God would inevitably send them.

And then the trouble came. "Oh, that horrible, horrible year," Erzsi thought.

Viktor and Iren's son, Samuel, had been a beautiful child with long blond curls and a pleasant disposition. Everyone loved Samuel. The grandmothers fussed over their first grandson, putting him on display whenever the opportunity presented itself. "Did you ever see such a beautiful child? The curls, the eyes, they are the eyes of an angel." The little boy was inseparable from his father, crying when Viktor left in the morning, toddling into his arms when he came home at night.

When the boy was almost two, diphtheria spread through their village, devastating families. Iren had been the strong one caring first for her parents and then her little brother. Her efforts to nurse them, her fervent prayers, were of no avail. When they succumbed to the illness she collapsed in grief and exhaustion. Viktor felt helpless, unable to comfort her, unable to take away her sorrow.

Then he had watched with trepidation as his precious son developed the now familiar sore throat and cough. He would not eat; it was difficult for him to breathe. His tiny body shook with chills and fever. There was no doctor in the village. The midwife came but could not help. Samuel's fever grew worse. Viktor paced the floor cursing God. He would do anything to save his son. "Why is God so cruel?"

He held him in his arms throughout the night. Night after night, he refused to rest or leave his son. Helplessness and anger had filled his heart as the sweet blue eyes of his son had lost their sparkle and pale, lifeless skin replaced the once rosy cheeks. When the child's cries ceased and his suffering ended, Viktor gave the child to Iren and left the house. His face had hardened as his child, his precious little boy, was lowered into the ground.

Now as the wagon passed the small wooden church with its graveyard, Erzsi said a silent prayer for her loved ones who were buried there. Viktor just looked straight ahead.

The church bells were ringing, announcing to the village that she was leaving. Friends had gathered to wave to her and wish her well. The women in their babushkas, many with tears, thought of others who had left the village never to return. The men, holding farm implements, watched solemnly, anxious to get back to work. Children ran after the wagon waving good-bye. They knew she was going far away; perhaps someday they too would go on such an exciting adventure.

A friend held out a small bundle. "Some cheese and ham for the trip," she said, lifting her skirts slightly as she ran towards the wagon. It was Bianka, Erzsi's childhood friend. Bianka and Erzsi were the same age. They had played together as children, went to school together, and when they were older they talked of the handsome young men they planned to marry. When Bianka got married it was Erzsi who had gathered the flowers for the elaborate headpiece the bride would wear. With tears in her eyes Erzsi reached out for the bundle. "Thank you," she said to her friend, their fingertips touching briefly. "We will miss you," Bianka called after the wagon. Viktor had not bothered to stop the wagon; there was no time to waste with sentimental good-byes. Erzsi smiled and waved, for the moment she buried her trepidation in her heart. "I want them to remember me smiling, happy. They will tell each other how brave I was."

Viktor just kept looking forward. "Your friends," he mumbled, "they will forget you tomorrow."

Mr. Balog, the carpenter, stood at the door of the shop waving a friendly good-bye. Mr. Breiner and his wife, the only Jewish family in the village, stood in front of the tavern they owned. There was sadness on their faces; their own children had left for America years ago. On the outskirts of the village was the blacksmith shop owned by the Gypsies. "I wonder if they have Gypsies and Jews in America," she mused. She tried to imagine what life would be like in America. Would she live in a village like this one or in a big city like Kosice?

The wagon moved slowly, steadily forward, down the dirt road leading to the city of Kosice. The rows of tiny homes that lined the street in the village were replaced by seemingly endless fields of wheat, sugar beets, and potato crops. Apple trees lined the road, rolling hills stretched out to the horizon, and the mountains leading to Poland were in the distance at their backs.

"I will miss all of this," she said, trying to make conversation with the irritable man next to her.

"Just fields, where we work, sweat, and barely have enough to feed our families."

Again, the groaning of the wagon, Pista's hooves falling softly on the dirt road, and the jingle of the harness were the only sounds.

"I have seen post cards of New York. The buildings are made of stone and marble, many six stories above the ground. Maybe I will have the chance to ride one of those iron cages so you don't have to walk up the stairs." She could not imagine how such a thing would work. "I know I will be dizzy," her voice reflected her excitement as she thought of such an adventure.

"Then don't go up."

"But Viktor, don't you want to see distant places? Have adventures? Don't you wonder about the world?"

"I have my family, responsibilities. Life is what it is," he shrugged his shoulders, slumping further forward so she could not see his face.

The sun was setting when they finally reached Kosice. The quiet country road was now a busy, noisy street, the open fields and scattered villages were replaced by city buildings.

"Go now," Viktor said, stopping at a narrow side street with rundown wooden buildings where Clara lived.

"Goodbye, Viktor."

"The horse is getting tired. I will leave you here." Erzsi knew that Viktor would be spending the night with his brother on the outskirts of the city.

Without ceremony Viktor stopped the wagon and waited for Erzsi to gather her belongings.

"Viktor, I want you to know how grateful I am for all that you have done for me."

"Yes, yes. I know. It was for Iren," his expression softened a little.

She gathered her skirts and climbed out of the wagon. Leaving her belongings on the dirt road, she reached in the basket for an apple and placed it in her pocket. It was time to say good-bye to Pista, to the sweet memories of childhood that he represented. The horse nuzzled her face with his upper lip and explored her hands for a treat. "So you are expecting something, are you?" She reached into her pocket, giving him the apple which he accepted gratefully, chewing, salivating, while savoring the sweet juices. She giggled, like she had as a child, and wiped her hands on her skirt, giving him a gentle kiss. He lifted his nose to her mouth, and she blew gently into his nostril. Nostril to nostril, one last time, showing the lasting affection they had for each other.

Erzsi stepped away from the wagon and silently waved to Viktor. She was working hard to look confident and strong.

"God be with you, Erzsi, I know Iren and the children will miss you." The wagon, a link to her family, moved steadily away.

5 A Chance Encounter

Kosice to Budapest
May, 1882

The mud from the street covered her shoes and darkened the hem of her skirt. It was late in the day and gloomy, threatening shadows filled the alley that led to her sister's tenement. Still, Erzsi walked with resolve, her destination was not far.

The bundle of clothes on her back caused her to slump slightly forward, the wooden handle of the basket cut into her wrist. Her pillow, usually a comfort, was now an awkward burden. "Am I really going to carry all of this to America?" she mumbled to herself, bending forward just a little more, adjusting the bundle on her back. "I will be happy for the warm clothes," she said, trying to convince herself. Robert had written about the cold winds and rain that had caused him much discomfort when his ship crossed the North Sea. "I would rather carry these clothes than be cold," she thought, walking a little straighter, her expression reflecting her strength and tenacity.

Reaching the wooden tenement where her sister lived, she stepped around an old man wrapped in a torn blanket sleeping on the ground. The smell of rotting garbage and animal waste filled the air; a rat startled her as it ran for cover beneath a porch. She did not envy Clara living in such a place.

She struggled with her belongings, nearly tripping on her skirt as she climbed the steep, narrow staircase. She heard them coming, the thud of their shoes on the stairs, the loud voices, laughter. But when boys from the tenement pushed past her, she was not prepared. In their haste, the boys shoved her against the wall. She lost her balance, everything she was holding tumbled down the stairs. The boys, focused on their game, ignored her, escaping down the stairs, vanishing out the door. Retrieving her belongings, envious of their energy, but disapproving of their behavior, she resumed her climb.

She could hear a man shouting, a baby crying. A door opened, watery old eyes peered at her from under a black babushka. A few strands of white hair fell carelessly down the wrinkled face. "Not so different from the widow Benes," Erzsi thought. The widow Benes lived alone in a shack not far from the Gypsies in her village. "Witch," some called her, with disdain. But it didn't prevent the villagers from asking her for potions when they were ill. Now Erzsi gave the woman in the doorway a reassuring smile. Curiosity satisfied, the old woman retreated to the safety of her room. The door slammed shut. Erzsi was alone again in the stairwell.

The smell of soup simmering on a stove, the laughter of children, a familiar voice, it was Elmer. "We thought we heard you coming," he said, hurrying down the stairs. "Welcome," he said reaching for the basket and bag. With relief she allowed him to help her take the heavy bundle from her back. An instant later, Erzsi climbed the last few stairs. Clara was at the door holding the new baby.

The bond the sisters shared since childhood was still strong and evident on their faces as they embraced, the tiny form of the new baby between them. Erzsi stroked the infant's pink cheeks, marveling at the softness of the baby's skin. A tiny hand wrapped around her finger. As always, when she held a new baby, her emotions were conflicted. Tenderness and love for the infant predominated, but deep in her being was regret that she did not have a child of her own. "Someday," she thought, smiling down at the baby in her arms.

"She is a good baby, a real blessing." Clara looked down at her baby and then over to the other children. "Stefan, Matilda, come and give your aunt a kiss."

Two-year-old Matilda, shy with the aunt she had only seen on a few occasions, was holding her brother's hand. Her six-year-old brother, Stefan, was looking at his aunt with curiosity. He had heard his parents talking. She was leaving her home and going far away.

Erzsi knelt down giving each of the children a hug. "Are you going to America?" Stefan asked as Erzsi let go of him.

"Yes, it is going to be a long journey," Erzsi said, her expression solemn.

"Are you afraid of the ocean?" asked the little boy. "It is very big and very deep."

"Yes, a little. But it will be a fun adventure as well. Maybe I will meet pirates," she said raising her eyebrow in mock excitement. Stefan's eyes opened wide as he pondered this thought.

"Pirates! But who will keep you safe?" he asked, his face showing a mixture of awe and concern. "The captain of the ship will protect me," Erszi responded with a reassuring tone. Stefan nodded his head up and down in silent understanding.

"That's enough, Stefan, your aunt is tired," said Clara putting an end to the discussion. "Go and play with your sister. Stefan took Matilda by the hand and led her to the corner of the room where the children played. "I am a pirate and you are my prisoner," they heard him say his tone serious and authoritative as he led the little girl away.

"Now look what you started," Clara said, shaking her head in mock disapproval. Erzsi just smiled, remembering the games she had played with her cousin Peter when they were children.

"Elmer, put her pillow there," Clara said pointing to the bed she shared with Elmer and Matilda.

"No, no. Where will Elmer and Matilda sleep?" Erzsi protested, knowing that Matilda shared the bed with her parents. Stefan had a small iron cot tucked in a corner on the opposite side of the room. The baby slept in a cradle near her parents' bed.

"Don't worry about me. Clara will make a bed for me near the window. Matilda will sleep with Stefan." Elmer smiled at his daughter who was tightly holding her doll, protecting her from the pirate who was brandishing a sword above their heads.

"Tell me, how is Iren? How are the children?" Not waiting for an answer Clara continued, "What about Viktor!"

"Still the same."

"How does she put up with him?"

"She is a saint."

Clara led her sister to a small wooden table near the stove. "Mama's dishes," Erzsi touched the rim of the bowl in front of her. "I am glad you have them."

The family lived in one room cluttered with the necessities of family life. There was a stove, a sink, no running water. Bright reds and greens decorated the room, touches of their Hungarian heritage, brought vibrant color into the room. Clara had used her talents to keep the small space organized and inviting. Clothes and cooking pots hung neatly from hooks Elmer had installed on the walls. A pot for making coffee sat invitingly on the stove. Colorful plates with elaborate flowers were carefully arranged on a shelf.

"Stefan, bring Matilda to the table. We are ready to eat," Clara called to her children.

Reluctantly Stefan put down the stick that served him well as a sword. He took Matilda's hand and the children settled at the table.

"Let us pray," said Elmer.

With a touch of envy Erzsi watched the small family. Elmer was so different from Viktor. He obviously loved his children and adored his wife.

"Clara, you are truly blessed."

"God has been good to me." Clara smiled at her husband and children.

After the meal, the dishes were cleared away, the children put to bed. Elmer settled near the window enjoying a final cigar.

The sisters talked late into the night. It was nearly dawn when their eyes finally closed in sleep. They were holding hands as they had done when they were children.

Josef was waiting for the train. He lit his cigar, placed his cap far back on his head, and lowered his back against the hard wooden bench.

From his vantage point in front of the small ticket office, he observed the crowd assembling on the platform. An army officer in a perfectly tailored blue uniform, medals on display across his chest, a sword at his waist, and white gloves in his hand, stood apart from the crowd. He was impatient, pacing, the train was late. His aloof stance contrasted with the raucous laughter of a group of infantry soldiers standing nearby. They looked young to the twenty-six-year-old Josef. "I wish you well," he thought.

A tall, well-dressed man protectively guided his wife along the platform, moving her away from the rowdy soldiers. A governess followed behind, holding the hands of their children, while a porter balanced a cart piled precariously high with hatboxes and leather suitcases. "They won't be traveling in third class," Josef thought.

A woman, a rather handsome woman, wearing city clothes of the working class variety, was pushing a baby carriage. Walking next to her was a woman wearing the heavy clothes and white apron of a peasant, her hair covered with a scarf. She was bent slightly forward from the weight of the bundle on her back and was clutching a pillow. "Like a child, holding her most precious possession," he thought. The women were standing close together in what appeared to be a sad, intimate conversation. A little girl clung to the skirts of the woman pushing the carriage. A young boy trailed behind, ignored, his impatience obvious as he idly swung the stick he was holding.

They stopped. Josef watched as the woman put down her pillow, turning to adjust the bundle on her back. Their eyes met. Blond curls had escaped from the confines of her scarf, her face was flushed. With an approving smile he touched his cap. She smiled faintly, reflexively, and quickly turned away.

"Where are you going, pretty lady?" he thought to himself. "To meet a husband? Perhaps a soldier," he speculated. "Lucky man!"

The train whistle blew in the distance. The clanging of bells, the black and grey smoke billowing from the stack as the large black locomotive made its appearance on the horizon. The crowd, passengers and spectators, moved closer to the tracks.

Josef watched the third class passengers. Women with scarves and heavy shawls marking them as peasants carried crying babies and held the hands of toddlers. Behind them men, husbands, fathers, brothers, pushed carts filled with bags and boxes, feather pillows, and mattresses. "Off to America like me?" Slowly he got up from the bench, picked up his cardboard suitcase and joined the crowd.

He caught a glimpse of the woman with the curls. She was on the platform of the train and had turned to wave a final good-bye. He studied the curve of her bosom and the shape of her waist. She was petite, delicate; the bundles she was carrying looked far too heavy for such a tiny person. She was very different from his Maria, with her full figure and strong arms.

The last passengers were boarding the train. Through the third class window he could see the woman settling into a seat. The conductor signaled that the train was about to depart. "It's time. This is it," he said to the man next to him. His casual, confident demeanor was replaced by excitement and anticipation of the adventures to come.

Hurriedly, he worked his way through the crowd of onlookers, pausing for a brief moment to touch his cap with his free hand as he passed an attractive woman. "I'm going to America!" he proclaimed, his face beaming with excitement. It didn't matter that she ignored this rude man pushing past her.

He took the stairs two at a time, landing on the platform as the train started to move. He looked back, one more time, the exhilaration of the moment reflected in his face.

"Off to America!" he shouted. "I'm going to America!" He was waving his cap to the crowd and many responded with cheers, wishing him well. The train whistle blew as if to acknowledge the hope and courage of those on the train traveling to places far from home, possibly never to return.

The train jerked forward; he caught his balance and moved into the third class coach. He saw her. She was sitting at a window, both hands pressed against the glass. Her belongings were on the floor in front of her, the feather pillow on her lap. The seat next to her was empty.

Without asking, he placed his suitcase on the floor, taking ownership of the seat. She continued to look out the window; Clara was still there waving to her. The whistle blew, its melancholy sound reflecting her sadness. She felt the force of the train, its momentum building as it relentlessly carried her away from her home. She watched the station recede in the distance. "I will not cry," she thought as she hugged her pillow. "There will be no regrets, no doubts."

"Are you going to Budapest?" It was the voice of the man next to her. She felt him watching her but she continued to clutch her pillow, struggling not to cry.

"It's a good day to travel," his voice was casual, not threatening. It was rude to continue to ignore him. She turned and was surprised to see it was the man from the station.

"I'm going to Budapest," her voice was soft but confident. She was determined not to show the turmoil that was in her heart.

"It is going to be a long day."

"Yes," she nodded, turning away. She wanted to be alone with her thoughts.

Josef, feeling the steady rhythm of the train, rolled up his coat, placing it behind his head. Settling back, he pulled his cap over his eyes, crossed his arms, and fell into a deep, comfortable sleep.

She watched him sleeping. She didn't know him, there was no reason, but somehow it was comforting having him close to her. "He has nice eyes," she thought, remembering the way he had looked at her in the station. His eyes were self-confident, filled with optimism. "I wish I could feel like that."

Erzsi watched as white puffs of clouds formed over the grey-green mountains in the distance. "Fair weather clouds," she thought. "It is going to be a beautiful day."

The train slowly picked up speed as it passed an endless expanse of fields. A symphony of green and gold played out in front of her. Yellow gold squares of wheat were intermingled with the green leaves of corn and potatoes. Orange poppies dotted the landscape mixing with the wild grasses growing near the tracks. Forests filled with densely packed dark green trees wound their way around the fields, eventually blanketing the distant hills. Erzsi was thrilled to be moving so fast. She watched in awe as trees and fences close to the track sped past her, while distant mountains seemed to amble slowly. She imagined galloping on a young horse trying to keep pace with the train.

Villages, not so different from her own, nestled among the trees. The crimson roofs of the small houses contrasted with the white churches, the tallest buildings in each village. Old women would be in those churches tonight, chanting the rosary, creating a bond with each other while they worshiped. She pictured the children playing with the farm animals, running through the fields, or helping with chores to keep the household in food for another week.

The train whistle blew, the brakes squealed, the train stopped. A sign said they were in Miskolc. The man next to her woke, looked out the window, adjusted his cap, put on his coat, picked up his suitcase and left the train. He didn't say a word to her, just touched his cap and left. Through the window she watched him light his cigar and talk to a vendor. "Maybe, this is the last time I will see him," she could not explain her disappointment. "I don't even know his name."

Sadness enveloped her. She was alone. New passengers were boarding the train. A woman started to sit in the seat next to her. Erzsi lifted her bag and protectively placed it on the empty seat. "For my husband!" she lied, wondering why it mattered if this woman sat next to her. The woman scowled and moved away.

The whistle blew, she saw him coming. "Hurry!" she almost shouted through the window. She watched him running to the train, it started to move. "He missed the train," she hugged her pillow wondering again why she cared.

"Is this seat open?" the voice was behind her. She turned, an involuntary smile on her face. Nodding her assent, she removed her bag from the seat. She watched as he pushed back his cap, took off his coat, and without further ceremony sat down. It was impolite to stare; she turned back to the window. But she was thinking about his large strong hands, calloused, rough. She wanted to touch them, to soothe them. She wondered what it would feel like to move her fingers through his thick black hair. "What is the matter with me?" She felt her cheeks flush and hoped he hadn't noticed.

When Josef had left the train he had not considered whether he would get his seat back. But in the station, he saw an old woman selling apples and got off to buy two. Now, he pulled them from his pocket and offered one to the lady who had saved his seat. It seemed the polite thing to do.

"Want one?"

She hesitated and then shook her head no.

"You must be hungry. Here, take it!"

"Thank you."

As she reached for the apple, Josef noticed her hands. They were rough and red from work, like most village women, but also delicate and graceful. He was mesmerized by their movements as she opened her basket and offered him some cheese.

"Are you meeting someone in Budapest?" he asked, taking the cheese.

"My cousin and his family."

"No husband?"

She didn't answer. They ate in silence, watching the endless expanse of open fields.

"My father would take us to get mushrooms in the forest," Erzsi said softly, almost to herself, as she watched the changing landscape. "And blueberries, Mama would make pies."

Josef didn't respond. He didn't want to talk about his family.

"I'm going to America," he volunteered after an extended pause.

"I wish you good fortune," she said, not offering to share her own plans.

"Look there!" Erzsi almost shouted as she saw horsemen in electric blue tunics and sweeping black hats herding their long-horned cattle toward the water. They had reached the Great-Hungarian Plain, the Puszta.

Erzsi imagined she could hear their whips cracking and the horses' hooves thundering as the men maneuvered their horses around the dangerous looking horns. The horsemen snapped long whips several feet in front of their horses' noses. Erzsi feared each crack would land on some helpless animal rather than harmlessly in the air. She remembered trotting her Pista around the field; it was nothing like these open plains. She watched one rider gallop off after an errant cow. Pista could never have run at such speeds and Erzsi wondered what it would be like with the wind in her hair, the ground racing below her from the back of a horse instead of this train.

Josef bent forward, his body gently pressing hers as he tried to get a better view of the scene outside the window. His body reacted to the softness of hers and he quickly sat back in his seat.

"That's something I will not see in America!" he said with confidence.

Josef settled back in his seat, pulling his cap over his eyes. He thought about the woman next to him. She was like a vulnerable child clutching that pillow, her smile was endearing. There was pain as well as determination in her eyes. It would have been nice to know her better.

Erzsi felt comfortable and safe with this strong, rugged man sitting next to her. "Perhaps in America I will meet a man like this. Someone strong, filled with optimism, willing to work hard," she thought, conjuring up an image of the man she hoped to marry.

Neither could know that this chance meeting would change their lives forever.

6 Pearl of the Danube

Budapest, Hungary
May, 1882

The whistle blew. A belch of black smoke and the squeal of brakes announced their approach to the terminal. The locomotive slowed to a crawl, the whistle blew again. The train jerked to a stop in front of a sign with large black letters BUDAPEST.

Travel-weary passengers scrambled to gather their belongings. Husbands and fathers lifted the bags, boxes, and bundles that had been strewn around their seats. Mothers gathered their children, firmly holding the hands of the youngest.

Josef stretched his cramped legs, put on his jacket and lifted the cardboard suitcase that contained his belongings. "Good journey," he touched his cap to Erzsi, and without waiting for a response, joined the passengers moving toward the exit.

Passengers from every car were debarking, some greeted by acquaintances, others walking confidently toward the entrance to the terminal. Josef made his way around a family with wide-eyed children encircled by what looked to be all their earthly possessions. He didn't have a destination in mind. Tonight he would find an inexpensive hotel or sleep on a park bench, it didn't matter. Tomorrow he would explore the city, perhaps joining a card game in a tavern. In a day or two he would travel to Vienna and then to Hamburg.

Reaching the entrance to the terminal he glanced back at the train. The woman he had sat next to was scanning the crowd, her arm tightly clutching the pillow, the heavy bundle on her back causing her to stoop slightly forward. She looked lost, hesitant. Perhaps he should offer to help her.

The expression on her face suddenly changed. A man was waving to her, calling her name. For a moment Josef felt let down, disappointed. "Just as well," he turned back to the door, dismissing the woman from his thoughts.

Erzsi had watched with interest and trepidation as the train approached the city. Fields, farms, and narrow dirt roads had been replaced with warehouses, factories with smoke billowing from their chimneys, and cobblestone streets. The track their train was using had been joined by others, all leading to the city. They passed other trains moving in the opposite direction. "How can they move so fast?" she wondered, fascinated and a little afraid as a blur of windows rushed by close enough to touch.

She heard the whistle announcing their arrival in Budapest and felt the locomotive slow to a crawl. A large black sign announced their arrival in BUDAPEST.

"Budapest! I am in Budapest!"

The train passed under an archway entering the terminal. A high ceiling, black with soot, covered the tracks, blocking out the sky. She felt panic; it was dark, shadowy, and noisy, like nothing she had experienced before. Closing her eyes, she imagined the open fields, blue skies, and the quiet streets of her village. "What am I doing here? I don't belong here." She wanted to retreat, to turn the train around and go back home. Erzsi stayed in her seat while the families moved toward the exit. "Better to wait. I won't be in everyone's way."

There were three tracks in the station, each with its own platform. People were waiting on the platforms, so many people. "How will Peter know where to find me?" Her legs felt weak, she wondered if she would be strong enough to walk off the train.

Through the window she watched the man who had been sitting next to her. He was walking along the platform. "He is so self-confident, so sure of himself." She reached into her pocket and felt the reassuring presence of the prayer book. "You can do this," she told herself.

Adjusting her belongings, attempting to show confidence she did not feel, she made her way through the cabin to the exit. As she paused on the landing, the smell of smoke, steam, coal, and oil bombarded her senses. The squeal of brakes from another arriving train startled her; she wanted to cover her ears, to run away. Crowds of people were disembarking from the train, everyone was in a hurry, everyone knew where to go, what to do. "Where is Peter?"

"Erzsi, here! Over here!" Peter was calling to her, waving frantically as he made his way through the crowd. Struggling to hold onto her belongings, she awkwardly rushed toward him, precariously balancing her load. Finally, dropping her belongings to the ground, she fell into his open arms.

"Peter! Oh Peter, I have missed you!"

He lifted her off the ground in a bear hug as he had when she was a child. "Welcome to Budapest!" They were both laughing, their faces displaying the pure joy of the moment.

When he finally put her down she stood back from him, admiring. "I have not seen you since Clara's wedding."

"Have I changed? I feel the same."

"Your clothes!" She looked approvingly at the waistcoat under his black coat, the bowler hat worn by working class men in the cities. "Will I embarrass you?" She adjusted her scarf and ran her hand down her apron.

"Never! You are perfect." He hugged her again.

Childhood friends, reunited, the pair walked to the entrance of the main terminal.

"Are you ready?" Peter pushed open the door and watched Erzsi's expression as she walked through the terminal building. Her eyes opened wide, she moved through the room trying to see everything at once.

The room was massive, ceilings higher than any of the buildings in Kosice, walls decorated with murals and tall pillars trimmed in gold. The floor was made of marble and there were too many ticket windows to count.

"OOH!" she inhaled, speechless. "I have never seen anything so beautiful."

"More wonders still to come."

"I will need to write Clara every detail."

He understood her reaction; he remembered the first time he came to Budapest, arriving at this station. The building was magnificent, the architecture like nothing he had ever seen. There were so many people crowded into one building. Some, with serious expressions, were hastily moving toward their destinations. Important work was waiting for them. Others, reunited with loved ones, were laughing and embracing. He had known on that first visit that he would make Budapest his home.

"This way," Peter pointed to a large wooden door. A beautiful fan-shaped window above the door let in rays of sunlight, beckoning the travelers to leave the terminal and enter the city.

"That exit will take us to the boulevard where we will catch the trolley."

When Peter opened the door, she was speechless. Before her was a vast plaza with gardens, statues, and walkways. A wide tree-lined boulevard filled with trolleys and carriages of every type bordered the park. Tall buildings stood shoulder to shoulder like soldiers in a parade. Pedestrians moved along the sidewalks passing storefronts with awnings to shelter them from the weather. A woman, a governess, Erzsi supposed, was pushing a child in an elaborate wicker pram while her other charges skipped ahead of her.

But it was the noise that caused her to pause, commanding her to listen. It was at once deafening and exciting, unlike anything she had ever heard before. The sound of construction, hammers pounding, men shouting, announced a dynamic city undergoing rapid growth. The squeal of brakes from a trolley mingled with the more familiar cacophony of hooves on stone and made it clear that this was a city where commerce flourished.

"I told you there were more wonders to see," Peter said, watching her expression as her eyes darted from one marvel to another.

A vendor pushing a cart with postcards stopped in front of them. "A postcard to send to a loved one?" he asked.

"You should send postcards to your sisters." Before Erzsi could respond Peter was giving the vendor money. "Send one to Iren and one to Clara. I'm sure they will be glad to hear you arrived safely in Budapest."

"These will be perfect," she said, selecting postcards showing photographs of the station and the boulevard. She stood on her toes giving him a sisterly kiss on the cheek. "Thank you, Peter."

They sat on a bench while Erzsi wrote on the back of the postcards. "She looks so fragile, so defenseless," Peter thought, watching her as she addressed the postcard. "What does she know about the world?" Erzsi stood, giving the postcards to the vendor. "I wish I could protect you," he thought. "It was easier when we were children and life was simple."

"Over there," he said picking up the bundles. "We want that trolley."

Laughing, they ran across the boulevard and boarded it just in time. Bells clanged as the trolley worked its way through the streets of Budapest. Holding the pole for support, feeling the gentle breeze on her face, Erzsi felt young and free and alive. Peter watched her, the smile, the flush in her cheeks, the sparkle in her eyes; this was the Erzsi he remembered. But despite her smile he could see that hard work and disappointments had aged her. There were tiny lines around her eyes that spoke of sadness; her hands were red and sore from endless toil. "Perhaps in America she will find happiness."

"Next stop is ours. Be ready." With a helping hand from Peter, Erzsi landed safely on the cobblestone street. They were on a tree-lined residential street with rows of neat apartment buildings painted in soft pastels.

"We are on the second floor of that building." Peter was pointing to a handsome tan stucco apartment building with a Dutch gambrel roof line, five stories high. "We were fortunate to get a flat. With the influx of laborers, housing is hard to come by. I have a friend with connections who found this place for us." Peter did not mention that he had been promoted to supervisor and his salary had greatly increased with his increasing responsibilities.

"So much nicer than the old wooden building that Clara lives in," Erzsi thought.

Reaching the landing on the second floor, the darkness of the staircase was broken by soft rays of sunlight filtering through a dusty window. Erzsi could smell chicken soup simmering on a stove, and she could hear the muffled sound of children laughing and playing. "The smells and sounds of home," she thought, wistfully.

"Construction dust," Peter commented, pointing to the window. "When the windows are clean, we can see the dome of St. Stephen's Basilica. At times it seems that the entire city is under construction."

Peter put down the bundles he was carrying and opened the door. Erzsi was stunned by the grandeur of the room she was about to enter. There were no beds in the room, only a comfortable couch, a plush chair, and a desk piled high with papers. A stove and a cabinet for storing dishes occupied the back wall of the room. There was a table big enough to accommodate the entire family, no one needed to sit on benches along a wall holding plates in their laps.

The room came alive with excitement when Peter's daughters saw him. "Daddy," four-year-old Dora ran to her father, throwing herself into his waiting arms. Two-year-old Jolàn, not to be left out, dropped her doll and ran as fast as her little legs could carry her. Within seconds Peter was holding them both, one girl on each hip, little arms wrapped around his neck. "Where is your mama? Where is Bernadette?"

"Here, we're here, Peter." Yolanda came out of the bedroom holding a blue ribbon that was meant to be a bow in her daughter's hair. Eight-year-old Bernadette followed proudly, a big smile on her face. Her cream-colored dress with a big blue sash around her waist was obviously new and she was expecting complimentary words from her father.

"Come in, come in," Yolanda said, draping the ribbon on a chair, her arms open to welcome Erzsi. "We are so happy you are here."

Bernadette's smile faded from her face, no one seemed to notice her new dress. Peter saw the change in her expression and gently lowered Dora and Jolàn to the floor. "Mama, is that our little Bernadette? She looks far too grown up to be our little girl." His brows were furrowed; a frown on his lips, but there was a twinkle in his eyes.

"Oh, Daddy, do you like my dress?" Bernadette said laughing while throwing her arms around her father's neck.

"You look beautiful, my princess," he said, giving her a hug and stroking her long auburn curls.

"There is so much love here," Erzsi thought, watching her cousin and his family. "Peter is a wonderful father." Again she felt the pang of her own loneliness. "I will have a family of my own someday," she reassured herself.

"Peter, bring Erzsi's bags into the girls' bedroom." Yolanda had taken control.

"You must be hungry," she said turning back to Erzsi. "I have made some soup, and cheese Kolash for dessert."

"I could smell the soup coming up the stairs, and the cheese Kolash will be a treat."

"But you need to get settled before you eat. Peter, bring her things to the girls' room. Bernadette, show her where she will be sleeping."

Bernadette took Erzsi's hand and together they walked to the tiny bedroom. The room had one large bed with a linen cover embroidered with rich colors of red, green, and blue and matching pillowcases. There was a child's doll resting on the pillows giving the bed an inviting look. The large feather comforter that kept the girls warm in the winter was stowed away for the summer in a wooden box in a corner of the room. Hooks on the walls held Sunday dresses and winter coats. "Peter must be doing well to provide all of this for his family." She was happy for her cousin. He was clever, handsome, and well-liked by everyone. Moving to the city had been the right thing for him to do.

"I sleep in here with my sisters. Tonight Jolàn will sleep with Mom and Dad, and you will sleep with me and Matilda."

Erzsi sat on the bed. "It is very kind of you to let me sleep here."

"It is nothing, Erszinéne," said Bernadette using the title of respect. "Jolàn kicks us during the night and sometimes cries, waking us up," she paused for a moment, looking intently at her aunt. "Mama says you are going to America." The little girl didn't know where America was but it must be very far away. "Papa is sad that you are going. He is afraid that he might never see you again."

"That makes me sad, too."

"You are very courageous, Erszinéne."

"Not so courageous, dear Bernadette."

"But you are leaving your family," the young girl frowned. To Bernadette leaving her family simply was not an option.

"It makes me sad to leave, but it is for the best."

"America is so far away. Aren't you afraid?"

"Yes, I am afraid," she paused for a moment. What should she say?

"I really have no choice, Bernadette. We need to follow the path God puts before us."

"How will I know what God's plan is for me?"

"What would you like it to be?"

"I would like to marry a man like Papa and have lots of children."

"Then I am sure that is what will happen." Erzsi stood and gave Bernadette a reassuring embrace. "With your sweet manner and beautiful face I am certain you will have no problem finding the perfect husband."

"I hope you are right, Erszinéne."

"I am. Now go. Help your mother."

Bernadette left the room and quietly closed the door. Erzsi found a much needed chamber pot. There was a wash basin on the dresser with a towel next to it. She smiled when she noticed it was her initials embroidered on the towel. The stitches were large and crooked, the work of a child. "It must be from Bernadette," she smiled.

She glanced in the mirror above the basin. Her face looked tired, her hair in disarray. She washed her face, combed her hair, and straightened her apron. "I wish I could take off these shoes!" But that wasn't a possibility. "What would Yolanda think if I came to the table without shoes?" She smiled at the thought of the shocked expressions at the table if she showed up in her stocking feet.

Now, she was ready. Her face was clean and her hair was pulled back in a tight bun with only a few ringlets escaping. With satisfaction, she looked at her reflection in the mirror. "You look fine!" She tilted her head from side to side checking out every angle. "What man wouldn't be happy to have me as a wife?"

Well, there was the issue of her nose not being as perfect as Iren's, and her curls would not stay properly in place, but her complexion was good. She admired her bodice, satisfied that her figure was inviting. With a smile she remembered the admiring glances from the man on the train. She felt a warmth course through her as she thought of the strong male body that had been so close to hers. With a bit of longing and regret she thought of Robert and the kisses they had shared. "Enough!" She carefully adjusted her skirt and joined the family for dinner.

She spent a week with Peter and his family. On Saturday afternoon they explored the city. The trolley took them past Saint Stephen's Basilica, the tallest building in Budapest, and the Hungarian Royal Opera House on Andrássy Street. Both were still under construction but their grandeur was already apparent.

They strolled along the Danube. The air was cool, but the midday sun was warm on her back. It was a Saturday, the sounds of hammers and men working were replaced by the laughter of children. Erzsi was happy, content being here with Peter and his family. Peter always made her feel safe. Even as a child he was always there to protect her. When she fell off Pista he carried her home; when she was frightened by a barking dog he calmed her fears.

Peter was leading the way along the promenade, little Jolàn perched proudly on his shoulders, Dora holding his hand. Bernadette, wearing her new dress, walked demurely between Yolanda and Erzsi.

Bernadette was filled with questions. "Do you have a river as big as this one in Kosice? Swans like those? Castles like the one on top of Castle Hill over there?" The questions came in rapid succession.

"Yes, we have a river in Kosice, but not one as grand as this. And we have many swans, as well as storks that build their nests in chimneys. Someday I will tell you the story of the beautiful Baroness who lived in the castle near my home." Wistfully, Erzsi looked back toward the distant hills in the north. "Home," she thought, "home is back there. It is not so far away."

Church bells could be heard in the distance. "The bells are coming from Matthias Church, over there." Bernadette was pointing to the hill on the other side of the Danube. The blue sky and dark green foliage of the trees provided the perfect setting for the church with its pale grey stones and richly colored diamond patterned roof tiles. The gargoyle-laden spires seemed to be striving to pierce the white clouds floating above.

"It was named after King Matthias, a great ruler of Hungary," Bernadette felt compelled to instruct Erzsi on history. "Kings were crowned there and Mama told me about the royal weddings." Erzsi imagined the processions with golden carriages, white horses, and soldiers dressed in perfectly tailored uniforms. Perhaps they passed by on this very street where throngs of their loyal subjects had gathered to wish them well.

"Shall we walk across?" Peter had turned to Yolanda. They were approaching the entrance to the Chain Bridge, the longest bridge in Europe.

"The children are getting tired," Yolanda interjected. "Walking to the landing in the middle of the bridge will be enough. The view is beautiful there."

Erzsi was relieved, not sure that crossing the bridge was something she wanted to do. She had been admiring the bridge as they approached, but its span across the Danube was so great she was hoping they would not need to walk all the way to the other side. The source of her trepidation was not the length of the bridge but its height and the strength of the current flowing beneath. She feared if the bridge collapsed she would be swept away, perhaps crushed on rocks beneath or carried out to sea. "I can't swim," she thought as she pictured herself falling into the cold water. As they got closer to the bridge and these thoughts had time to settle in her mind, her nervousness grew. Rational thoughts were not possible.

There was no way around the situation. Peter and the children had already reached the bridge. Dora, having let go of Erzsi's hand, was running ahead leading the way. The women followed at a more dignified pace. Yolanda was watching her children; she didn't notice that the color had drained from Erzsi's face.

The entrance to the bridge was guarded by massive stone lions crouched on their pedestals. To Erzsi, already tense from her fear of the bridge, it felt like the lions were looking down on her, ready to pounce if she should venture too close. Their mouths were slightly open, exposing powerful teeth ready to pierce her skin. She shuddered as she moved past them. "Legend has it that they have no tongues," Yolanda said. Erzsi decided the legend might be true as she looked up once more at the mouth of the stone lion near her.

More to her liking was the magnificent stone arch that boasted the Hungarian coat-of-arms. There was no doubt to whom this structure and the buildings beyond belonged.

With wobbly legs and moist palms, Erzsi continued to walk up the bridge, with each step she was moving further from solid ground. Nothing was beneath her except the water, currents seeming to move in all directions. She wanted to look out at the vista unfolding before her. The hills of Buda on one side of the Danube, Pest on the other, but she could only look at her feet, willing them to keep moving forward.

Finally they reached the landing in the center of the bridge. Looking down from this great height, the current flowing faster here, her breathing became heavy, her stomach queasy and her legs weak. Fear that the bridge would collapse, crumbling around her, consumed her. She would fall until her body crashed into the cold water of the Danube.

She watched a boat moving under the bridge. "How will I survive on a great ship in the middle of a vast ocean if I cannot manage this?" she asked herself. She turned away from the water, focusing her gaze on the hills of Buda on the other side of the Danube. She could see The Royal Castle with remnants of ancient fortifications that proclaimed the strength of the empire and the importance of the city through the ages. For a moment she forgot her fears as she marveled at the magnificence of the structure before her. "This is my heritage," she thought proudly, "my Hungarian heritage." To the right of the bridge she could see Matthias Church with its colorful roof and impressive spires standing proudly as a testament to the faith of the people. "I have my faith to give me strength," she whispered to herself her hand reaching for the prayer book in her pocket.

With relief Erzsi took Peter's arm and the family left the bridge and returned home.

As promised, Yolanda and Peter helped her make plans for the journey and her new life in America.

Yolanda gave her a letter of introduction to give to her friend in America.

Peter purchased tickets for a steamship leaving from Hamburg. He told her the ticket agents would advise her of available accommodations in Hamburg.

"When I am settled in America, I will return the money."

"Not a concern. Start your new life. Be happy."

"Peter, you and Yolanda are making it so easy for me."

"It will not be easy, Erzsi," Peter looked at her with concern. "You don't need to do this. You can stay with us and find employment in Budapest. You will be with family."

"No, I have made a decision. This is what I need to do. If it doesn't work out I can come home." In her heart she wanted to stay. She wanted to run home to Clara and Iren and the village where she had always lived. But the carefree life she had known as a child was gone.

She looked at Peter and Yolanda with a confidence she did not feel. "I will be all right. You mustn't worry."

"Be careful, Erzsi, don't be too trusting," her worried cousin advised.

"God will protect me." Peter knew this might not be enough, but he didn't want to frighten her. He simply gave her a hug.

The morning she was leaving, Yolanda took Erzsi's basket from the shelf where it had been stored and filled it with bread, cheese, sausage, preserved pears, and a Kolash, this time with a poppy seed filling.

"How will I ever be able to repay your kindness?" Erzsi said, taking the basket.

Knowing the tears would start if she lingered, she gave Yolanda and the girls a final kiss. She lifted Jolàn, "Oh, sweet baby, will I ever see you again?"

"Erszinéne, you will come back to visit us," Bernadette said with confidence.

"If God wills it, but I can promise that I will write."

"Erzsi, it is time to go," Peter was ready, waiting at the door.

"You have the letter for Adel?" Yolanda, a mother of three children, considered it her responsibility to be sure everything was in order. "It has the address of the Rondout Boarding House. I have written to her, so she will be expecting you."

Peter and Erzsi made their way to the train station. This time there was silence between them. Peter was worried. She would be so far away; he would not be able to protect her.

Erzsi was building her courage to face the moment she would say good-bye to her dearest friend.

They entered the station. Erzsi found a seat on a bench and watched as Peter waited in the long line at the ticket counter. He had grown older; streaks of grey hair were visible when he was not wearing his hat. But he was still tall and lean like the boy she remembered. She struggled to conceal the sadness that she felt, anticipating the loneliness that would be hers.

"Here are your tickets." She looked up to see Peter, looking concerned, staring down at her. "Are you all right?"

"Yes, yes, fine. I was just thinking how much I am going to miss everyone." Peter sat next to her holding her hand. "Peter, I am all right, truly." She reached out for the tickets in his hand.

"Your first stop will be Vienna where you will change trains to Prague. You will catch another train, making one more stop before reaching Hamburg. If you have concerns, just talk with the conductor. You will sleep on the trains. In Hamburg there will be people to help you. Here are the tickets for the steamship *Closinda.*"

"I understand." There was so much she wanted to say but the words wouldn't come.

They could feel the rumble of a train entering the station. The whistle blew; even in the terminal they could smell the smoke rising from the locomotive. Her heart raced, her palms were moist, but her face was set, determined, and strong. Together they walked to the boarding platform. Peter boarded the train with her, carrying everything except the basket and the pillow. When she was settled, surrounded by her sack of clothes, the basket and the pillow in her lap, she smiled up at Peter.

"Thank you."

The train whistle blew; Peter kissed her one last time.

In an instant he was gone and she was alone.

7 Gypsies and Such

Budapest to Prague
May, 1882

Erzsi felt fortunate. The third class cabin was crowded, stuffy, a musty odor predominated, but she was sitting by a window. Nearly all the passengers had boarded and the seat next to her was still empty. "Perhaps I will have room to spread out and maybe even take off my shoes," she smiled at the thought of the small luxury.

The conductor was about to close the door when a portly old woman, with little concern for others, pushed her way into the cabin. With difficulty she stepped around the feather quilts, pillows, and other baggage that littered the floor. A crate with a scrawny red and white chicken swung at her side, bumping anyone who was in her way. A pungent odor filled the space around her.

With a groan she lowered her massive body into the seat next to Erzsi. The folds of her skirt, the smell from the dirty cage, and the woman's corpulent body intruded into Erzsi's already limited space. Erzsi tried to pull her own skirts out of the way but she was too late. They were firmly anchored beneath the woman's leg. Annoyed, Erzsi moved closer to the window. Her belongings were on the floor in front of her; there was no room left to stretch her legs or reach her shoes. "They will be staying on," she sighed, trying to wiggle her toes inside the shoes. With difficulty she opened the window, thankful for the air and the illusion of open space.

With grunts, moans, and deep sighs the woman finally settled into her seat. She spoke to the clucking chicken in soft reassuring tones. "Hush now, my sweet, we will be home soon." Moments later Erzsi heard a snore that rivaled those from Viktor. Reluctant to turn from the open window, curiosity prevailed. She glanced in the woman's direction.

The chicken crate was precariously balanced on the woman's lap. Her legs akimbo blocking the aisle, her eyes closed, now from her toothless mouth came a soft rhythmic whistle. As Erzsi watched with dismay, the woman's body became limp. Her head fell to the side landing on Erzsi's shoulder. With a sigh of resignation Erzsi accepted her fate. "Pleasant dreams, old woman."

Just then the train jerked forward, the whistle blew. The startled chicken began to cackle and flutter in fear. To Erzsi's astonishment the woman continued to snore while feathers flew in every direction.

Erzsi silently brushed away the feathers that had landed on her pillow. "They are only feathers," she consoled herself, "be patient."

Heavy breathing, a snort, a loud sneeze and the feathers were everywhere again. The woman shook her head, opened her eyes and sneezed.

Erzsi, no longer feeling tolerant, glared at her. Feathers were everywhere, on top of the crate, on the woman's ample bosom, and between the folds of their skirts. With a frown that made her annoyance obvious, Erzsi brushed the feathers from her skirt.

"Don't you like chickens?" the toothless woman said while ignoring the feathers and smiling at Erzsi.

"Yes, but," Erzsi again pointed to her pillow and the feathers on her skirt.

"Isn't she beautiful? She lays good eggs."

"Yes, very beautiful," Erzsi gave up. She brushed the remaining feathers from her skirt and pressed even closer to the window. She sighed in acquiescence when the woman simply expanded into the space, moving closer to her.

Wistfully she thought of the man who had been next to her on the train from Kosice. She hadn't minded the confined space, the way his body brushed against hers. The smell of his cigar lingered on his clothes, reminding her of her father. "I wonder where he is now."

The train moved steadily toward its destination. "Vienna, imagine that!" She tried to picture the city. "Will the station be as beautiful as the one in Budapest?" She no longer felt overwhelmed by what she anticipated would be a magnificent building. "I will send postcards to Iren and Clara." The thought was comforting, a connection to her sisters, to her home. "Vienna!" She settled back against the hard wooden seat. "Someday I will share all of this with my children and my grandchildren."

Sitting quietly, the old woman's head resting on her shoulder, Erzsi had time to reflect on where she had been and where she was going. With Peter's help, arrangements for her trip had been made. Tickets were safely tucked in her pocket next to the letter of introduction Yolanda had given her. "At least I will have a safe place to stay." The thought was comforting.

Reflexively she reached into her pocket. "Just checking," she reassured herself. It was all there, the tickets, the money, and the letter. Her fingers lingered on the prayer book. "I will be fine." Her eyes closed, she yielded to the rhythmic motion of the train and fell asleep.

The train whistle blew. She was jolted awake, startled, pulled abruptly from her dream of home. The locomotive slowed as they approached the station. A sign, VIENNA, announced that they had reached their destination.

"No one will be here to greet me. I am on my own." She took a deep breath. "I can do this." Lifting her belongings, she waited for the chicken lady to vacate her seat. "I have tickets, money, and a destination. Everything I need." She reached once again into her pocket, everything was there.

Walking with confidence, she followed the other passengers to the entrance of the terminal. She was an experienced traveler now. Instead of being overwhelmed by the enormity of the building or the crush of people moving toward their destinations, she felt elation. She was self-reliant, capable. "I am in Vienna, on my way to America."

Entering the terminal, her confidence evaporated. She looked around, trying to determine where to wait for her train. The signs were in German, everyone around her was speaking German. She placed her bags on the floor to retrieve her tickets, perhaps a policeman would be able to show her where to go.

A woman, dressed in rags, speaking a language Erzsi did not understand, was suddenly in front of her. With tears in her eyes, her arms outstretched, the woman was trying to place a baby into Erzsi's arms. "No," Erzsi backed away. "No, I can't take your baby!" The woman grabbed Erzsi's arm and pulled her towards the baby. Other children surrounded her, she didn't know how many, she could feel them tugging on her skirt. Erzsi felt uneasy. She wanted to back away from this strange lady and her children but she was trapped. She didn't want to be rude. Something wasn't right. It was all happening so fast. The woman was tightly holding her arm. The children were tugging at her skirts. The baby began to cry. The woman drew her even closer, pleading. Erzsi could feel the heat from the woman's body, the tightness of her grasp on her arm. "NO!" Her heart was racing, there was no escape.

"*Stoppen*! Halt!" a policeman was running towards them. A crowd started to form, curious spectators. The woman and her children vanished. Erzsi couldn't move, her eyes were wide with shock, confusion, and embarrassment.

What had happened? She looked at the policeman. He pointed to her pocket. Her money, still wrapped in the cloth, was visible, no longer tucked deep in her pocket. She turned pale, as she began to understand.

The policeman looked angry, scolding her in German. She didn't understand but nodded *"Ja! Ja!"* He took the ticket she was holding. "*Dieserweg*, over there," he pointed to the gate she needed.

"Danka, thank you," her voice was soft, almost a whisper. Her hands were shaking, her palms moist as he handed the tickets back to her.

The crowd dispersed, the excitement was over. Erzsi, still shaken, picked up her bags and walked slowly to the gate. She was early. A washroom was close. Splashing cold water on her face, she thought about what had happened. "The money, I need to protect the little money I have." She took the money from her pocket tucking it inside her dress. "The pocket is too obvious; let them try to get it out of here." She smiled, touching her bosom.

Leaving the washroom she settled down on a bench. She continued to think about the beggars. "Why me? Because I was alone? Because I looked vulnerable?" She visualized again what had happened. "How could the situation have been avoided?" There were no easy answers. "I am alone, but I don't need to be a victim." She felt the money that was now tucked inside her undergarments.

She studied the train tickets, verifying again that she would travel through the night arriving in Prague just before dawn. From there she would change trains one more time, arriving in Hamburg in the afternoon. "I am all right," she reassured herself again. "I have my tickets, my money is safe." She reached into her pocket and touched the prayer book, drawing strength from the familiar object, a link to her family, to her past.

When she boarded the train to Prague, there were no window seats available, but she did manage to find a seat next to a young woman about her own age. Erzsi stretched out in the seat, preparing to settle in for the long ride. She reached down, finally able to take off her shoes. She wiggled her toes in relief. The woman next to her moved aside the blanket that was covering her legs. Her toes were also free of the confines of her shoes. The women laughed and instantly became friends.

8 Port of Departure

Hamburg, Germany
June, 1882

The sky was still dark when the train from Vienna stopped briefly at the small station in the outskirts of Prague. Passengers, who had reached their destination, or like Erzsi, were changing trains, prepared to debark. Children were gently nudged awake, an infant cried.

Moving quietly, not wanting to disturb the woman sleeping next to her, Erzsi attempted to make herself presentable. She adjusted her scarf, brushed the curls off her face, and wiped bread crumbs from her skirt. With an inaudible groan, she forced her swollen feet into her shoes.

Still sleepy, she stepped carefully over the boxes and bags, which littered the space around the benches. Moving around a large trunk her foot landed on something that moved. She struggled to maintain her balance; the weight on her back had shifted. A loud unintelligible mumble told her she had stumbled on a person sleeping on the floor. She pulled back, tried unsuccessfully to regain her balance and landed in the lap of a startled old man.

"So sorry," she said her face crimson with embarrassment. In her attempt to stand, her hand had found his knee. He gave her a big smile. His tobacco stained teeth and foul breath gave her the strength she needed to get back up. "So sorry," she said again turning to him one last time before she hurried off the train.

The uncovered platform, dimly lit with a few scattered lamps, was nearly deserted. Passengers debarking from the train either disappeared into the darkness or settled on the wooden benches waiting for their connecting trains.

There was a chill in the night air. A family huddled close together, the mother expanding her shawl to envelop her children. A little girl slept in her father's arms, her head resting on his shoulder. A man, head lowered, an unlit cigar in his hand, nodded his head as he slept.

Erzsi headed toward the terminal to find a washroom. A single ticket agent sat in his booth, his cap pulled over his eyes, his legs comfortably resting on a wooden crate. "Excuse me," Erzsi said. There was no response from the man. "Washroom?" her voice was louder. "*Waschraum?*" she tried using her limited knowledge of German. Head still bent, eyes closed beneath his cap, he slowly raised his arm and pointed. No sound was uttered.

"*Danke,*" she said curtly, and left him to his slumber.

Finished with the washroom, she heartily drank her fill from the water pump next to the platform. Finally, settled on a bench, she took out the last slice of sausage. Eating slowly, making it last, she thought about the people she had met on this journey. A blush formed on her face thinking of the man on the train who had aroused her body as he sat close to her. "Will I find someone to love in America? Will I find a husband?" She thought about how he might look. "He must be strong. Dark hair and blue eyes would be nice. He will need to be a good father to our children."

There were others who she would remember in her prayers. The old woman, with her wide toothless grin, content with her chicken and the "good eggs" that were provided. "Sweet Jesus, protect that woman."

The image of the beggar woman, her tears, her ragged, hungry children who needed to steal for food, filled her with sadness. "Please dear Savior, help that woman, help her children. She is desperate, her children are starving. In your mercy forgive her."

Except for an occasional snore and the cry of a baby, the dimly lit platform was quiet. "I'll just rest for a minute," she whispered to no one as she leaned her head against the wall behind the bench. Her eyes closed, her breathing deepened, she was in her old bed sleeping with Clara. A train whistle blew, the platform rumbled, she jumped, dropping the basket and pillow she had been clutching in her lap. The train that would take her to Hamburg was pulling into the station.

It was afternoon when the train arrived in Hamburg. A letter from Robert, dimly remembered, had not fully prepared her for the throngs of emigrants she would encounter.

Hamburg, Germany
March 12, 1876

Dear Erzsi,

I arrived in Hamburg this afternoon. I have never seen so many people in one place. Many languages are spoken, some I recognize, German, Hungarian, Slovak, Polish. It sounded like market day in Kosice. A photographer took a photograph of emigrants outside the train station. The photograph was in the newspaper the next day. I am sending you the picture. You can see me standing right in the middle. I was unprepared for the cold and damp air that morning. I envied the women wrapped in winter scarves, heavy shawls, and winter coats buttoned tight against the cold.I asked the photographer why he took a photograph of such a humble group. He said he was struck by the faces. Excitement, sadness, determination, wariness, each face told a story. Everyone was tired. You could see it in their faces. Many have been traveling for weeks, on foot, on the rivers, or, like me on the newly built railroads. I will be in Hamburg for a few days before boarding my ship.
My next letter will be from New York.

Yours Forever,
Robert

Hamburg officials, with German efficiency, had a system for organizing and assisting the emigrants. Men and women, some who looked like volunteers, others wearing clothing that identified them as employees of steamship companies, were ready to help the throngs arriving on the trains.

"May I help you?" A neatly dressed man, speaking perfect Hungarian, approached her. With surprise and relief she saw his badge.

Hamburg-Amerika Linie
Magyar Volunteer

"Welcome to Hamburg. I am here to assist emigrants from Hungary."

"I am traveling on the *Closinda.*" She showed him her ticket.

Putting on his spectacles he consulted an official looking notebook. "The *Closinda* is scheduled to leave tomorrow afternoon." He flipped some pages. "You will need to be at the dock at 8:00 AM for processing. Boarding for steerage passengers will be at 10:00 AM. Do you have lodging for tonight?"

"No."

"The agent at the Hamburg-Amerika Linie desk can direct you to suitable housing." He pointed to a row of desks, each occupied by an agent from a different steamship line. "You can see the sign for Hamburg-Amerika Linie?"

"Yes, thank you."

"Can you help us?" A man holding a small child was walking rapidly towards them. "My son is not well."

"Certainly." The volunteer was now focused on the man with the child.

Before joining the long line at the agent's desk she stopped at the canteen. "I'll buy some fruit, maybe some postcards."

She purchased an apple, some crackers, and three postcards. For Clara she selected one with soft colors and a pleasing view of the Elbe River. The one with a picture of a transatlantic steamer with the Hamburg-Amerika Linie logo emblazoned across the top would be for Iren. For Peter, a picture of massive warehouses lining one of the many canals found in the city. Purchases made, washroom visit done, she was ready to join the line at the agent's desk.

"Excuse me, Miss," a tall man, with a rugged face and scruffy beard was standing in front of her, blocking her path. Erzsi backed away. He was standing too close.

"I run a boarding house for Hungarian emigrants." He was speaking Hungarian. Erzsi relaxed a little hearing the words spoken in her native language, but she was still wary of this stranger.

"The agent will help me find suitable lodging." Her voice was strong, steady, not reflecting the unease she was feeling. She started to walk away, she didn't like him. He had a foul smell about him.

"Be wary," the man called after her. "The agent will cheat you." She stopped, looked back, hesitating. "He will send you to his friends," he said softly, shaking his head sadly.

He walked up to her. "Miss, I am trying to help you." His voice was polite, sympathetic. "My family is from Hungary. My dear mother, rest her soul, is buried here, far from her home." He made the sign of the cross and lowered his head respectfully while saying this. "I understand how difficult it is to make this journey." He managed to look sincere as he tried to create a bond between them. "The agent will charge you three Marks for a crowded, dirty room. I will charge you only two Marks."

She wavered, thinking of the money tucked inside her dress. There wasn't very much, she needed to be frugal. She bit her nail, wondering what to do. He saw her vulnerability. "All right," he said with a sigh of acquiescence. "For you, for a fellow Hungarian, I will charge 1 Mark and 50 Pfennig."

She turned to look at the agent at his desk. There was a long line. She was tired. Could she trust the agent? Could she trust this man? He spoke Hungarian. His family was here. He obviously loved his dear mother and he practiced his faith. "All right, go with the agent." He shook his head as if to say I tried to help you. Looking defeated he slowly turned away from her. "I have others waiting to leave," he pointed to a family sitting on a bench near the exit.

She watched him go. He approached another family, a husband and a wife with what appeared to be an infant in her arms. She watched as the husband argued with the man, presumably about the price. Finally the wife warily reached into her bag retrieving some money. The husband shook hands with the man. Everyone was smiling now; a satisfactory arrangement had been made. Now there were two families on the bench waiting for the ride to the lodging.

"Am I being foolish?" she thought about the money in her dress. "There are two other families going with him." She looked at the families on the bench. The men looked strong, capable, the women friendly. "I will be safe." She ran after him. "Yes, yes, I will go with you."

"Good. One Mark and seventy-five Pfennigs." He held out his hand, no longer making an effort to be pleasant.

"But you said…"

"That is the price."

"I only have Hungarian currency." She held out some of her money, her hand shaking. He took what he wanted.

"Wait with the others on that bench," he said, pointing to the families.

When it was time to board the wagon, the family with the infant was not there. Erzsi's face turned red as she realized she had been tricked. "I have so much to learn," she thought. She had never before encountered such evil. Even Viktor would not have done something like this.

Everyone was quiet in the wagon as it bounced over the cobblestone streets. The woman looked apprehensive as she held her child. The husband gave her a reassuring smile. To distract his son, he pointed to a barge moving through a canal. "That boat is headed for the Elbe River. Our ship is waiting for us there."

They watched as a crate hanging from a rope, was slowly lifted from a barge. The boy's eyes widened as the crate disappeared in an opening on the sixth story of the warehouse. Erzsi understood the wonder on the boy's face. "If he is from a small village like mine he has never seen a building so large."

Erzsi's heart sank when the wagon stopped in front of a rundown wooden building. The air was heavy with smoke, the sound of machinery was oppressive, the horn from a ship could be heard in the distance. Sailors and workman were shouting obscenities, a drunk nearly fell into their wagon. Women, in less than modest clothing, were smoking cigarettes and leaning against a building.

"*Ausschalten*, off," said the man, giving his brusque command in German, Hungarian forgotten.

"*Siewohnenhier*, you will stay here."

The husband moved toward him, his face angry. His wife reached for his arm, "No, István." His face red, his muscles taught, he fought for control. "Help us down, István, it is only for one night."

The mother, holding her children close, the father balancing a heavy trunk on his shoulder, walked toward the building. No one helped Erzsi as she lowered herself from the wagon. With her belongings firmly held, her face stoic, she followed the family moving towards the building.

The emigrants, tired, hesitant, entered the large open dormitory. István entered the room first, prepared to protect his family. The mother pulled her children back, tightening her grip on the little ones. Erzsi stood behind them, her eyes for the first time showing fear.

The smell of urine, cabbage soup, smoke, and mildew stung their eyes. People were everywhere, sprawled on bunks, sitting around the tables, children were playing on the dirty floor. Bunk beds, with flimsy mattresses, were stacked one on top of another. Men playing cards and smoking cigars sat at wooden tables that spanned the length of the room. The bare wooden floor was littered with crates, trunks, sacks, and the contents of a box that had spilled unnoticed by its owner.

Erzsi could feel the moisture on the palms of her hands as she walked into the crowded room. Unprotected, vulnerable, she clutched her pillow tighter. Her nails pinched her hand as she squeezed the handle of the basket.

No one greeted them when they entered the room or told them where to go. It was obvious they were to fend for themselves. István swore quietly, condemning the man to hell who had taken them to this place. He guided his family to bunks that appeared to be unoccupied. Erzsi was left standing alone.

Four young men, standing on the opposite side of the room, noticed her. One, more brazen than the others, winked at her, tipped his hat, and mockingly bowed. His friends laughed at his boldness. She lowered her eyes, just enough to show indifference, but felt his mocking gaze. A shiver ran down her back, a warning. She had never experienced such a strong suggestion of evil intent. With retreat impossible, she walked into the room, ignoring the men and their laughter.

She passed a family, a mother on a lower bunk, feeding her infant while two little boys were on the floor at her feet playing marbles. On the bunk above her, a man, possibly her husband, was snoring. The woman smiled weakly at her as she walked past. Erzsi smiled back, envious of the woman who was with her family.

An old woman was sleeping on the next bunk but the one above her was empty. "Perfect!" Erzsi glanced at the woman with the children and pointed to the bunk. The woman nodded "Yes."

Erzsi glanced furtively in the direction of the young men. They were still watching her. The upper bunk promised refuge.

Throwing the cloth bag up into the bunk, she claimed the premium space. She felt the gaze and heard the taunts of the men as she awkwardly struggled up the ladder, hampered by her skirts and the heavy weight on her back.

Reaching the bunk she sat still, hugging her pillow, calming her fears. "They are rude for sure, but harmless," she tried, unsuccessfully, to reassure herself. This time she didn't try to stop the tears. She let them roll down her cheek onto the pillow. "Why did I come here?" Her shoulders shook in quiet sobs as she thought of home. It had been difficult at Iren's but she had never felt this afraid.

Eventually the fear subsided and the tears stopped. "You can't sit like this all night," she chastised herself. "Get busy, get organized. Nothing is gained by feeling sorry for one's self." She reached in her pocket and stroked the tiny book. The letter Yolanda had given her was still there as well as her tickets for the steamship. Her money was still safely tucked inside her dress. "I have everything I need."

Following the example of others she hung the cloth bag from a wood beam above her bunk. She took off her shoes but decided to keep them close. There were boots and shoes hanging from the rafters above other bunks but she would keep her shoes near. They could be used as a weapon if needed in the night.

She fluffed her pillow, spread open the blanket, and stored the winter clothes in a neat pile at the foot of her bunk. Suddenly she was hungry. There was an apple in her basket, crackers she had bought in the canteen. That would suffice.

While she ate she listened to the little boys in the bunk next to hers.

"We are going to America!" the older boy informed his brother.

"No we are NOT! We are going to New York," the younger brother said with defiant authority.

"We are going to New York, which is in America," interjected their father as he tried to settle the boys in the crowded bunk.

"See, I was right!"

"I was right!"

"Enough now. Tomorrow we will be on the ship. Now you need to sleep."

Erzsi finished her apple and crackers and settled back on her pillow. She had planned to stay awake but it wasn't long before her eyes grew heavy and she drifted into a restless sleep.

Voices, angry voices, men arguing, made their way into her dream. Erzsi pulled the blanket over her head, snuggled deeper into her pillow. Straw from the mattress poked her leg, reluctantly she changed her position.

"Robi, Pali," a woman was calling for her children. "Robi, Pali, come here now!"

The noise around her made it impossible to sleep. She could hear the boys laughing. "Probably wrestling, like Iren's sons," she thought. A tin cup clanged against a pot. The smell of coffee, someone had used the stove in the corner of the room.

She urgently needed to leave the relative safety of the bunk to use the washroom. Were the men who had leered at her last night still there? She pulled her blanket up around her chin. "The washroom, Erzsi, you need the washroom," she scolded herself. "You cannot hide in this bunk forever."

Reluctantly she forced her feet into her shoes. With a tug, the bag Clara had given her fell from the rafters. Quickly rolling up the blanket, she picked up the winter clothes. She needed to change into the heavy traveling clothes but undressing in the exposed bunk was simply not an option. "The washroom, Erzsi, hurry already."

Putting her hands inside her dress, she was satisfied that her money was still secure. The tickets, Yolanda's letter, and the prayer book were still in her pocket. Her fingers lingered on the prayer book, "Lord Jesus, Holy Mary, protect me." Inhaling deeply, she cautiously climbed down the ladder.

The family that had occupied the bunks next to hers were sitting around a table. Erzsi could see steam coming from mugs of coffee. The boys she had heard earlier were quiet now, their mouths full of bread, tin mugs in their hands.

"*Jó reggelt*, Good morning," the mother, her infant asleep in her arms, smiled at Erzsi.

"*Jó reggelt*," Erzsi was pleased that the woman had greeted her in Hungarian.

The door to the room slammed open. The men she had seen the night before were staggering into the room. One had his arm around the waist of a woman whose breasts were exposed over her low cut blouse. He stopped to kiss the heaving mounds of flesh. The others laughed, swaying, holding on to each other for support. The woman kissed him back touching parts of his body that Erzsi never thought a woman would touch. The raucous laughter increased. Erzsi turned away, her face crimson; glad she would not need to pass the men to reach the relative safety of the washroom.

There was little privacy in the small dirty washroom. A washbasin, a dirty lavatory, a mirror, and a small table were all that was available to the women using the room. Erzsi squeezed herself into a corner, quickly changing from her summer dress into her heavy traveling clothes. Robert had written about the damp, cold weather he had experienced while crossing the North Sea. The heavy wool dress would protect her.

In an attempt to subdue her unruly hair she pulled it tightly to the back of her head, tying it into a bun. A few stubborn ringlets fell onto her neck and around her face. With the addition of the scarf tied neatly under her chin, she was ready.

As she walked out of the washroom a new worry surfaced. "How do I get to the dock where the *Closinda* is berthed? I need to be there by 8:00 AM." Once again she realized how foolish she had been not to go to the agent's desk in the railroad station as she had been instructed.

The door of the boarding house opened, an agent of the Hamburg-Amerika Linie entered the room. He was carrying a sign:

**_Closinda_ Passengers
The departure of the _Closinda_
has been delayed by a week.
New Departure Date June 9, 1882**

The notice was in German but Erzsi could make out the date, it was not the same as her ticket.

"*Elnezést*, excuse me," her voice was anxious. "June 2," she said pointing to the date on her ticket.

"*Nicht.*" He took the ticket, corrected the date, turned away from her to change the dates on other tickets.

"Seven more nights in this place," she shivered as she reclaimed her bunk.

The room which had been cool during the night grew warmer as the day went on. It soon became apparent that the wool dress was no longer needed. A more immediate concern was food. She was afraid to leave the lodging, deceivingly called a hotel. "Whatever is out there might be more dangerous than here," she thought. She planned to stay close to the family in the bunks next to hers.

Eventually she was able to purchase food from vendors but she was quickly running out of money. She made friends with the family who occupied the bunks next to hers.

The woman, whose name was Amalia, prepared coffee every morning, and invited Erzsi to join them. After the children were fed the women would talk. They talked about the loved ones they had left behind, their plans for their new life in America.

The room was large but claustrophobic with so many bodies crammed into the space. The smell from the filthy lavatory and unwashed bodies was oppressive. It was inevitable that Erzsi would eventually feel the need to escape.

"Just a little air," she thought while walking to the door. "I won't go far." She was walking with a determined step, almost to the door when it happened. A man grabbed her from behind. Strong hands squeezed her breasts, cutting into her ribs. Her feet were floating in the air. She was kicking, screaming, her arms flailing, but she was unable to break free. She was moving through space, her body no longer in her control.

"That a boy, Karl," she heard a male voice jeering.

"She needs a man, traveling alone and all," said another.

"Maybe more than one," said another voice, this one ugly, threatening, evil.

She had never been so frightened.

Suddenly she was sprawled on the floor. She had landed hard when the man holding her had let go. Everything hurt, her face, her body, it was difficult to breathe. She was disoriented, confused, everything was happening so quickly.

There was noise all around her, shattering screams, children crying, male voices shouting. Punches, flesh hitting flesh, the smell of blood, a loud thud, a table had turned over. Erzsi, still sprawled on the floor, protected her head with her arms. She was crying, sobbing in pain and confusion. "Who had done this to her? Why?"

And then it was over. The room was silent. Strong arms lifted her gently. She was in a bunk; Amalia was wiping her face with a towel. "They are gone," Amalia whispered gently. "It is over, you are safe."

Book 2

The Voyage

9 The *Closinda*

Hamburg, Germany
June, 1882

The morning was cold and damp, the harbor obscured by a dense fog. Erzsi pulled her shawl tighter against the bone-chilling dampness. Amalia stood near her, comforting the baby she held in her arms. The boys, restless as always, were firmly under the control of their father. Amalia's mother was sitting on the only bench, fingering a wooden rosary, her mouth moving in silent prayer. They were waiting for the tram that would take them to the ship. Erzsi looked back at the lodging one last time. She wanted to forget what had happened there, what might have happened. She would never share this secret with her sisters or with Peter.

"It's over now," Amalia whispered, watching Erzsi's expression.

"I know," Erzsi said softly, a sad smile on her face.

Amalia's husband, along with other decent men, had come to her rescue on that awful day. He had been injured in the fight, his hand cut with a knife. Now, Erzsi looked at his bandaged hand with sadness, she would never be able to repay his kindness. She was filled with guilt, embarrassment and shame. "Did I encourage them?" she had asked Amalia.

"You did nothing wrong," Amalia said, trying to comfort her friend.

Nothing helped. She had stayed in her bunk for days, nursing her sore ribs and her shattered self-confidence. Amalia brought her food, but she wasn't hungry. She thought about going home.

Slowly Erzsi began to heal. She sipped tea and managed to eat some stale bread. Holding Amalia's baby helped her break through the melancholy and regain her strength. When the baby returned a smile, Erzsi was comforted. Her resolve and inner strength started to return. Lessons had been learned. Knowing the dangers, she would now be prepared. Amalia's husband gave her a small knife. "Jesus, Mary, and Joseph, protect me," she prayed as she placed the knife in her pocket.

The tram arrived. Erzsi found a seat next to Amalia. With the clang of a bell the tram began to move. The little boys were bursting with excitement while the adults were quiet, reflecting on what was to come.

The tram stopped to pick up a family who had stayed at another hotel. They were a noisy bunch, a husband who seemed preoccupied with his own thoughts while his wife settled their five restless children. They were pretty, dark-eyed children, "But oh, how dirty they are," thought Erzsi. She instantly regretted the thought. The poor mother must have been hard-pressed to manage her children, let alone keep them clean on their journey to Hamburg. Like many others, they may have traveled a long distance and suffered unthinkable hardships just to get this far.

Eventually the fog started to lift, revealing a panorama of industrious activity. Amalia's boys stood on the benches in the tram, their eyes wide with amazement. Large cranes were loading and unloading the transatlantic steamships, while smoke billowed from others, signaling their impending departure. Handling tenders were moving up and down the river guiding ships in and out of the harbor, while an older, but still majestic, sailing ship could be seen moving down the Elbe River headed for the North Sea. Erzsi had never seen a river like this or ships so big. She felt small, insignificant. "How will I ever be able to explain all of this to Iren and Clara?" Without conscious thought her hand had reached into her pocket and she was clutching the prayer book. The prayer book, her link to her home and to the life she was leaving.

Erzsi held her breath as they approached the dock where the *Closinda*, the ship that would take her across the Atlantic Ocean, was waiting.

"Look Daddy, is that our ship?" Amalia's boys were pointing to the *Closinda*. The vessel was majestic with its graceful lines, long black hull, tall masts rigged for sail, and the large black and white stack that stood between them.

Instantly all the children on the tram, filled with excitement, were fighting each other for the most advantageous spot on the bench from which to see the ship. The adults were more subdued and reflective as they viewed the vessel that would be their home for the next two weeks. Amalia's mother worried, not for the first time, that the ship might sink in the mighty ocean. She could not even imagine what a great ocean might look like. Fear of the unknown, fear of drowning, had filled her thoughts since she first learned the family was going to America. Now, seeing the ship, she was sure her fears would be realized. Amalia worried about caring for her children, would they get sick? Would there be enough food? Her husband thought of the hardships of the journey, wondering if he had done the right thing for his family.

"*Wir sin dhier*, we are here," the driver informed them as he stopped the tram. "*Gehen sie es*, go there," he said pointing to a large brick building with the words Hamburg-Amerika Linie in large letters above the door.

As they entered the building their tickets were checked. Erzsi was directed to a line with other single women. Families were in another line, single men in still another. Erzsi glanced over at the long line of men all in dark somber clothing. One, carrying a cardboard suitcase, looked familiar, but she could not see his face.

There was an agent of the shipping company at the desk. He was asking questions of each woman in the line and recording the information in a ledger.

"Name?" he asked without looking up.

"Erzsi Viarka," she replied meekly.

"Age?" his tone was distracted, indifferent.

"Twenty-five."

"Occupation?"

"Servant."

"Nationality?"

"Magyar."

"What is your destination?" She handed him the letter from Yolanda.

A few more questions, he stamped her ticket, and pointed dismissively to another line. "Medical examination," he offered, seeing her questioning frown.

Dutifully, quietly, fearful that she might be turned away, Erzsi joined the line of women. She shivered, wondering exactly what would happen in the room she was about to enter.

A man dressed in a somber black suit, probably the doctor, was gruffly inspecting a young woman's throat. Erzsi cringed at the thought of this man touching her, looking at her in that unemotional, clinical manner. She had only known the caring touch of the village midwife or her family when she was ill. Her body tensed when, without a word, his cold hands touched her face, her eyes. When he tried to open the lids of her eyes they reflexively clamped shut. Her cheeks flushed with embarrassment knowing she was being difficult.

"*Öffnen*, open!" he commanded, making a perfunctory effort to peer under her lid.

"*Husten*, cough."

She obeyed.

"*Öffnen*, open!" He examined her mouth and throat.

A woman, in a crisp white uniform, took her measurements. "Five foot, two inches," the measurements were recorded.

She was told to roll up her sleeve, the vaccination was next. She watched with horror as the large needle was inserted into the arm of the woman in front of her. "How can anyone do that? I would faint." She closed her eyes, unable to watch when the needle was plunged into her arm. The inspection card was stamped and marked vaccinated. With a sigh of relief, Erzsi rolled down her sleeve, the examination was over.

Walking onto the dock she squinted, temporarily blinded by the bright sunshine. The warmth of the sun enveloped her body. Unfamiliar sounds, the screech of gulls, clanging of machinery, the lapping of water against the pier, reminded her she was far from home. Everything was strange, unsettling. The smell of low tide and rotting fish, accompanied by anxiety, caused her stomach to churn. "How will I survive an ocean voyage, if I am sick before I even board the ship?"

One hundred women filled the small space. Even in the open air the smell from bodies that had not been properly washed in days was oppressive. Erzsi felt a trickle of moisture forming on her face and neck. She regretted that she had changed into her woolen dress and coat.

A sailor from the upper decks called to the crew on the dock. A rope that had blocked the gangplank was removed and officers of the ship stood at attention to welcome the First Class passengers.

"They are boarding," an excited murmur came from the women in front of Erzsi.

Using the full force of her tiny frame she pushed her way forward to get a better view. "Clara will want to know every detail."

An aristocratic gentleman wearing a perfectly tailored grey frock coat was approaching the gangplank. A lady, wearing a soft green summer dress, was ever so gently holding his arm.

"I will need to tell Clara that corsets are very much in style," mentally noting the lady's fashionably corseted silhouette.

The parade up the gangplank continued with a swirl of color; magenta, blue, yellow, on soft summer dresses adorned with ruffles, pleats and flounces.

"Oh, Clara," she thought, "you should see the hats and bonnets! Some are truly peculiar, decorated with birds, fruits and vegetables, feathers and ribbons. Imagine!"

Erzsi watched as a boy and a girl followed their parents up the gangplank. "Clara," she would write, "your little Matilda would look so adorable dressed like the little girl. She is wearing a traveling coat, leather gloves, bonnet, and knee-length boots. Her brother, I assume he is her brother, is wearing knee-length breeches and a jacket. The little girl is standing near her mother, walking like a perfect lady.

The boy is busy throwing something over the edge of the gangplank, he reminds me of Stefan."

A commotion behind her caused her to turn away from the scene on the gangplank. Steerage passengers, families, were exiting the processing building joining the women on the dock. Gulls that had been peacefully sitting on pilings and ropes suddenly circled overhead, screeching, agitated. Erzsi protectively pulled her bag and basket closer to her body.

"What caused that?" she asked to no one in particular. The woman next to her shrugged.

"There," another pointed to a little boy.

A child, perhaps three years old, wearing a cap identical to his father's, was holding a pretzel. As the women watched, a gull swooped down, snatching the treasure from the little boy's hand. The boy cried out, a look of surprise, fear, and loss flashing across his face. Tears rolled down his cheeks as he stared at his empty hand. A man, probably his father, Erzsi assumed, quickly lifted the boy. He tenderly kissed the tiny hand that had held the pretzel. When the tears had subsided, the man hugged the boy, who then rested his head on the man's shoulder.

Watching the tender scene Erzsi felt a premonition. One day she would watch her own son held protectively and lovingly by his father. She smiled at the thought.

Finally, the wait was over. One hundred cabin and saloon passengers watched from the upper decks as the densely-packed crowd of six hundred anxious steerage passengers prepared to board.

Representatives from the steamship company directed the women toward the gangplank. Walking single file, many struggling with bags and boxes, the women approached the ship. Erzsi paused as she reached the gangplank, looking at the ship that would be her home for the next two weeks. She whispered a silent prayer, "Lord Jesus, Blessed Mother, keep me safe." She could feel the woman behind her, moving closer, nudging her, impatient to board the ship. There was no turning back. The only way to go was up the steep slope toward the deck that waited at the end of the climb.

Josef patiently waited to board the *Closinda*. First and cabin class passengers had already boarded. Steerage passengers had been separated into three groups. Women without escorts boarded first followed by families, single men would board last.

Josef didn't mind. He was content to smoke his cigar and watch the activity on the dock. "I will be on the ship long enough."

Yesterday he had sent Maria a postcard.

Hamburg, Germany
June 7, 1882

Dear Maria,

I arrived safely in Hamburg. Tomorrow I will board the steamship Closinda. The ship will take about fourteen days to reach New York. I will write when I can. I am well.

Love,
Josef

He thought of Maria now, strong, capable, the woman who would be the mother of his children. He missed the warmth of her body at night, the way she looked at him with love.

The crowd of men moved closer to the ship. Josef watched the women, a sea of babushkas, slowly climbing the gangplank. At the top, stewards were directing them, encouraging them to keep moving, so as not to slow down the boarding process.

A woman, bent over with a heavy bundle on her back, looked familiar. She was looking down but he could see blond curls coming loose from under her scarf. A feather pillow was held protectively under her arm. He smiled as he remembered the woman he had met on the train. Could it be her?

Reaching the deck, slightly winded, Erzsi was greeted by a crew member. "*DieserWeg*, this way," he pointed to an open door leading to a large room.

"This is probably where we will take our meals," the girl behind her whispered.

"*Willkommen*, welcome," an official standing perfectly erect, his face reflecting authority, greeted them in German. He was standing inside the room, a short distance from the door, so that he could see each woman as she entered the room.

"*Deutsche*, German" he pointed to a desk where a line of German women was forming.

"*Hebräer*, Hebrews," he pointed to another desk.

"Magyar." Erzsi followed his direction.

At the desks each woman was given her stateroom and berth number. The noise in the room grew steadily louder as friends and relatives learning they were in the same stateroom hugged each other in excitement and relief. One-hundred women, all talking at once, their voices echoing from the wall, the noise was deafening.

A shrill whistle blew. A severe looking matron was calling for their attention. "Look at her arms," someone said. "I bet she could fight with my brother and win," the women around her giggled. The whistle blew again. She stood there, an ominous expression on her face, until she was sure she had everyone's attention.

"*Junge frauen,* young women," she paused for effect. Her voice was stern, demanding respect, if not fear.

"I am Frau Mueller. I will be in charge of you until you depart from this ship. Now you must follow me, Germans first, Magyar next, Hebrews at the end of the line." She turned and walked to the door. Not everyone understood her German but it was clear what was expected.

Erzsi found it difficult to descend the steep, poorly lit staircase. She bit her lip as she held her skirts with one hand, the cloth bag and basket in the other. The clothes wrapped in the blanket on her back swayed as she moved, challenging her equilibrium. She was dimly aware of the ache in her arm from the vaccination. The heavy, oppressive air that greeted her as she descended deeper into the bowels of the ship made it difficult to breathe. The smell of disinfectant and lingering odors of passengers from earlier voyages stung her nose.

Pausing on the stairs to adjust the bundle on her back she saw the German women entering the compartment where their staterooms were located.

"They get special treatment," a woman whispered in Hungarian.

"Germans! They think they are superior," whispered another.

"Like this?" a woman around Erzsi's age put her nose in the air, walked down a stair and pretended to trip. "Oh my," she sighed putting her hand delicately over her mouth. Those who were near enough to see her giggled.

Frau Mueller was waiting for them at the bottom of the staircase. "Hebrew, go to the compartment at the end, the rest of you will find your staterooms here. You are expected to be in your rooms by nine o'clock each night." With that, she turned and walked down the hall.

Eight women, mostly strangers, would share the tiny room for the next fourteen days. The iron berths were arranged in two tiers, four berths along each wall. Each woman was provided with a straw mattress covered with white canvas, a blanket neatly folded, and a life preserver that could be used as a pillow. Ominously, there was a can for seasickness placed near each sleeping area. A single chair, a small mirror, and some hooks for hanging clothes completed the meager furnishings in the room. On the wall next to the door was a copy of the passenger act of 1882 in German and English. It was supposed to increase the safety and comfort of steerage passengers. Since no one in the room could read German or English the notice was ignored.

The women entered the stateroom, filling it with feather pillows, blankets, parcels, baskets, coats, shawls, dresses, and oddly, an empty bird cage. Erszi found her berth and began to organize her belongings in the small space. A young girl, not more than sixteen, Erszi imagined, began to climb up into the berth next to hers. "Hello," Erszi gave her what she hoped was a reassuring smile. The girl nodded in acknowledgement and continued her climb. Erszi returned to her task of arranging her belongings in the small space. There was a card on top of the life preserver.

Welcome to the *Closinda*
Today's schedule
12:00 noon Departure from the Port of Hamburg
1:00 PM Dinner
3:00 PM Lunch
6:00 PM Supper
9:00 PM Return to your stateroom.
Today's menu
Dinner: Lentil soup, meat, boiled potatoes, pudding with plum sauce
Lunch: Coffee and coffee cake
Supper: Bread, butter, tea, meat

You have been assigned dining room A.

"Hello, up there." Erzsi felt something poke her mattress. "Hello," another poke. She dangled her head over the side. A pretty woman, about her own age, was looking at her with mischievous eyes, and a wide grin.

"My name is Agnes."

"I'm Erzsi, pleased to meet you, Agnes."

The ship's whistle sounded, once, twice. The rumble of the steam engines was felt by all as the massive vessel prepared to steam out of the Port of Hamburg. Everyone in the room was suddenly silent. The chatter between women who had just met, the noise from baggage being moved, pillows being fluffed, bottles being unpacked, everything stopped. The ship's whistle sounded again.

"We're leaving," someone said, excitement in her voice.

"I'm going on deck to watch," another said, heading for the door.

Erzsi scrambled down from her berth.

"Let's go," said Agnes.

"Wait," Erzsi turned to look for the girl in the berth next to hers. There was no noise from her berth, no excited laughter, only a tiny form under a thin blanket.

"Are you coming?" Erzsi stood on the frame of the lower berth so she could see the girl.

"No," a quiet whisper from under the blanket.

"Are you ill?"

"No! Go away!"

"Come on. You can come with Agnes and me. It will be exciting."

Silence as the girl moved further away.

"Come on, Erzsi. You don't want to miss this. It will be magnificent. We can wave to everyone on the dock." Agnes started to leave, she didn't want to miss anything.

Erzsi glanced at the girl one last time. There was nothing she could do for her right now.

"We are going to America!" Erzsi proclaimed, following Agnes out the door.

The ship's whistle sounded again, smoke billowed from the black and white stack. Steerage and upper-class promenade decks were filled with passengers shouting farewells to friends and families on the dock. White handkerchiefs were waved like flags by the women, while men raised their hats in salute. The ship's whistle sounded again and the jubilant roar from the crowd made Erzsi's heart race. She raised her hand and waved her handkerchief, a last good-bye to the life she had known.

Gradually, as the ship moved from the pier, slowly turned, and began to move up the Elbe River, the people on the dock grew smaller and the steerage passengers grew quiet. A gentle breeze wafted across the deck, gently moving the curls that framed Erzsi's face. She tightened her shawl across her shoulders. The waves created by the wake of the ship reminded her that she was relentlessly and inescapably moving away from her past toward her future.

Her thoughts drifted to memories of the family and friends she was leaving behind, possibly forever. A deep sense of loss consumed her. There would be babies she would never hold, holidays she wouldn't share. Weddings and funerals would happen without her. She would not share joyful moments or help comfort those in need when there was sorrow.

"Come on, Erzsi, it is almost time for dinner. I'm starving." Her new friend Agnes took her arm and pulled her away from the railing.

10 Agnes

At Sea
June, 1882

Josef saw her, the woman he had met on the train from Kosice. She was leaning against the railing of the ship, slowly waving her handkerchief.

The ship's whistle, loud, jubilant, announced the moment of departure had arrived. The engines rumbled, a whirlpool of water formed at the stern, the ship began to slowly move away from the dock.

Josef threw his cap in the air, his jubilant yell as loud as any man around him. The men, most still strangers, cheerfully slapped each other on the back. They shared a bond. The adventure had begun, their dreams were about to be realized.

The ship glided over the water, gradually accelerating as the passengers watched. The buildings of the city, the piers, and the vast number of ships that lined the shore seemed to grow smaller and smaller, proving that the ship was really underway. Josef watched the wake of the ship. "Like a road leading back home," he thought, "but the road will fade away." It was an uncharacteristic, melancholy thought.

Josef turned to look at the woman from the train. She was still by the railing but now appeared thoughtful, perhaps a little sad. For a moment he thought he might stay and talk with her but quickly changed his mind. A bell rang, he was hungry. He followed the others to the dining room reserved for single men.

"That must be the dinner bell." Agnes gave her new friend a gentle tug on her sleeve. "Hurry now." They headed for the line forming at the entrance to dining room A.

"Who uses dining room B?" someone in the line asked.

"Single men," answered a steward who was standing nearby. "Women traveling alone and families use this one."

"They want to keep us safe," Alice said. "A long voyage like this, you never know what might happen." Erzsi shivered remembering her ordeal at the lodging in Hamburg.

They entered the room where they had been given their berth and stateroom numbers. It had been transformed. Long wooden tables covered with white muslin cloths spanned the length of the room. Heavy white ceramic plates, cutlery, bread, salt, pepper, and mustard had been placed on each table.

"Let's sit there," Agnes said, pointing to a table where other women from their stateroom were already seated.

A very handsome, very young, man wearing a white apron, approached their table. He was carrying a heavy tray with ten bowls of lentil soup. With precision, he put down the tray and placed a bowl in front of each woman at the table.

Agnes was sitting next to Erzsi at the end of the table. When he reached her, she gave him her most enticing smile and a suggestive wink. His hand shook and some of the soup spilled on the table.

"So sorry, Miss," he said, using the napkin on his arm to clean up the spill.

"What is your name?" Agnes asked while gently placing her hands near her bosom.

"Ludwig, Miss." He was just a boy obviously inexperienced with women who were so bold. His face turned bright red as he watched Agnes. He could not remove his eyes from her ample bosom. She was adjusting her blouse, pushing her chest forward, causing the outline of her breasts to press against the cloth.

"How fortunate you are, Ludwig, serving a table with only women. It is so much harder to serve families with children."

"Yes, Miss, I mean no, Miss. Excuse me, Miss," Ludwig stammered. He turned away, quickly disappearing into the galley.

"You were such a tease, Agnes. He is just a boy."

"He is probably in the galley bragging about the woman at his table."

Erzsi did not know what to make of Agnes. "So different from Iren," she thought. "Even Clara would not be so bold." But she was glad she was sharing this voyage with Agnes. "It's not going to be boring." She smiled at the thought.

The other women at the table had various reactions to the behavior of the young woman flirting with the steward. Some smiled, some frowned. Some remembered a time when a look from them could make a young man stammer and blush. An old woman was fingering her rosary beads, perhaps asking for forgiveness for the temptress.

"Shall we introduce ourselves?" suggested a confident woman of around forty years of age.

"She must have been a school mistress," whispered Agnes. "She even looks a little like Mrs. Szabo, my teacher."

"I'm Rosa. I'm going to meet my husband who works in the mines in Pennsylvania. My children are married so I am traveling alone."

"I'm Franciska," the woman with the rosary volunteered. "I'm going to America to be with my daughter and her family." She paused for a moment, giving Agnes a stern glance. "I promise you, we are assured safe passage. Members of my church are offering weekly Novenas on our behalf." Many of the women nodded with understanding and appreciation. They also had families praying for their safe journey.

"My name is Agnes. I'm going to join my husband who left for America two years ago. He has settled on land in Iowa."

"My name is Erzsi. I have been promised employment in a boarding house in New York."

Other women volunteered that they were going to meet sisters, brothers, family members who were already settled in America.

Ludwig, having gained his composure, and perhaps some advice from comrades in the galley, quickly served the rest of the meal. He avoided looking at Agnes and she left him alone.

"And what would your husband think about the way you flirted with the steward?" Erzsi whispered to Agnes when Ludwig was safely back in the galley.

"He knows me. He knows I love him and would not betray him. A woman needs to have some innocent fun." Erzsi and Rosa nodded in agreement while Franciska frowned. She did not approve of this young woman's forward behavior.

"Want to explore the ship?" Agnes had finished eating and, as always, was looking for the next adventure.

"What about the girl who stayed in her berth?"

"What about her?"

"I don't think she left the stateroom. She must be hungry. Let's bring her something."

"Sure."

"Ludwig, could we ask you for a favor?" Agnes asked the young steward when he returned to clear the table. She gave him her most attractive smile but this time kept her hands folded in her lap.

"Of course," he stood a respectful distance from Agnes, his eyes on the floor.

"We have a sick friend in our stateroom. We would like to bring her something to eat."

"I will gladly ask the cook."

He returned with a tin of broth and some bread. "The cook says this is good for persons who are suffering from the ship's motion."

"Thank you, Ludwig. I am sure this will improve her spirits." With a smile Agnes took the food.

"All right, Erzsi, let's go see the girl."

Although families ate in the same room as single women, Erzsi did not see Amalia or her family. "I will check on them later," she promised herself.

Agnes was animatedly telling a story about one of her many romantic encounters when they reached the door of the stateroom. Still talking, she opened the door.

It was dark in the room, the only light coming from the two tightly closed port-holes. Sunlight, reflected from the ocean waves, filtered through the dusty windows, and danced on the curves of the girl still huddled under the blanket in the upper berth.

Erzsi stood on the lower berth, "Hello there."

"Hello there," Agnes echoed, climbing next to Erzsi.

No response from the girl.

"You can't stay here for the entire voyage," Erzsi climbed into the berth, bumping the girl's legs in the process.

"Ouch."

"Sorry."

"Go away."

"There is no air in this room. I need to open the port-hole," Erzsi reached over the girl and pulled on the latch holding the port-hole closed. "There, that's better."

"I'm coming up, too," Agnes pulled herself up into the tight space.

"I can't move. Go away."

"We brought you some food. You must be hungry."

Silence.

"We'll go away when you come down and talk with us."

Silence.

They stayed there for a long while. Agnes and Erzsi were on top of the blanket, their legs dangling over the edge of the berth. Occasionally there was a sob from under the blanket.

"Come now, that's enough. You need to get up. You need to eat," Agnes spoke in a stern voice. She was out of patience.

Silence.

"Let's go, Erzsi. I don't want to spend the day sitting in this room," Agnes said while climbing down from the berth. Erzsi followed her and the women moved to the door.

"I need to use the washroom," a tiny voice could be faintly heard under the blanket. "I don't know where it is."

"We'll show you." Agnes was almost out the door but Erzsi could not leave the girl. She was so young to be making a journey like this on her own.

The girl sat up, her hair matted, her eyes red from crying. Erzsi smoothed her hair and used her apron to wipe away a tear. Warming to the motherly touch, the girl rewarded her with a faint smile.

"I am hungry," she confessed, looking at the tin with the broth and the bread waiting on the small table in the corner. She had not eaten since yesterday.

"We can sit on the deck while you eat. The fresh air will do you good. First, the washroom."

The air on the deck of the ship was cool, refreshing, a welcome relief from the stale air in the stateroom. They sat on a hard wooden bench, the girl between them scooping the meager meal into her mouth. She was quiet, but the tears had stopped.

"Well, young lady, do you have a name?" Agnes was still impatient with the girl.

"Ilona."

"Beautiful name," Erzsi smiled at her. "Where are you going in America?"

Thoughtful silence followed while Ilona finished the broth. She was unsure what to make of these women. What did they want from her? Should she trust them?

"I'm going to live with my brother and his wife."

"It can be a little frightening traveling alone. Is that why you were crying?"

"No."

"Your brother and his wife must love you very much to send for you. You will have an exciting new life in America."

"No! My life is over. I will do what they expect of me, nothing more."

The women were surprised to hear such despair in one so young.

"Why do you say that?"

"I will never see Rudi again," Ilona said as tears started to form in her eyes. "We were in love. We wanted to be married."

"What happened?"

"Our families forbid it."

"But why?" Erzsi asked.

"He is Jewish. We were going to run away but Rudi's father sent him to Pressburg to live with an uncle. Then my mother became ill. My father died when I was a baby and my brother left for America years ago. My mother was worried there would be no one to look after me. When my brother sent for me, my mother insisted that I go to America."

"You are fortunate to have such a good family," said Agnes.

"They don't understand. No one does."

"They want what is best for you, I am sure."

"I will never love again. My life is over."

"All right, your life is over," Agnes had no more patience. "Do you want to explore the ship with us or go back to your stateroom?"

"I...I don't want to be alone."

"Well then, come with us," Agnes said, turning to go.

There wasn't much to see as they were limited to the decks reserved for steerage passengers. They did peek into the galley, where Agnes waved to Ludwig who blushed crimson when he saw her. Erzsi found

Amalia and her family and introduced them to Agnes and Ilona. Agnes played a game of hide and seek with the little boys, Ilona fussed over the baby.

After supper they returned to their stateroom where many of the women were already propped up in their bunks, knitting or writing letters. Others were early victims of seasickness, holding the sickness cans at the ready. Most of the women had come prepared, they thought, for the anticipated travails of an ocean voyage. Remedies for seasickness, all of which would prove useless, included patent medicines, lime-drops, apples, and raw onions. It would be apparent before long that none of the remedies would work.

Erzsi sat in her bunk writing to her sisters. Ilona, again feeling melancholy, was curled up under her blanket. Agnes, already bored anticipating the long days at sea, was planning an adventure. In the morning she would inform Erzsi and Ilona of her plan to explore parts of the ship outside the purview of steerage passengers. They could spend the day working out the details. Smiling, she drifted off to sleep.

It was their second day at sea. Erzsi, Agnes, and Ilona spent the day preparing for their evening adventure. "We will need to wait until Frau Mueller has made her rounds," Agnes instructed them. "After dark we will make our way to the ropes that separate steerage from cabin class passengers." The women walked the route they planned to take. They discussed strategies to avoid the night watchman, seeking out places to hide, planning for a quick getaway if they were spotted.

"What if we are caught?" worried Ilona.

"Then they will throw us overboard," responded Agnes, looking serious. Ilona did not believe her of course, but nevertheless she shivered thinking of falling into the cold black ocean.

"Don't worry. They will just take us back to our stateroom," Erzsi consoled the nervous girl. But Erzsi was getting excited thinking about their plan. It had been a long time since she had felt the freedom to break the rules.

When the warning bell sounded at 9:00PM steerage passengers slowly, reluctantly began to move to their staterooms. No one was in a hurry to return to the stuffy, airless rooms below deck. A night watchman made his rounds searching for young lovers, troublemakers, or anyone else who might try to shirk the rules. Frau Mueller waited with her usual stern expression, nodding as each of her charges descended the staircase. Soon she would complete her rounds, confident that everyone was in their assigned rooms. She was ever diligent that her girls would not be victim to unseemly advances from men on the ship.

With the lack of privacy in the small room all of the women slept in their clothes. This worked well for the friends who planned a daring mission into forbidden territories. They settled into their berths waiting for everyone to be asleep. In the darkness they heard women whispering, praying, stifling sobs. A soft voice sang a sad song reminding them of home. Eventually the gentle rocking of the ship, the rhythmic waves splashing against the port-holes, lulled everyone to sleep.

The door opened quietly, a light shown in the doorway. It was Frau Mueller checking their room again. All was quiet, the room was dark, and everything was as it should be. Her work for the day was done.

As planned, Agnes poked the berth above her. It was time. Erzsi signaled to Ilona. Stealthily they slid from their berths, and in stocking feet, made their way to the door of the stateroom.

"Where are you going?" a sleepy voice asked.

"We need to use the washroom," Erzsi responded in a hushed voice.

The heavy door resisted, the rusty hinges squeaked as Agnes pulled it open. They stood still for a moment, fearing they would be discovered. All they could hear was the heavy breathing of contented slumber. They quickly slid through the open doorway.

Ilona reached for Erzsi's hand. The hall was dimly lit. Agnes was confidently leading the way. That afternoon they had seen a maid leave the galley with a tray. "That fancy tray certainly isn't for someone in steerage," Agnes had remarked. So they had watched as the maid carefully made her way to a staircase blocked with a heavy rope. Moving past the rope didn't seem like it would be difficult. "We can do that, even in the dark." A plan had formed for their late night exploration.

The women climbed the stairs leading to the steerage deck, past the dining room, past the galley.

Noises, pans, dishes, loud voices, they were still working in the galley. The door to the galley started to open. Erzsi pushed Ilona deeper into the darkness. The trespassers held their breath squeezing their bodies against the wall. A man, carrying a large pail, walked onto the deck, dumping the contents into the ocean. When he turned he saw the women. Startled at first he just stared at them. Then, with a shrug, he walked back into the galley. It wasn't his concern if these women wanted to walk the decks.

Erzsi's heart was pounding. "What if we are caught? What are the consequences for breaking rules?" Confinement to their berth, embarrassing interrogations, perhaps they would be accused of stealing, these were all possibilities. "Too late to worry about that now." Somehow, the knowledge that she was breaking the rules and risking the consequences was exhilarating. She was breaking rules, being true to herself, and enjoying her new freedom. "I will do penance tomorrow," she quietly promised.

With Agnes leading the way, the three rule breakers cautiously made their way to the stairs leading to the upper decks. Carefully, watchfully, they climbed over the rope. Reaching the top, Agnes signaled to her companions to keep their heads down while she scanned the deck to be sure they were alone. She could see a young couple, occupied with each other, a safe distance away. She climbed onto the deck, waving for the others to follow.

Before them was a broad deck painted bright white, immaculately polished brass railings separated the deck from the dark ocean below. A row of lounge deck chairs, looking irresistibly comfortable, spanned the length of the deck.

What a contrast from the unpainted deck and hard benches they had sat on earlier that day. Laughing softly, pretending to be fine ladies, they arranged their skirts and settled themselves into the chairs. They were quiet for a moment, feeling the cool air on their faces. A shooting star fleeted past. "A good omen," Ilona whispered. "Maybe it means my Rudi will find me someday." The night was suddenly filled with optimism.

Erzsi pointed to a row of small round windows, trimmed in shining brass that lined the wall one after the other. With a gesture to be quiet, she started to walk to the windows. Agnes and Ilona followed. As they approached the windows, they could hear voices in animated conversation, followed by an occasional hearty chorus of laughter.

Bending down and moving slowly, cautiously, they approached the portals. Now there was the faint smell of cigar and pipe smoke.

Exchanging a look, they slowly raised their heads and looked through the portals into a smoke-filled room. "This must be the smoking-lounge," whispered Agnes.

Well-dressed men wearing dark jackets, waistcoats, and white bow ties were sitting in plush leather chairs around highly polished tables. They were intent on a game of cards. There was a bar on one end of the room, a fireplace with an elaborately carved mantle and dark blue tiles on the other. Four men were sitting on plush leather chairs in a small alcove. Smoke wafted from their pipes and cigars, the men engrossed in animated conversation.

"What do you think they are discussing?"

"Politics, I am sure."

"I am certain they are not talking about the latest fashions?" Ilona giggled.

"Perhaps they are discussing an opera," Agnes wasn't sure exactly what an opera was but it might be a suitable conversation for gentlemen.

A waiter came into the room. He carried a silver tray with a crystal decanter that reflected the light from the immense chandeliers scattered around the mahogany paneled room. The men in the corner signaled to him to bring the whiskey.

Piano music could be heard from a room further down the deck.

"Shall we dance?" Agnes asked moving away from the port-hole. The music grew suddenly louder. A door was opening. A young man in a tuxedo had his arm around the waist of an attractive young woman. His eyes were riveted on hers as he guided her onto the deck. They were whispering softly.

With no place to hide, Agnes pointed to the stairs. Everyone nodded and this time without fear of detection they ran to the stairs that would take them safely back to the steerage deck.

Finally, safely in their stateroom, they collapsed onto Agnes's berth amid a torrent of giggles. This, of course, brought complaints from the other women in the room. It did not matter. It took some time for them to quiet down.

During the night, as the passengers slept, the ship was engulfed in a thick fog. The ship captain, as required by law, sounded the steam whistle at regular intervals to warn oncoming ships of its presence. The sound of the whistle made it into the dreams of the women, being interpreted by some as an omen of impending doom and others as a call to a new life with endless possibilities. Agnes dreamt of her husband and the family they would have, Erzsi dreamt of a voyage on an unearthly vessel relentlessly transporting her to a remote as yet unidentified new home. Ilona dreamt of Rudi, holding her, kissing her, vowing eternal love.

11 Temptation

At sea
June, 1882

Her bed was rolling, one way, then the other, slowly, rhythmically. Was this a dream? Was she being transported by some strange magic to an unknown universe? She opened her eyes. Pre-dawn light filtered through the porthole. Everything in the room was swaying, the clothes on the hooks, shoes tied to the metal rods separating the berths, the mysterious bottles the old lady had hung from a hook on the wall.

A wave of nausea started low in Erzsi's belly working its way into her throat till it presented itself as sour tasting bile in her mouth. She sat up quickly, reaching for her basket, regretting that the sick can was on the floor. The nausea subsided. She fell back onto her pillow, too weak to reach for the blanket that was dangling from the edge of the bed.

The stuffy, stale air in the tiny room now reeked of vomit. She glanced at the port-hole above her berth. The latch had been pulled tightly shut for the night. She could see waves crashing against it in rhythm with the rocking of the ship. She needed air, fresh air. She glanced at Ilona who was propped up in her berth, a pail in her lap.

"I'm going on deck," Erzsi whispered to the sick girl.

"I'm afraid to move," whispered Ilona, her voice hoarse, her face pale.

Erzsi nodded in understanding. She glanced at Agnes. Somehow she was still peacefully asleep.

The knuckles of Erzsi's fingers were white as she clutched the handrails that lined the corridor. The rocking of the ship made progress difficult. With trepidation she slowly climbed the steep damp staircase, slipping more than once as the ship continued to rock.

Opening the hatch, a gust of moist, salty air hit her face stinging her eyes. With damp curls dangling on her neck and her scarf in disarray, she pushed against the door opening it wider. With difficulty she climbed onto the deck.

The boat was rocking precariously. The deck was slippery from the spray of salt water coming from the angry ocean. Grasping the railing with both hands Erzsi made her way to a wooden bench partly sheltered in a small alcove.

With relief, she lowered herself onto the bench and closed her eyes. Erzsi shivered in the cold damp air, her hair and clothes soaked with salt water. The nausea had subsided but she was afraid to open her eyes. She was sure that the sight of the swaying ship would bring it back.

She felt someone sit next to her.

"Are you all right?" a male voice, strong, confident, concerned, asked her.

The voice was familiar. Odd, she didn't know any men on this ship. She was about to respond when the ship rolled steeply to the right; a large wave crashed over the bow. Strong arms caught her as she was about to slide off the bench. His body sheltered her from the torrent of water rushing past them. She could smell his wet woolen clothes; the cigar on his breath, his mustache tickled her face when she turned to look at him. His dark brown eyes were looking at her with an intensity that spoke of more than just concern for her welfare. It was the man she had met on the train.

"So sorry," he backed away from her, removing his arms, but continuing to look into her eyes.

Embarrassed, she tried to adjust her soggy scarf, pushing the damp curls off her face.

"I'm fine, thank you." She turned away from him, unnerved by the ardency of his gaze.

"It was unbearable in the stateroom," she stammered, feeling that she needed to justify her presence on the deck under such dangerous conditions.

"You are not the only one. Anyone strong enough is somewhere on the deck."

"Thank you for catching me." She was feeling more confident now and remembered to be polite.

He smiled at her. She looked so defenseless; her tiny frame no match for the powerful waves pounding the ship.

"Would you mind if I stayed here for a while? It is one of the few places left on the deck where there is some protection from the waves."

"No, please stay." He was not a stranger but a connection to home. They had spent a day together on that train. She felt comfortable with him. As she had on the train she felt drawn to him.

"How nice it would be to rest my head on his shoulder," she thought.

It was difficult to talk with the wind and the waves but somehow just sitting there together was enough. An hour passed, maybe more. The seas had quieted, Erzsi's nausea had subsided.

"I need to find my friends. They will be wondering where I am." She stood, straightening her damp skirt. "Perhaps we will meet again before we reach New York," she said, looking up at him, their eyes meeting. She shivered, reacting to the force of his gaze.

"Perhaps," he answered, standing very close to her. His eyes traveled from her flushed cheeks to the wet blouse that clung seductively to her bosom. Reflexively her hand touched her breasts following his gaze. She knew the way he looked at her was not proper yet she wanted to stay. Her body was drawn to his, her breath quickened. "Good-bye then," she said gaining control, quickly walking away.

He watched the movement of her skirts as she turned. His imagination aroused, he pictured her naked. "You're a married man Josef, leave the woman alone." He shrugged his shoulders and walked to the men's dining room.

Agnes was already in the dining room heartily devouring a bowl of vegetable soup, when Erzsi arrived.

"Where have you been?" Agnes asked as her friend approached the table. "You look as though someone pushed you overboard and then dragged you back."

"I've been sitting on the deck. I wasn't feeling well, I needed some fresh air."

"I can understand that! The smell, nearly everyone in our stateroom is sick. No one came to clean it up," Agnes wrinkled her nose to show her disgust. "Rosa went to find the doctor but seasickness is not considered an emergency so he didn't come to help."

"Did you get sick?"

"No, not really, well, just a little. I've been here in the dining room all morning. Ludwig has been very attentive," she added with an impish grin. "He brought me some tea and crackers, a hot towel for my forehead."

"How is Ilona?"

"Still sick. She won't leave her berth. I asked Ludwig for some broth that we can bring her. Maybe we can convince her to sit on deck now that the storm is past."

"Agnes, I met someone," Erzsi interrupted. She spoke softly in a conspiratorial tone. "We sat together on the train from Kosice and now he is on this ship. We spent the morning together."

"So, I get Ludwig and you get who?"

"His name is Josef, he comes from a village near mine."

"What does he look like? Is he handsome?"

"Yes, in a way. His hair is thick and dark, his eyes warm. I felt safe sitting next to him."

"Did he try and kiss you?" Agnes asked warming to the possibility of a shipboard romance.

"No, but," Erzsi told Agnes about the way he had shielded her from the wave and how he had stared at her wet bosom.

"Be careful, he might have unseemly intentions," Agnes was a little concerned by the forwardness of this Josef.

Erzsi's face turned pale thinking of the attack in Hamburg, what might have happened if not for Amalia's husband. "No, he isn't like that. He is kind. I can see it in his eyes."

"Well then, I will need to meet him so I can give my approval."

It rained for the next three days. The women who were not sick spent their time in the dining room, knitting, playing games with the children, writing letters home. By the third day, boredom and melancholy pervaded the atmosphere.

On the fourth day, the clouds finally parted, the sun came out, the decks dried off. Everyone well enough escaped the confines of the steerage compartments and the dining room. Erzsi looked for Josef but did not find him.

"If he is interested he will find you," Agnes counseled her friend.

After the evening meal, while mothers were putting their children to bed and fathers were playing cards or sleeping in their berths, young men and women gathered on the steerage deck. A bottle of whiskey was shared, there was laughter, and new friendships were forming.

A young woman began to sing. It was a melancholy song, a song of home, of longing. Tears were wiped away with tattered handkerchiefs. Lovers sat close together, finding solace in their embrace. New friends joined together in a line, their arms interlocked, each understanding the somber mood of the others.

When the song ended, someone began to play a violin. The rhythm was slow, teasing, filled with anticipation that something else was about to begin. As the tempo of the music slowly increased, the mood of the group changed, hands began to clap, and young couples began to dance.

Agnes was pulling Erzsi in the direction of the music, Ilona was reluctantly following behind. She was still not well but her friends would not let her stay any longer in the cabin.

A young man approached Agnes giving her an elaborate bow. She smiled and nodded. He put his arm around her waist and swung her around in a vigorous, improvised version of the Csárdás.

Josef was about to join a card game when he heard the music and the laughter. "It won't hurt to get out of this smoke filled room for a while," he reasoned, adjusting his cap and throwing away what was left of his cigar.

There she was, the woman from the train, clapping and laughing watching the dancers whirling around the deck.

"What harm," he reassured himself, "just one dance to pass the time?"

Her face lit up when she saw him. He was flattered, encouraged.

"Join me?" he asked, offering her his hand.

Standing proudly as the dance required, Josef placed his arm around her waist, pulling her toward him. Their eyes locked on each other. He moved slowly, guiding her, his movements reflecting the rhythm of the violin. Slowly the tempo of the music increased, his boots struck the deck in an ever increasing rhythm.

The strings of the violin were being worked into frenzy. Erzsi was being whirled around the deck at an exhilarating speed. Her skirts twirled around, exposing her dainty feet and ankles. She was laughing with delight feeling Josef's arms controlling her movements. She did not dare take her eyes away from his; he was watching her, laughing with her, her heart was beating fast, she could hardly catch her breath. One last swing around the deck and the music stopped with a flourish. They were alone in that moment looking at each other laughing. For Erzsi it had been a long time since she had felt this happy. Josef hesitated for a moment and then slowly stepped back from her and made a small bow. Erzsi, still laughing and flushed from the dance, wasn't sure what to do next. She wanted to keep him close to her; she didn't want this happiness to end.

"Come and meet my friend Agnes," Erzsi said taking Josef's hand guiding him. While Erzsi was dancing she noticed that Ilona had left.

The evening was perfect. Agnes, Erzsi, and Josef sat together enjoying the music until darkness fell and the night watchman sent everyone off to their compartments. Josef offered his hand to help Erzsi stand and then wished the women a good night. He stood there watching Erzsi move away into the darkness.

That night Josef dreamed of Erzsi. She was in his bed, her soft curls falling down on the pillow. He held her hands, fascinated by the long delicate fingers. Their love making was passionate, satisfying. Suddenly Maria was in the room, hurt, angry, telling him she was leaving him. He woke in a sweat, his heart beating fast.

"I am just lonely, far from home, it is normal for a man to be tempted."

The fifth day at sea, the women were finishing their noon meal. A plum sauce was dripping off Erzsi's spoon when Agnes nudged her.

"Ouch," she frowned, the sauce dripping on her apron.

"Over there, by the door," Agnes whispered. It was Josef. He was leaning against the wall opposite the open dining room door.

"Oh," she caught her breath. "What should I do?" She was looking at her pudding, her eyes averted from the door.

"Well go and talk with him of course." Agnes could not believe her friend was suddenly shy. "It is obvious he came here to see you."

"Josef, you are far from the men's dining room. Are you lost?" Erzsi said with a teasing look in her eyes, a broad smile on her face as she approached him.

"I thought you might like to take a walk on the deck."

There wasn't much to see or do on the limited space allotted to steerage passengers but they could stand by the ships railings and look out over the vast ocean. They were quiet most of the time, just standing there, enjoying the fresh sea air. There was a comfortable silence between them as though they had spent a lifetime together and words were unnecessary.

It became a daily ritual. He would meet her in the dining room hall at noon; they would walk to the railing, Erzsi talked of her family, of the job she was promised in Rondout. Josef talked about America, the opportunities there but he did not have specific plans. He did not talk about his family.

When they were alone in their bunks Erzsi thought about Josef and wondered if he was the man God intended for her. Josef thought about Maria and made excuses for the time he spent with Erzsi. "It is a harmless shipboard flirtation. Maria need never know."

Eleven days at sea, tomorrow they would arrive in New York. It was a beautiful evening, the sea was calm, the air cool, a gentle breeze drifted over the bow of the ship. The sunset stretched in an endless expanse from one end of the horizon to the other.

Leaning against the rail, puffing on his cigar, Josef was thinking of the erotic dream he had the night before. "The woman certainly is invading my thoughts and my dreams in a not unpleasant way." He was thinking of Erzsi and how she had looked while they were dancing. "I am human after all, just a man. We will part in New York. No harm will be done."

Laughter from women deep in some secret conversation interrupted his thoughts. They were moving in his direction. Vaguely curious, he turned to see who was approaching.

"Josef!" the woman said as their eyes met.

"Hello, Erzsi," he spoke softly, their eyes locked on each other.

"I think I'll go back to the music," said Agnes understanding that she was not to be a part of this conversation.

"I think I should go with Agnes," Erzsi's voice was hoarse, without conviction.

"Wait," Josef moved toward her and touched her arm. The touch was electric. He quickly removed his hand.

"I've been watching the sunset and thinking about America," he said, pausing for a moment. "I was thinking about you." He turned back to the railing. He had not planned to say that and was not sure what her reaction would be.

Erzsi's cheeks flushed crimson as her body reacted to his words. She moved closer to him but did not know what to say. She wanted to touch his arm, to tell him she had also been thinking of him. They stood there for a long while, watching the sunset, listening to the rumble of the ship's engines, feeling the gentle movement of the ship.

As they stood there, all thoughts of their past or their future melted away, it was just the two of them together in the moment. Slowly, cautiously, Josef reached for her hand. Erzsi did not move. He knew that if he let this go on he would be crossing a line he never thought he would cross.

Erzsi turned towards him and heat rose in her cheeks as their eyes met in silent communication. Gently he moved a curl from her face, she felt a weakness in her knees. Surely she would collapse if he did not hold her.

The moment was abruptly interrupted by the night watchman sounding his bell. It was time for steerage passengers to return to their compartment. Erzsi, embarrassed, moved back from the railing. Josef reached for her, putting his arm around her waist. He looked into her eyes moved forward, slowly, as though time stood still, their lips met. Erzsi felt her body melt into his.

"I need to go," Erzsi said lowering her eyes. "Agnes will be worried about me."

Reluctantly Josef released her. She placed her hands on his shoulders and gave him a slow, sensual kiss before turning away.

Josef stood there, watching her leave. He wanted to touch those curls that were escaping from her scarf, put his arms around her waist. He wanted to kiss her again.

As she moved toward the steep stairs that would take her down into the stifling compartment, her knees felt weak and she could hardly breathe. Somehow she made it back to her berth where Agnes was waiting. "Well, tell me, tell me everything," Agnes pleaded, anxious to hear all the details of the encounter.

"I don't quite know, honestly. We were talking, and then he kissed me." Erzsi relived every moment as she shared even the most passionate details with Agnes.

Agnes, being an experienced married woman, understood the power of a physical attraction.

"Be careful, Erzsi. You are a woman traveling alone without the protection of family."

"There is nothing to worry about. After tomorrow I will probably never see him again." In her heart she believed, she hoped, otherwise.

Later when the room was quiet, everyone asleep, Erzsi lay in her berth thinking about Josef, the night they danced, the kiss. How happy she was when she was with him. Tonight, the few minutes alone with him watching the sunset, she had wanted to touch him and she knew he felt the same. When he kissed her, she knew his desire matched her own. How wonderful it would be to be married to such a man. But she hardly knew Josef and tomorrow they would arrive in New York. Would he even bother to say goodbye?

12 First Glimpse of the New World

New York Harbor
June, 1882

Notices had been posted; the *Closinda* would sail into New York Harbor at daybreak on Tuesday, the twentieth day of June.

Preparations began the day before. Mothers were on the deck washing their children's hair, the youngest nearly naked as they were thoroughly scrubbed for the first time in over a week. Undergarments were washed and hung in every corner of the staterooms. Best dresses, saved for the disembarkation, were unfolded, wrinkles lovingly smoothed with work-weathered hands. A few fancy hats and bonnets that had been hidden in boxes suddenly appeared.

During the voyage, modesty and limited space had caused many of the women to give up trying to stay clean. The washrooms were small, often crowded spaces that smelled of disinfectant. The deep sinks, made of coarse metal, were used to bathe children, shampoo hair, and wash diapers, soiled handkerchiefs and clothing.

There was no shower or bathtub available to steerage passengers. Stoppers were used to partially fill the deep sinks, but the number of sinks available was inadequate to meet the needs of all the women. The hot water faucet only produced tepid water. Enterprising women could bring warm water from the galley, but they needed their own pot and the distance to the galley did not make it convenient. The women used small towels to wipe away at least some of the dirt and smell from their bodies.

"A self-respecting person can't wash properly in a room that is being used by others," complained Franciscka, storming out of the washroom early in the voyage. "Only my husband has seen me without my clothes!"

Now, the day before landing, Franciscka gave up on modesty, commandeering a washbasin. "I must be clean and presentable before I meet my daughter and her children," she said, forcefully pushing a younger woman out of her way.

Erzsi had unfolded her summer dress, shaking out the wrinkles. She didn't have an iron, it would have to do. Her heavy wool dress had served her well on the cold nights at sea but now, approaching the harbor, it was time for the lighter dress.

"When I am settled this dress will need to air outside for at least a week," she frowned, smelling the wool dress she had worn for twelve days. In the morning she would roll it into the blanket before she debarked.

Sleep did not come easily to the women in the dark, stuffy, stateroom. Franciscka could be heard saying her rosary, as she had every night, but this time she was thanking the Blessed Mother for the safe passage on the treacherous seas.

Other women, who had become friends during the voyage, talked softly about their loved ones who would be meeting them at Castle Garden.

"It has been three years since my sister left for America. I have only seen pictures of her daughter, a beautiful child. "

"My husband said he has shaved off his beard. I will miss the softness of it when we kiss."

"I don't care if my husband has a beard or not. All I want is to be in his arms again."

Others were troubled because their travels would not be over when they reached New York. Rosa would be taking a train to a place called Hazleton in Pennsylvania. "What if I get lost or take the wrong train?" her voice was filled with dread. "Will anyone understand me? I don't speak English. How will I ask for help?"

Ilona had become sullen again. She had gone to her berth right after the evening meal and refused to talk with anyone. "My life is over," she sulked, taking refuge under her blanket.

"Best to leave her alone now," Agnes was sitting with Erzsi on the lower bunk. "She won't be able to stay in her berth much longer."

"Will Josef forget me when we reach the port?" Erzsi whispered to Agnes.

"Of course he will you silly woman. It was just a flirtation. He will have other things to think about when he leaves this ship. Anyway, he might be meeting a girlfriend or a wife. You really don't know anything about him."

"But that kiss! Surely he felt the same as I did. I saw it in his eyes."

"Maybe he did."

Erzsi and Agnes were awake long before dawn. "We need to get to the washrooms before the others," Agnes had urged. "Clean washbasins, soap, maybe even fresh towels. It will be a luxury to have the room to ourselves."

Properly cleaned for the first time in days, summer dresses, fresh undergarments, hair combed and colorful scarves tied into place. The young women were ready to see New York Harbor.

Steerage passengers had been given disembarkation information the night before. There would be a hearty breakfast of cereal, corned beef, bread, and coffee at six a.m. At seven a.m. they were to report to their assigned areas for disembarkation.

Six hundred steerage passengers, including Erzsi, Agnes, and Ilona were standing on the deck as the ship entered New York Harbor. Six hundred souls, faces filled with hope, anxiety, and exhaustion, looked out over the blue-green water, toward their new home.

The morning fog was lifting; the buildings of New York City were visible in the distance. A silence fell over the ship as the passengers watched the approach to the harbor.

"Over there, look over there! Isn't it magnificent?" a young boy called out to anyone who would listen.

Many on the ship, coming from inland countries, had never seen such an impressive harbor.

Mothers held their babies and pointed to the horizon. Husbands put their arms around their wives, holding them close. Tears of joy were evident on many faces. The voyage was almost over and the realization of their dreams was about to begin.

Erzsi had looked for Josef among the passengers, carefully checking out each man dressed in the now familiar brown jacket and cap. She thought she saw him, started to call to him, but stopped abruptly. A woman, with a child in tow, took the man's arm as she looked to the horizon. It wasn't Josef.

If Josef wanted, he would find her. Perhaps, Erzsi thought, she had read too much into the kiss.

The emotion and desire aroused by the kiss were still there when Josef awoke from a fitful night's sleep. He wanted, needed, to see her one last time. A kiss, perhaps on her hand or her soft inviting cheek, would be enough. Then he would give her a polite bow, say his farewells and move to the section of the deck where he had been told to wait. No harm would be done; it was just the conclusion of a shipboard flirtation.

As the ship approached the harbor he searched for her. Steerage passengers crowded together watching the horizon to get a glimpse of their new home. He stood on some crates searching, looking, and hoping for a glimpse of the woman who had entered his dreams.

Finally he saw her standing near the railing. Blond curls were escaping as always from the confines of a lavender scarf, a pillow clutched under her arm. She had her arm around a young girl and they were looking out over the harbor. Her friend, Agnes, was talking excitedly pointing toward the still distant city.

"Excuse me, Miss," he stepped over a pile of bedding.

"Excuse me, Sir," he pushed a small trunk out of his way.

"My wife," he pointed in the direction of the railing. He explained as he received more than one annoyed look.

Finally he was behind her. "Erzsi," he said, resisting the urge to wrap his arms around her waist. She turned, surprised.

"Josef," she said, her voice filled with relief.

"May I stand here with you until we reach port?" he asked. "I was assigned a place on the other side of the ship but you have a much better view."

"Of course," Erzsi moved aside, making a place for him. Her legs felt weak as she felt his body next to hers. "Why does he have this effect on me? Is this love?" She hoped he hadn't notice the heat rising in her cheeks.

Josef touched his cap, smiling at Ilona and Agnes.

Ilona, for the moment, forgot to sulk. "We do have the best view on the ship," she said turning back to the railing.

The approach to the harbor was imposing. The busy port was filled with vessels large and small, each with its own rigs and flags. Some appeared to be standing idle waiting quietly while others, with thick clouds of black smoke coming from their stacks, were moving steadily toward their destinations.

There were exquisite pleasure crafts and a white river steamer, with paddle wheels spinning. From their vantage point on the deck of the *Closinda* passengers watched as their ship glided past two islands that contained the remnants of old forts. On the mainland they could see churches, public buildings, factories, and stores.

"New York! Have you ever seen such a place?" a passenger shouted waving his cap to the great city.

With Castle Island in view, the ship's whistle blew. Accompanied by cheers from passengers and crew, the *Closinda* dropped anchor. The voyage was over. They had reached the New World.

"Look at the palace!" said a Russian peasant standing next to them.

In the distance was a large circular building. Wooden walls topped with a magnificent domed roof rose proudly from a sandstone base. Several large granite sheds abutted the main building, adding to the imposing size of the structure. The American flag, reminding them that they were approaching America, flew proudly above the majestic building. Erzsi understood why the peasant had mistaken it for a palace, but she knew America did not have royalty. Life would be different in America.

A ferry came alongside the ship. The steerage passengers watched, and waited, as the upper class passengers and American citizens were transferred from the *Closinda* to the ferry. They had been processed on the ship and were free to disembark. Later, a tender would take the immigrants to Castle Garden for processing. The moment of parting was approaching.

13 Welcome to America

Castle Garden, New York
June, 1882

Suddenly, silence. The groaning of metal chains and the shouts of seamen had stopped abruptly when the gangplank was finally secured to the tender. Everyone seemed to be listening to the creaking of the gangplank bobbing above the water, the lapping of waves against the wall of the pier. Even the children were quiet, sensing the tension in the crowd as the immigrants waited for permission to disembark. Erzsi thought she could hear her heart racing.

A clerk from the Health Department scanned them for signs of contagious illnesses; a family with a sick baby was separated from the rest. As the family was led away, confusion and fear passed like a wave through the crowd of steerage passengers. Would they too be taken away, refused entrance into the country they had struggled to reach?

A signal was given, a barrier removed. Slowly everyone began to move toward the gangplank with their bundles, boxes, and suitcases balanced on their heads or thrown over their shoulders. A wide-eyed baby rocked to and fro on its mother's back, while a boy clung tightly to his father's shoulders as they marveled and worried at the chaotic scene about them.

Erzsi pursed her lips as she approached the gangplank. Ten steps she counted, it would take ten steps to walk down the short gangplank, ten steps and she would be in America. She took a deep breath then quickly let it out.

The tenth step. One more step and she would be in America. She could feel Josef's presence close behind her. A wave of sadness coursed through her body. "How will I say good-bye to him? What if I start to cry?" Tightness formed in her stomach, a lump in her throat.

"Are you all right?" Josef could see, but misinterpreted, the worry on her face.

"Yes," she hesitated. "Yes, I'm fine." Her voice quavered slightly.

She looked so vulnerable, yet so determined, the heavy bundle on her back, her pillow clutched under her arm. Her eyes, warm and filled with emotion, melted his resolve to say good-bye. He wanted her, wanted to protect her, wanted to stay with her a little longer.

"Would you like me to stay with you until you are safely on your way?"

"That really isn't necessary," she spoke bravely but regretted the words as soon as she said them.

"It really is no problem." His confident, casual tone did not match the turmoil he felt, the growing need to touch her, to be with her. "We both need to go through processing. It would be nice to have company."

"I would be very grateful to you if you would." She felt like she would collapse with relief. The inevitable good-bye was to happen sometime in the future. Or, maybe, there wouldn't be a good-bye.

Police were on the pier diligently watching for anyone who would try to take advantage of the immigrants. Erzsi shivered remembering the beggars in Vienna and the despicable scoundrel in Hamburg. New York City would be no different. She moved a little closer to Josef, thankful that he was with her.

Officers of the Immigration Commissioners and the Custom House were guiding the new arrivals, making order out of the chaotic scene. "Baggage, over there!" Bags, boxes, trunks, suitcases, and various other objects, some of mysterious appearance, were being loaded onto carts to be taken to a warehouse.

Erzsi accepted brass tokens from the Customs Clerk for the bundle she carried on her back and for her basket but she would not relinquish her feather pillow or the cloth bag Clara had given her. Josef gave them his suitcase.

"Do you see Agnes and Ilona?"

"Over there!" Agnes and Ilona were supervising the placement of their belongings on another cart.

"Looks like another line is forming," Josef said as they joined their friends.

"Well hurry then, we want to be at the front of the line." Ilona, with the exuberance of youth, did not have the patience for the adults who did not seem to understand the importance of being first in the line.

"There's Amalia," Erzsi saw her friend approaching the gangplank. The baby was secured in a shawl tied around her neck, her fidgety sons, who would have preferred to make a mad dash down the gangplank, were controlled only by their mother's stern commands. Her husband was behind them bent slightly to the right under the weight of the trunk he had balanced on his shoulder.

"She looks tired," Erzsi said, worried about her friend.

"We are all tired and it's getting hot out here." Agnes was loosening the top buttons on her jacket. The breeze from the water was not enough to tame the heat that was building on this cloudless June day.

"And I'm hungry," Ilona complained. "We have not eaten since breakfast."

Ilona's efforts to hurry the proceedings did not achieve their purpose. They waited, like the others, in the heat of the June afternoon with no shelter from the sun, many still wearing their heavy traveling clothes, coats, scarves, shawls, and woolen hats. Everyone was exhausted and hungry. They had not eaten since breakfast on the ship. Many were clutching tired children, but still they waited patiently.

The line was forming outside a narrow passage-way, where they would again be examined for disease and their ability to care for themselves. Those who might be compelled to resort to charity or were showing signs of illness would be taken to Ward Island for further investigation. Some would be sent home on the steamer that brought them to America. It was considered to be the responsibility of the steamship companies to pay their return fare since they had not been properly screened before embarking on the voyage.

Erzsi moved through the line with the others.

"Do you have money?" she was asked when she reached the agent.

"Yes," she said showing him the coins she still had.

"Friends in the city?"

"No."

"Anywhere in the country?"

"Yes, Rondout, New York."

"What do you expect to do?"

"Work in a boarding house owned by a family friend."

The agent was satisfied with her answers. Josef was next.

With relief they all passed the inspection and entered a massive circular room but again they waited. They were held behind a maze-like barrier while a crew of scowling workmen mopped the floors.

From behind the barrier they could see the room that signified for them the grandeur and promise of the world they were about to call their home. Beams of sunlight filtered down from a large glass dome to the large circular space in the center of the room. To Erzsi it looked like the hand of God was welcoming them to America. Thin, tapering columns with fluted tops appeared to hold up the dome, elaborate moldings graced the ceilings. Under the glass dome were multifarious enclosures, where sat money changers, agents of the railroad companies, telegraph operators, and registration clerks. Officials speaking every language and dialect of Europe were ready to assist the immigrants.

The apprehensive, tired, excited immigrants waiting behind the barriers finally were allowed to enter the Rotunda. It was a heterogeneous mass of people that entered the Rotunda. They came from Southern Italy, the Russian Empire, Austria-Hungary, Greece, Romania, and the Ottoman Empire to find a better life in America. Irish girls, with their light hair and soft brogues, Russians with long wooly grayish overcoats and fur hats, Italians with dark hair, lustrous eyes and gay colored scarves, Slavs and Greeks, all crowded into the room waiting to be given permission to enter their new country.

Babies were crying, children playing, men talking loudly in a myriad of unintelligible languages; the discordant babel assaulted their ears. Mothers with pinched, long-drawn faces rocked their infants to and fro as they found seats on the wooden benches that circled the room.

"Look, look over there, under the dome, in the center of the room," Ilona was pointing to a group that had gathered in what was apparently a solemn ceremony.

"It's a wedding," Agnes said in disbelief.

A priest, a long green stole with embroidered Latin crosses draped around his neck, a black book in his hand, was prepared to conduct the sacrament. In front of him stood a young man and woman desiring, it would seem, to join in Holy Matrimony.

The bride, a woman of perhaps twenty years of age, her face radiant with happiness, stood tall, expectant as she clutched a bouquet of daisies. Light from the glass dome glittering off her long flaxen hair gave the impression of angel dust sprinkling from the heavens. Next to her, a young man, holding his cap tight in his hand, looked awkward and clumsy next to his radiant bride.

A shrewd looking woman, in an official looking uniform, stood near the girl. She had spotted the girl earlier and had taken her aside for questioning. Discovering that the unmarried girl had traveled with a companion with promises of marriage she had spoken to the Registration Clerk.

"You came across together didn't you?" the Clerk asked the young man while pointing to the girl.

"Yes, Sir."

"Do you intend to marry her?"

"When we are settled," answered the young man, looking embarrassed, shifting from one foot to the other as his treachery was revealed.

"Better have it done now," responded the Clerk. A priest, from a nearby parish, was called for. Rings were borrowed. This was not the first hasty marriage to be performed at Castle Garden.

"The groom looks rather solemn," observed Erzsi.

"Or perhaps trapped," Josef spoke with a laugh in his voice. "I'll wager the crafty young man had made promises of marriage before they began the voyage."

"She looks lovely," Ilona said, ignoring Josef's comments. She was standing on her toes to get a better view of the bride. "Look at her bouquet!"

"Someone must have picked them for her when they went to fetch the priest," a woman standing next to them observed.

"The daisies are a perfect flower for the bride. I wonder if she will press them and place them in a book to cherish forever." Ilona was wistfully thinking of the wedding plans she had made with Rudi before his parents sent him away.

A bell rang. The clerk at the registration desk was ready, a line was forming. "I'll go first," volunteered Erzsi with a look of confidence she did not feel.

The Clerk sat on a small stool behind the counter looking very official under his cap. His ledger was open and his pen was poised to write down the information given to him.

"Nationality," he asked when Erzsi approached the desk. He did not look up from his ledger.

"Magyar," she responded.

"*Hajó*, ship," he asked in Hungarian. The clerks spoke many of the more common European languages.

"The *Closinda.*"

He selected a page in his roster. "Name."

"Erzsi Viarka." The clerk found her name on the ship's roster.

"Destination."

"Rondout, New York."

He compared the information to the ship manifest made a few notes and nodded.

Trying to contain a giggle, Erzsi observed that his mustache twitched as he asked her the questions. You could tell from the look on his face that he was bored, and he wrote quickly so as to move on to the next immigrant.

"Next!" he said without looking up. Erzsi was dismissed.

Registrations complete, it was time to say good-bye. Agnes went to catch her train for Iowa. She had sent her husband a telegram so he would know when to expect her. Amalia and her family were reunited with relatives. Josef stayed with Erzsi. He was feeling awkward standing there while the women were saying their good-byes but he was not ready to leave Erzsi. Pushing any uncomfortable thoughts from his mind he just watched her and knew he needed to stay with her for just a while longer.

Ilona's name was called, her brother was here. "Erzsi, come with me. I want you to meet him." Without giving Erzsi a chance to respond, Ilona took her arm and started to guide her to the waiting area. Erzsi turned to Josef and gestured for him to join them. He shook his head no. "I'll go to the Labor Bureau and meet you here later."

Ilona pushed through the crowd, dragging Erzsi behind her. They were laughing, their pace quickened until it was almost a run. Then, abruptly, without warning, Ilona stopped. A tall handsome man dressed in the American style was standing in the doorway of the waiting room. An attractive woman stood next to him holding his arm.

"There he is." Erzsi was forgotten as Ilona ran to her brother. With tears of delight the reunited family hugged and laughed. In that instant all the heartbreak of a forbidden love, separation from home, and an ocean voyage melted away.

Wishing Ilona a lifetime of happiness in America, Erzsi set out to find the Money Exchange. She had coins that she could exchange for American money. Reaching into her pocket searching for the coins, her hand briefly touched the prayer book with the rose. She thought of her mother. "I know she would have liked Josef." Smiling, she handed the clerk her coins.

After the Money Exchange, she went to the Letter-Writing Department to purchase postcards to send to Clara, Iren and Peter. To her surprise Josef was there passing a postcard to the clerk.

"Josef," she called to him as he turned from the clerk.

"Erzsi," he looked startled, maybe even a little embarrassed. "I was sending a postcard to my sister," he said a little too quickly covering his guilty lie with a smile.

Erzsi was surprised. Josef had spoken of his brothers but never a sister. It reminded her how little she knew about him.

"I was going to buy postcards to send to Iren and Clara. I have so much to tell them, but perhaps for now a picture and a note is all I can manage."

Josef leaned against a pole and watched her as she carefully inspected the postcards looking for the perfect image to send to her loved ones. Watching her he wondered why he was staying with her, why didn't he just go on his way? His future was with Maria, he had made a vow. But when Erzsi walked to join him, her postcards mailed, all thoughts of Maria vanished.

"I got these on the way back from the Labor Bureau." He held out two apples and offered one to Erzsi. "There was an old woman, Irish I think, who was selling apples. I thought you would like one."

"Thank you. Did you have any success at the Labor Bureau?" She took a bite out of the apple. She had forgotten she hadn't eaten since breakfast on the ship.

"There was a very persuasive representative from the Newark Lime &Cement Company," he said with a twinkle in his eye. Erzsi's heart sank. This was the end.

"Is the job here in New York City?"

"No, it is in a section of Kingston called Rondout. I think you know of the place?" he said teasingly.

Erzsi's heart was pounding. The boarding house where she hoped to work was in Rondout. She had told him where she was going the day of the storm at sea. She stared at him for a moment, not believing what she had heard. He had chosen to go to Rondout knowing she was going there.

At the labor bureau there had been many job opportunities. Josef considered staying here in New York City. As planned he would work here for a year and then take a ship back home.

Then he was approached by the representative from Rondout. He thought of Erzsi. "We are friends. I like being with her. What harm will it do?" He accepted the offer without further thought. "We have no power over fate," he rationalized.

"I have tickets for the riverboat *Mary Powell*. I told the representative I needed a ticket for my wife. If you want to come with me, the *Mary Powell* is leaving for Rondout tomorrow afternoon."

She threw her arms around him and without thinking kissed him passionately on the mouth.

"I guess that means yes," he said laughing as she pulled away.

As evening approached they found a space on the floor where they could lie down for the night. Some of the immigrants found rooms in boarding houses or inexpensive hotels but those without money simply stayed at Castle Garden.

Erzsi had her pillow and Josef folded his coat and used it as a headrest. As she was getting settled he reached out his arm for her. She hesitated for a minute and then accepted his embrace. Her body was close to his, nestled in his arms, her head resting on his shoulder.

There was a loud clap of thunder followed by a flash of lightning. The rain fell with heavy drops on the glass dome. Erzsi, listening to the rain, felt safe and content in Josef's arms. But there was a new feeling of doubt, a warning that she kept pushing away, refusing to acknowledge. She kept thinking of Agnes telling her to be careful. What did she know of Josef? He had a secret. She had seen it on his face when she had asked him about the postcard he handed to the clerk. He was always evasive when she asked him about his family. Perhaps he had left a woman at home waiting for his return. Maybe he had made promises that they would be married. She didn't want to think about it now.

Safe in his arms she could hear his heart beating. She closed her eyes and drifted off to sleep. She dreamt of home. She was bringing fresh water from the well to her father while her mother was tending the vegetable garden, Iren was in the kitchen and Clara was playing with her doll. In the dream her world was safe, familiar, she was content.

With Erzsi so close to him Josef was filled with desire. He wanted her but knew that he could not have her. He thought about the lie he had told when asked about the postcard. He had not planned to lie. Now it could not be undone. Erzsi was with him tonight, Maria was far away. He rationalized that fate was guiding events; he did not want to hurt anyone. For now he just needed to sleep.

Tomorrow they would board the *Mary Powell* and by evening they would be in Kingston.

14 A Day Trip on the Hudson

Castle Garden to Rondout
June 21, 1882

A ship's whistle sounded, it was loud, giving warning. She could feel the hard floor beneath her, she was uncomfortable, stiff, sore, but still could not open her eyes. All around her she could hear whispering, groaning, friendly greetings, bodies moving and scraping against the benches and floor.

Erzsi sat up abruptly, eyes wide, momentarily disoriented. The stale smell of cigars and tobacco and the stink of unwashed bodies saturated the room, she gasped for air. She was alone.

Josef? Where was Josef?

Last night they had settled onto the floor, between the benches. His arm had reached out inviting her, tempting her to nestle her head on his chest. She had accepted the invitation, shyly at first, but then with gratitude. It had been comforting to feel his arms around her, to listen to his heart beating steadily. She had drifted to sleep, oblivious of the unrelenting drone of soft voices comforting children, the earnest exchanges of men unable to sleep, discussing their options.

He was not next to her now. His cap and jacket were gone. There was just a cold empty space, a hard floor, where there had been warmth and comfort. Where did he go? Had he left her? There was no reason for him to stay. "I barely know him," she reminded herself, blushing at the realization that she had spent the night asleep in his arms. Shame, embarrassment, a sense of loss, and a tumult of emotions clamored for recognition as she assessed her circumstances.

She scanned the room looking past the families, past the benches with sleeping men, past the clerks settling at their desks. He wasn't there.

Then she saw him. He was making his way through the crowd, walking in her direction. He was skillfully navigating the benches, stepping gingerly over parcels, and barely avoided a potentially disastrous collision with a running child. He saw her watching and gave her a smile, almost tripping on the feet of a man sleeping on the floor. She lowered her gaze, stifling a laugh. All thoughts of facing the day alone vanished.

"Thought you might be hungry," he said producing a warm muffin from his pocket. "There is a canteen on the other side of the Rotunda," he said while splitting the muffin offering half to her. She took it with a smile. Breaking off a small piece she savored the warmth and sweetness of the gift.

Josef watched her, his thoughts conflicted. Her clothes were rumpled; her tangled hair loose around her shoulders, her eyes still puffy with sleep. He wanted to kiss her.

He had never seen Maria looking like this. Maria was always gone from their bed when he awoke. He would find her in the kitchen, her hair neatly pulled back in a bun, her apron in place, her face slightly flushed from the heat of the stove as she prepared breakfast. She was efficient, capable, humble, and she adored him. Maria was everything a man could hope for in a wife. He pushed the memory away and looked again at the woman who sat next to him.

She was delicate, rumpled, vulnerable, a pillow from home resting on her lap, yet she had courage, and resilience. She had left the safety of her home and braved a long arduous ocean voyage. He wanted to wrap his arms around her. He wanted to make love to her.

"When will we board the *Mary Powell?*" she asked, breaking the spell.

"Boarding begins at 2:30 this afternoon," he said finishing his half of the muffin. "I'm going for a walk." He stood, adjusting his cap. "Do you want to come?" he said, almost as an afterthought. Erzsi nodded her head with a glance at her pillow. "You can check that. We will get it later."

Unencumbered by their belongings, they spent the morning exploring the beautifully landscaped park outside the rotunda. They were like young lovers on holiday. Josef offered Erzsi his arm and they followed shaded promenades through flower-filled gardens, looked with curiosity at the old salt baths, and stopping briefly to admire the swans and deer kept safely in an enclosure.

"Do you smell garlic and onions? It smells like my sister's kitchen."

A German immigrant was selling sausages from his cart. The familiar food reminded them of home and their expressions showed that they shared a common memory. A smile was exchanged and Erzsi nodded her head yes. They bought the sausages and settled on a nearby bench overlooking the harbor. Eating in silence, sitting as close together as propriety would allow, they listened to the waves pounding gently on the seawall.

A ship's whistle sounded and a seagull screeched. A cooling mist formed when a wave crashed against the seawall bringing the briny smell of the salt air to them. Erzsi was filled with a peace she had not known for a long time.

"I think the Russian Czar must own that yacht," Erzsi said pointing to an exquisitely appointed vessel that was slowly making its way towards the Atlantic Ocean.

"Perhaps he is here with his mistress," Josef said with a mischievous grin.

"You mustn't talk like that," Erzsi laughed shaking her head.

"It's time to go back. The *Mary Powell* is waiting." Josef allowed Erzsi to take his arm as they walked back to the Rotunda.

"Oh, I am happy today," Erzsi thought as she held Josef's arm. "I will remember this day forever." She glanced at Josef, the love that was growing in her heart was evident in her eyes. Josef was looking at the ships in the harbor and didn't notice.

The *Mary Powell* was waiting proudly and patiently at the pier. "Beautiful, she is absolutely beautiful,"

Erzsi's eyes sparkled with delight. The steamboat was majestic, her large white side-wheel hinting of her power, and the spacious breeze-swept decks promising spectacular vistas for passengers to enjoy.

Smoke from her stacks and the sound of the ship's whistle signaled onlookers that soon she would be leaving New York Harbor.

Erzsi, hampered by the pillow, the basket, the cloth bag, and the bundle on her back, found it difficult to keep up with Josef who was walking ahead, anxious to join the crowd going up the gangplank. Turning, he saw her distress, took the bundle off her back and slung it over his shoulder. Released from the awkward weight she quickened her step, this time outdistancing Josef.

"All right," he laughed catching up to her. "I can see you can outrun me if the need should arise."

There was a holiday mood shared by everyone walking up the gangplank: families with baby carriages, toddlers in the arms of their fathers, boys anxious to run but restrained by a glance from a parent, young men pushing bicycles, and dogs enjoying the adventure with their owners. Young ladies with parasols held the arms of their beaus while elderly couples, supported by their canes, walked with slower, more deliberate steps.

Music wafted from the ship, a rollicking upbeat song was playing and men were singing:

> *'Twas Friday morn when we set sail,*
> *And we had not got far from land,*

When the Captain, he spied a lovely mermaid,
With a comb and a glass in her hand.

As the passengers walked up the gangway a few picked up the chorus and a festive mood prevailed.

Oh the ocean waves may roll,
And the stormy winds may blow,
While we poor sailors go skipping aloft
And the land lubbers lay down below, below, below
And the land lubbers lay down below.

Working slowly through the crowd Erzsi and Josef pushed their way to the stern of the ship. They wanted the best possible view of New York City as their boat left the harbor. They stood close together at the ship's railing high above the wharf with its bustling activity. "Perfect! For this moment in time everything is perfect!" thought Erzsi as she slipped her hand under Josef's arm. "New York City is not as beautiful as Budapest with its palaces and grand buildings," she said smiling. "But the Hudson River is surely much grander than the Danube."

Promptly at 2:30PM the ship's whistle sounded, the engines came to life, a puff of steam escaped from the stacks and the huge paddle-wheels began to move. The *Mary Powell* left her berth and headed for destinations along the Hudson River. With the cool, refreshing breeze from the water gently caressing her face, Erzsi sighed with contentment.

The *Mary Powell* with unrelenting purpose navigated the blue waters of the Hudson. She was known to be the fastest steamboat on the river and she always arrived at her destination exactly on time. Her reputation would not be tarnished on this day. Often referred to as "Queen of the Hudson" she proudly glided past yachts, transatlantic steamships, sailboats, tugs, and freighters. She sounded her horn and passengers waved, acknowledging a steamer on its return trip to New York City.

The busy harbor was left behind. The passengers watched as the city skyline was replaced by the steep cliffs of the Palisades which rose nearly vertically from the edge of the river. Gradually the river widened and the ship was in the broad, blue Tappan Zee. There was little conversation on the deck; even the children were momentarily quiet, enthralled by the spectacular, ever changing landscape.

They passed a lighthouse under construction in a place called Tarrytown and again the scenery changed as the river narrowed and wound through a rugged mountainous landscape.

Approaching a bend in the river, the ship's whistle announced their arrival at West Point. In front of them with a backdrop of high, rocky, mountains were gray buildings nestled on top of a hill. As the steamer prepared for landing, bell signals were heard, letting the pilot know when the gangway was lined up with the dock. Erzsi marveled at the power of the ship and the skill of the pilot. She listened to the rumble of the reversing engines and watched the foam from the paddle wheel as their ship made a perfect landing.

On the dock, cadets in their blue-grey uniforms waited for family and friends making a long anticipated visit. They welcomed the warm hugs given by their mothers and the proud handshakes of their fathers. Erzsi watched with a smile as a slender woman in a lace-trimmed pastel dress with a full skirt gathered at her slim waist twirled her parasol as she beamed at her cadet. A young boy of maybe eleven or twelve years of age proudly saluted a cadet.

Always on time, the *Mary Powell* did not tarry at West Point. The ship's whistle blew, signaling an imminent departure, goodbyes were hastily said to those staying behind. Passengers continuing to destinations up the river boarded the ship.

They passed a small island with what appeared to be an old fortress made of stone. Erzsi was reminded of the castles she had seen in Europe, but large concrete letters pronounced it to be BANNERMAN's ISLAND ARSENAL. The *Mary Powell*, its large paddle wheels moving with purpose, passed wooded shores with magnificent mansions, and a large railroad bridge that was under construction.

Beyond the bridge they made a stop at the Poughkeepsie wharf. While the ship was docked, Erzsi and Josef took the opportunity to explore the ship. They watched the musicians who were playing *My Bonnie Lies Over the Ocean* while passengers with much drama and laughter were swaying and singing.

Erzsi didn't understand the words but she hummed the tune and her body moved in time with the music.

They found the restaurant and realized they were both getting hungry. Erzsi touched her scarf and absently tried to straighten her curls as she watched the well-dressed ladies enter the restaurant. The scarf, which had been so lovingly embroidered, was now an embarrassment. It marked her as an immigrant. Josef noticed and understood her discomfort.

"Let's get something from the cafeteria and bring it onto the deck where we can enjoy the fresh air." He took her arm, guiding her away from the restaurant. Erzsi didn't resist.

They ate chicken sandwiches standing at the railing on the bow of the ship. There was a lighthouse on a tiny rocky island in the middle of the river. "Iren's boys would love to climb those rocks," thought Erzsi. "Clara would appreciate the beauty of the white clapboard cottage with its tower and red roof." She felt a tug at her heart as she thought of the family she had left behind.

The voyage neared its end as the *Mary Powell* passed the Kingston Lighthouse and the pilot skillfully guided her into Rondout Harbor.

Erzsi and Josef lifted their belongings and headed for the gang-plank. Erzsi was aware of how different they were from the animated vacationers surrounding them. Their poorly made clothing and heavy bags marked them as immigrants. The conversations around her, animated, excited, were in a language she did not understand. No one would understand her if she asked a question. She had nothing in common with the vacationers on their way to the Catskills. She was here to work, to begin a new life. The excitement, anticipation, and freedom she had felt earlier in the day was being replaced by uneasiness. She glanced at Josef and he could see the worry on her face.

"Don't worry. Together we will be safe. We will look after each other." He gave her what he hoped was a reassuring smile. "Together we will be safe." The words echoed in her heart.

They knew nothing about the town they were about to enter. Erzsi tightly held the letter from Yolanda and showed the address to passersby who pointed in the direction they should go. Dark, billowing clouds were forming on the horizon; a summer squall was approaching. They quickened their pace, but it was not easy with their cumbersome belongings. With their final destination in view, a clap of thunder, a flash of lightning, and heavy raindrops hit their faces. They ran to the door of Mrs. Timko's boarding house.

Book 3

Seduction

15 Mrs. Timko's Boarding House

East Kingston, New York
Last week of June, 1882

The dark, forbidding door, offering their only shelter from the storm, was closed against them. Josef knocked while Erzsi clutched at her shawl, an inadequate shield from the pelting rain. Beyond the door could be heard the sounds of men talking and laughing. Dishes and cutlery clanked, followed by women's voices and more laughter. Then came another loud rumble of thunder and a flash of lightning. Erzsi moved closer to the door. Would anyone hear them? Were they even at the right house, would they be welcome? The letter from Yolanda was probably wet, ruined, and unreadable. Without the letter Erzsi had no proof of who she was or what she had been promised. They were too wet, too tired, too desperate to worry about being rude. Together Erzsi and Josef pounded on the door.

Slowly it opened. A somber looking woman dressed in black, wary of the unexpected visitors standing on her doorstep, stood behind the half-opened door.

"Yes?" she asked cautiously, ready to slam the door shut at the slightest provocation. The bedraggled couple, loaded down with parcels, the woman clutching a soggy pillow, looked like beggars or street people seeking shelter from the storm. She ran a respectable boarding house and had no room or patience for vagrants.

"What do you want?" the woman asked, her voice brisk, making it clear they were unwelcome.

"Please, my name is Erzsi Viarka." A razor sharp bolt of lightning flashed across the sky, Erzsi flinched, her words lost in the storm around them. Josef stepped behind her as though to protect her from the storm. The woman reflexively stepped back into the room. Erzsi was afraid she would close the door and leave them standing in the rain.

"*Bemehetunk?* May we come in?" Erzsi's voice was strong but desperate. Josef, pulling his cap further down over his eyes, was getting angry. He wasn't about to stand here much longer.

The woman's expression softened hearing the words spoken in Hungarian. She looked again at the girl, but the presence of the man was unsettling. She expected a young woman who was in need of employment. A letter from Hungary, from their dear friend Yolanda, had asked that her husband's cousin be welcomed into their house. "She is trustworthy and will work hard for you," Yolanda had written. Her sister Adel had insisted it was the right thing to do. Ethel was not sure they were in need of additional help.

"Erzsi?"

"Yes."

"Erzsi, yes of course, of course, come in. Come in quickly." Looking at Josef with suspicion, Ethel opened the door a little further and gestured for them to enter the hallway. "Hurry." She backed away, not wanting their wet clothes to touch her dress, her eyes looking with disapproval at the water collecting on the floor.

"Stay here, I will get my sister." Adel had insisted on hiring the girl, Adel could deal with this problem. Ethel, holding her skirts so they would not touch the puddles forming on the floor, went to find Adel.

Relieved they were out of the storm but uncomfortable at the unfriendly reception, they dared not move from the spot where the commanding, unpleasant woman had left them. Their eyes followed the woman as she walked briskly down the long dark hallway. There was a worn, faded carpet covering the wooden floor. Steep, uncarpeted stairs led to the second floor where the flickering reflection of an oil lamp welcomed those who ascended. There was a musty smell in the hallway, cigar and pipe smoke mingled with the smell of work clothes and men who toiled for a living.

On their right was a long narrow room that, Erzsi guessed, served as a sitting area for the boarders. The room was filled with heavy, plush furniture. Ornate drapes, accented by gold fringe and tassels, cascaded gently to the floor. Even though everything in the room showed signs of wear, Erzsi was impressed with the warm inviting look of the room. "Clara would approve," she thought.

In a corner of the room a middle-aged man sat next to an oil lamp that Ethel had generously lit early due to the storm. The gentleman did not look like the laborers whom Erzsi had expected to see at the boarding house. He was wearing a waistcoat, jacket, and carefully pressed trousers. Spectacles were placed precariously on the bridge of his nose. His head was bent slightly forward. There was a frown on his face, perhaps caused by a story in the newspaper he was reading. He briefly looked up at the intruders, acknowledged them with a nod, adjusted his paper, and returned to his task.

Erzsi was miserable standing there; her skirt was rumpled and wet. Her curls, unruly most of the time, now clung in wet strands around her face. The feather pillow that always gave her comfort was now a soggy bundle steadily dripping water on the polished hardwood floor.

Josef held his cap restlessly in his hand and held his suitcase firmly. He was uncomfortable and did not want to stay where he was not wanted. These were friends of Erzsi's family. What would they say about this strange man traveling with her? Would they report back in their letters that Erzsi was traveling with a man? Would someone find out that he was married and report to Maria?

"I will go now. You are safe," he turned to walk toward the door.

"No! No, wait. You can't go back out there."

He hesitated as two old men entered the hallway from the kitchen. Erzsi was familiar with men like this, shoulders stooped from a life of heavy labor, leathery wrinkled skin, eyes dull with age and worry.

A deep, painful cough caused one of the men to hold his chest in an ineffective attempt to gain control.

The two men looked briefly, with just a little curiosity, at the man and woman standing near the door. One man mumbled a greeting, the other just continued to cough as he walked up the creaking stairs.

Male voices in a heated discussion followed by a quiet comment and raucous laughter could be heard in a distant room. The younger men, not in a hurry to go to their beds, were probably still in the dining room, thought Erzsi.

A rather ordinary, but not homely young woman came rushing from the kitchen, wiping her hands on her apron.

"Erzsi, my dear Erzsi, welcome, welcome," Adel took Erzsi's hands, gently squeezing them. "We are so glad you are finally here. Yolanda wrote letting us know to expect you."

Still holding Erzsi's hands, she glanced with a slight frown at Josef. She and Ethel had argued about him in the kitchen. "She is traveling with a man," Ethel had exclaimed, objecting to the impropriety. "We don't know the circumstances. Don't be so quick to judge," Adel had scolded her sister.

"Adel, let me introduce Mr. Josef Farkas."

"Josef, this is Miss Adel Toth."

Josef made a slight bow to acknowledge the introduction. Adel did not offer her hand to the rain-soaked man, she simply nodded. "Erzsi, come with me to the kitchen. You need to get dry. I will make us some tea. Mr. Farkas, thank you for bringing Erzsi safely to us." Adel moved to the door, pointedly dismissing the uninvited stranger who was standing in her hallway.

"Adel, Josef doesn't have a place to stay tonight."

Adel looked at the man standing in the hallway, his wet cap held in his hands dripping water on her floor. "I'm not sure we have room, this is unexpected."

"It's quite all right, Miss Toth. I will be on my way." Josef turned to the door, briefly touching his cap to indicate he was leaving. He had no interest in staying where he was not wanted.

"Josef, wait."

Adel heard the worry in Erzsi's tone. "This Josef is more than a kind stranger," she thought.

"Adel, please, Josef has been very kind to me. I'm not sure I would have found my way here without him," Erzsi pleaded knowing she was pushing the bounds of etiquette. Adel was under no obligation to welcome this man into her home.

"I don't want to impose, Miss Toth. Now that Miss Viarka is safe I will find lodging elsewhere."

Ethel was walking down the hall. She was carrying towels and a basin of water to be delivered to the upstairs bedrooms. With a frown she glanced from Adel, to Erzsi, and with a deeper frown her gaze rested on Josef. "He hasn't left yet," she was thinking.

"Ethel, have you been introduced to Mr. Farkas?"

Ethel just frowned.

"Mr. Farkas, this is my sister, Mrs. Timko."

"Pleased to meet you, Mrs. Timko," Josef made a polite bow of his head, his cap in his hand.

Ethel simply nodded acknowledgement.

"Mr. Farkas needs a place to stay tonight. Could he share a bed with Mr. Kulak?"

"I can pay and would be most grateful," Josef said. Despite his discomfort with the situation, it was still raining and he did not have any other place to stay.

Ethel stood there for a moment looking at the bedraggled couple who had shown up on her doorstep in the middle of a storm. She was not an unkind woman but she prided herself on running an efficient, clean and respectable boarding house. Again she looked down at the puddle of water forming on her floor. Clearly they could not stand here much longer.

"Just for tonight then, we will discuss compensation in the morning," Ethel reluctantly agreed. "I believe Mr. Kulak has already gone upstairs. You will find him in the first room on the left."

"Thank you, Mrs. Timko. Your kindness is appreciated."

"Adel, take his hat and jacket, hang them in the kitchen to dry." Ethel turned, resuming her task delivering water and fresh towels to her boarders. Josef gave Adel his jacket and cap and followed Ethel up the stairs.

"Come then, we need to get you dry." Adel led Erzsi to the kitchen.

"What wealth they must have," Erzsi thought as she followed Adel. "So many rooms in one house!" A whole family could live in the room where she had seen the man reading.

With efficiency Adel set up two large drying racks, the size of which amazed Erzsi who had never seen such contrivances. "We do a lot of laundry here," said Adel, noting Erzsi's expression. Adel draped Josef's jacket over one while Erzsi removed her scarf, wet shawl, and apron, draping them over the other. "Tomorrow we will hang the rest on the line." The smell of wet wool permeated the room.

"Sit down," Adel pointed to a chair at the square table in the center of the room. "Take off your shoes and your stockings as well," Adel ordered, but her tone was kind, solicitous. She put a pot of water on the stove to make the tea.

The rain had stopped. Adel opened the window, allowing the fresh evening air to drive away the odor of damp clothing. The breeze caused the curtains to flutter, reminding Erzsi of home.

"Tell me about Yolanda and her girls," Adel said while offering Erzsi a biscuit left over from the evening meal. "We were neighbors when we lived in Budapest. I adored the children, Bernadette and Dora were such beautiful and sweet babies. I never met little Jolàn, we left for America before she was born. We write letters, of course, and send pictures, but it isn't the same as being there."

"I have a photograph," Erzsi said producing a small portrait of Peter's family.

"The girls are growing so fast, soon suitors will be making their presence known."

"I'm not sure Peter is ready for that!" Erzsi laughed. "His girls are everything to him."

"Well, now you must tell me about your journey."

Erzsi recounted her adventure in Vienna with the beggars, the scoundrel in Hamburg and the horrible conditions in the lodging. The assault by the vulgar men was not mentioned, it was still too painful a memory.

She told her about Frau Mueller. "Her arms were as big as hams," Erzsi used her hands to demonstrate the girth of Frau Mueller's arms. "Her shoulders were like our neighbor's ox, she walked like this." Erzsi, walked across the kitchen imitating the confident, authoritative gate of the matron's stride. "I am Frau Mueller," she said, deepening her voice. "I will be in charge of you!" She looked sternly at Adel. "Now you must follow me," Erzsi waited until Adel realized she was meant to follow. "Germans first," Erzsi motioned for Adel to stand still. "Magyar next," her voice was stern as she nodded at Adel. "Hebrews at the end of the line," she pronounced the words as though they were an afterthought, Hebrews were barely to be acknowledged. The women marched around the kitchen until laughter required them to sit.

"And how did you meet this Josef Farkas?" Adel's tone was conspiratorial.

"Well it was a series of chance meetings, first on the train from Kosice and then on the ship," Erzsi spoke in a casual tone, not wanting to expose the depth of her attachment to Josef.

"So how did he come to be with you tonight?"

Erzsi did not mention that they were together at Castle Garden and spent the night together sleeping on the floor. "We met again on the *Mary Powell*. He offered to stay with me until I was safely here."

"Then I am glad he was with you." Adel was certain there was more to this story. She had seen how Erzsi looked at Josef. "I will thank him in the morning. I am sorry we were rude to him tonight."

"I am sure he was grateful you let him stay the night. Now tell me about yourself. Do you have a suitor?"

"No, no suitors. I am too busy; there is always so much to do. I'm glad my sister agreed to hire you. We can use the help and I could use a friend."

"So can I."

"We shall be friends then."

"Definitely." There was a pause in the conversation as the women smiled at each other, acknowledging the bond they were forming.

They talked about the boarders while they sipped their tea. One had lost his wife and daughter in a fire years ago. Mr. Bartos left a wife and three daughters in Budapest.

"Jimmy Chase, one of the younger men, likes the ladies. I am rather fond of Jimmy," Adel blushed just a little when she said this. "He has taken me on an outing from time to time, but I wouldn't call him a suitor. You are sure to like him, everyone does."

Erzsi smiled her encouragement and Adel continued.

"You probably saw Benjamin Sykes in the parlor reading his newspaper. Benjamin, never call him Ben, is a writer. He is smart, always neat and nicely dressed, very different from the other boarders. He works as a freelance writer for the Rondout Courier but he is also an aspiring novelist and poet. Sometimes, in the afternoons, he will read to us from a book of poems. Kipling, Longfellow, and Dickinson are his favorites."

Erzsi had never heard of any of them.

"Mr. Sykes has been with us for the past five years. My sister is very fond of him. He pays extra for the use of a small alcove in the attic where he keeps a desk and a wall filled with books. We don't know anything about his past but that doesn't matter. He has become family."

Finished with their tea, the oil lamp lit, Adel led the way to the small room behind the kitchen where she shared a bed with her sister. It was a modest room but clean and comfortable. The sisters slept on a large bed that nearly filled the room, Erzsi would sleep in a cot set up in a corner. Ethel was already asleep so Erzsi and Adel moved quietly around the room. Adel offered her a nightdress and a clean apron she could put over her dress in the morning. "It will have to do until we can get you some new clothes."

Lying still in her bed, Erzsi listened to the night sounds, Mrs. Timko gently snoring, Adel settling into her bed, an owl in a tree in the backyard. Her finger caressed the indented image of the crucifix on the cover of her prayer book as she said her prayers. She opened the book and let her hand rest on the yellow rose. They had been so happy the day the yellow rosebush arrived. So much had changed since then.

Her eyes drifted to the ceiling. Josef was up there, probably sleeping. She silently giggled at the not-unpleasant urge to sneak up the stairs and lie down next to him. Clutching her body with her arms, she imagined it was Josef's arms around her.

For his part Josef had fallen asleep as soon as his head touched the pillow. He had taken off his wet clothes and hung them from a hook. His cardboard suitcase had not offered much protection to its contents, but he would deal with that another day.

Tomorrow he would report to the cement factory. After the shift ended he would look for other lodging. But first, he would see Erzsi at breakfast. With that pleasant thought he fell into a deep, satisfying slumber.

16 Developing Friendships

East Kingston, New York
July, 1882

A woman was calling her name, "Erzsi, wake up."

"Not yet," she thought, it was still dark. She turned away from the voice, snuggling her face deeper into the pillow.

"Erzsi, the men will need their breakfast. I will meet you in the kitchen," the voice was authoritative. The door closed, she sensed she was alone in the room.

"I need to wake up." She fought the sleep that was pulling her back into her dream, struggled to force her reluctant eyes open.

Sounds from the kitchen, a door closing, water being poured into a basin, the clang of metal as a pan was placed on the stove. Erzsi opened her eyes. She heard voices in the kitchen, female voices, arguing, tense. Her name, Josef's name, the voices were suddenly soft, quiet. "They are talking about us," she realized, feeling embarrassed, humiliated. What were they saying about her? About Josef?

Scrambling to gather her belongings which had, for the most part, dried sufficiently, she quickly dressed, put on the clean apron Adel had given her, and headed for the kitchen.

"Well, it's about time. I was worried you would sleep all day," Adel said smiling, her tone teasing, as she chided Erzsi.

"At least she isn't angry with me," Erzsi thought.

"The men will be down for breakfast soon."

"What should I do?"

"Put these on the table." Adel handed Erzsi the cups and plates she was holding.

Ethel was in the hallway next to the stairs. It was her custom to greet her boarders as they came down for breakfast.

"Good Morning, Mr. Braun. How are you feeling today?" Ethel asked with genuine concern. She was very worried about Mr. Braun whose cough was steadily getting worse. He suffered from Black Lung Disease caused by coal dust. He worked on the canal boats shoveling coal that had been brought from Pennsylvania.

"Much better today, thank you, Ma'am." He usually felt better in the mornings. In the evenings, the cigar and pipe smoke in the dining room aggravated his cough.

"Good to hear, Mr. Braun. We will see you in the dining room."

"Josef," Mrs. Timko addressed him as he came down the stairs. "May I speak with you?"

"Of course," he said, putting down his suitcase. Uncertain of what she had to say, his expression was friendly but reserved.

"Erzsi spoke highly of you. She was very grateful for the help you gave her."

"It was nothing."

"She was concerned you may not be able to find suitable lodging."

"I'll find a place," Josef was feeling uncomfortable, a little defensive. He was more than capable of caring for himself, he didn't need the intervention of a woman.

"You are welcome to stay here."

"I would not want to impose," Josef was surprised by the invitation and the softening tone of Mrs. Timko's voice.

"You can continue to share the bed with Mr. Kulak. I assume that would be satisfactory."

"Very satisfactory, Ma'am," he said while looking politely at Mrs. Timko but thinking about Erzsi. He would be seeing her again, a very pleasant thought.

"You may join the others for breakfast if you like."

"Thank you, Ma'am." Leaving his suitcase near the stairs, he headed towards the dining room.

Josef was at the table with the other men when Erzsi brought out the coffee. "*Jó reggelt*, good-morning, Mr. Farkas." She poured his coffee but could not look at him. He might see the worry on her face. Would she ever see him again?

"*Jó reggelt*, Miss Viarka," he responded, his voice pleasant, unconcerned. He moved his arm so it gently touched hers. Her body instantly responded, she could feel the flush in her cheeks. She moved away, looking down at the carpet, hoping no one had noticed.

"*Jó reggelt,*" she said to the man sitting next to Josef while pouring his coffee.

"*Jó reggelt,* Miss Viarka," the man's voice was soft, friendly, instantly putting Erzsi at ease. It was Benjamin Sykes, she recognized him from the night before when she saw him reading the newspaper in the parlor.

"*Jó reggelt,* Mr. Sykes."

"You look very much like my sister," Benjamin said to her in English. Erzsi nodded, smiled, pretending to understand. Adel heard him. Strange, he had never mentioned he had a sister. Benjamin was a mystery. Always polite, impeccably dressed, he was the ideal boarder. Five years ago, he arrived in Rondout, started working for the newspaper, and moved into their boarding house. He never spoke about his family or about his past life.

"Good morning, Sweetheart," said a young man with a big grin and a mischievous look in his eyes. "A pretty woman like you is a welcome sight in the morning." Before she could move away he had his arm around her waist. "Come and sit with me a bit," he was using his arm to bring her closer; his other hand was tapping his lap. Erzsi nearly spilled the coffee she was holding as she tried to maintain her balance.

"Leave her alone, Jimmy, she will spill the coffee," Adel intervened; she had just entered the room with a basket of biscuits.

Erzsi gave him a sweet smile and quickly moved away. Adel had warned her Jimmy liked the ladies.

The other boarders either ignored her, preferring to spend the time talking with each other, or looked at her with mild curiosity. By her clothing, especially her scarf, which she wore even in the house, they assumed she was an immigrant who probably did not speak the language.

"I can finish in here," Adel said to Erzsi, when she had finished pouring the coffee. "Start cleaning the pots in the kitchen."

Erzsi wanted to say good-bye to Josef, but he was talking to the man who had left his family in Hungary. He didn't look her way.

"Yes, I came through Hamburg," she heard Josef say in Hungarian, "the *Closinda*, Hamburg Amerika Linie."

Filled with regret, this was likely the last she would see of him, Erzsi went to find the pot that needed scrubbing. Ethel walked into the kitchen. She had removed her apron and was pinning her hat into place in preparation for her daily trip to the market.

"Erzsi," Ethel went to the sink where Erzsi was struggling to remove the burnt oatmeal from the pot.

"Yes, Ethel," Erzsi's voice was polite; she hoped it was appropriately friendly. Ethel was her employer.

Ethel spoke when she was sure she had Erzsi's full attention. "I want you to know that I disapprove of your conduct last night. It was extremely rude of you to show up here, unannounced, with a gentleman. However," she paused for effect, "Adel explained to me how helpful Josef had been bringing you here safely." Again she waited, noting the concern on Erzsi's face. "I now understand it was never his intent or yours for him to enter the house. The storm changed everything." Erzsi nodded her head in agreement. She was too nervous to say anything. "I have agreed that he can stay here," Ethel's expression had softened, there was the hint of a smile on her face.

Erzsi nearly dropped the pot. She wanted to hug Ethel, to laugh, to run into the dining room to share the news with Josef. But she quickly composed herself. She didn't want Ethel to see her emotional attachment to Josef.

"Thank you so much, Ethel. I was so grateful to him for helping me last night."

"It is settled then. I am off to market. Adel will tell you what needs to be done." Ethel turned and left the room.

The house was quiet, the men had left for work. Ethel was at the market. "Ethel insists the floors upstairs are scrubbed every Thursday," Adel said handing Erzsi a bucket of water, a bottle of vinegar, and a mop. "If you take care of that, I'll do the laundry."

There were two bedrooms upstairs, four men to a room. "I wonder where Josef slept." She entered the room on the left. There were two large beds in the room separated by a small table with a lamp. On the wall were hooks where the men had hung their clothes and towels. There were trunks, boxes, and suitcases scattered around the room.

A brown, water stained suitcase with a rope holding it together caught her attention. It looked familiar. "Josef's," she thought as she carefully adjusted the sheets and fluffed the pillows on the bed where she assumed he had slept. "Silly girl," she thought to herself. When she was finished she went to find Adel.

"We can sit for a while before Ethel gets home. Would you like some tea?" Adel was already sitting at the kitchen table.

"I wouldn't mind sitting for a few minutes," Erzsi was rubbing her back, which was sore from kneeling on the hard floor.

"Here's a lotion for your hands. I always use it after doing the floors or the laundry. It will take away some of the redness."

"Ethel told me Josef would be allowed to stay. I am sure you had something to do with that."

"I spoke to my sister. Letting him stay seemed the right thing to do."

"It is kind of both of you," Erzsi said, attempting to keep her voice casual. She was trying to hide the relief, the excitement she was feeling knowing she would be seeing Josef every day.

Adel noticed. She felt certain that Erzsi had not told her everything about her relationship with Josef.

Some of the men returned for lunch and the dining room routine was repeated. Coffee was served and a huge bowl of sausages with sauerkraut was placed on the table. The men were already tired from the morning work, so there was little conversation. Their hands and clothing were dirty but no one seemed to notice or care. Only Mr. Sykes seemed concerned with his appearance and manners. He was wearing a bright crimson waistcoat over his clean white shirt. His hair, as always, was neatly combed, his face clean shaven. Except for the absence of a jacket there was no evidence in his appearance that he had spent the morning working in a small stuffy room on this hot July day.

"*Jó napot*, good afternoon, Miss Viarka," he said politely as she poured his coffee.

"*Jó napot*, Mr. Sykes." Erzsi decided she was going to like Mr. Sykes.

"I think Mr. Sykes is a very kind man," she said to Adel when they were in the kitchen.

"Yes, very kind, and also very handsome."

"Does he have a sweetheart?"

"No, at least not that I know of, he rarely goes out. Most of his time is spent reading or writing, although he does join us in the afternoons. He reads poetry or the newspaper to us while we are making doll shoes."

"Doll shoes?"

"We make a little extra money making doll shoes. It is easy work and gives us a chance to sit for an hour. Would you like to join us? It is not one of your responsibilities."

"Yes, yes, I would."

"It would be an opportunity for you to earn some extra money."

After lunch was served and the kitchen back in order, the women set up a table under the oak tree in the back yard.

Adel brought out the kettle of hot glue and placed it in the middle of the table. Ethel brought out the mold that would hold the upper part of the shoes while the soles were attached.

"This will be the inside sole." Adel demonstrated how to apply the glue to the sole of a shoe using a small paint brush. She handed the sole to her sister who put the sole on the mold preparing to attach the shoe upper. "Like this," Ethel said while demonstrating how to use the tiny tool to bend the edge of the shoe upper to the sole.

"Now you do one." Adel gave Erzsi the tiny brush. "This will be the outer sole."

Working carefully, Erzsi applied glue to the tiny piece of leather. She handed it to Ethel and the tiny shoe was made.

It took a few attempts for Erzsi to become proficient working with the tiny piece of leather and the thin brush. Excess glue dripped onto the table and on her fingers. A few of the soles needed to be discarded. "It's all right," Adel consoled her flustered friend. "It takes a little practice." First a tiny pink shoe was made and then a blue one. By the end of the hour they had filled two buckets with shoes. Progress had been slow at first, but eventually, Erzsi's skill improved and the production of the tiny shoes went smoothly.

"Tomorrow, with your help, we will fill four buckets." Ethel gave Erzsi a smile of approval.

So, on this beautiful summer day, Erzsi found herself in a garden under an oak tree with new friends making doll shoes. "This is a good place to be," she thought to herself. "I am safe, I have work, and tonight I will see Josef."

Benjamin watched them from the alcove window. Often he would join Adel and Ethel while they worked in the garden. He would recite poems from books he had found in the thrift shop or read to them from the newspaper. He enjoyed the break from his work; it was a pleasant way to spend a few hours on a summer afternoon. Over the years the sisters had become his family, the boarding house his home. Today he would not join them. It was Erzsi's first day, she would be nervous. His presence might make it more difficult for her to concentrate.

Watching her carefully applying the glue to the tiny piece of leather he was again reminded of his sister. "Celi would be about Erzsi's age," he thought sadly. He had not seen his sister since he was eighteen and that was twenty years ago.

Cecile had been eight years old when their father bought her the doll. He had just returned from a business trip in New York City. "The doll reminded me of you," their father had said when she opened the white box with the big pink ribbon. Like Celi, the doll had tender brown eyes, freckles along the bridge of her nose, and chestnut hair. The doll wore a dusty peach dress with lace trim, leather high button shoes and a straw hat. Celi was inseparable from the doll she named Catherin. Catherin had a place at the table where the maid was instructed to arrange a tiny plate and tea cup. On Sundays, Celi wore a dress identical to Catherin's. Everyone smiled at the little girl so lovingly holding her doll.

For Benjamin the memory was painful. "Cecile, will I ever see you again?" Probably not, he thought with deep remorse. He moved away from the window and returned to the article he was writing for the newspaper.

Josef returned to the boarding house tired and covered with splatters of cement. As Jimmy had warned him, the other men, mostly of Irish and Italian descent, were resentful of this stranger who didn't even speak their language. "Stupid hunky," they jeered among themselves. Josef had remained quiet, ignoring the taunts of the men. He would work hard, prove his worth, and go home.

At dinner he wanted to talk with Erzsi, to be alone with her for a few minutes. But it wasn't possible. She was working. He didn't want to embarrass her. He noticed that she looked tired; her hands were red and sore. But her eyes, those beautiful blue eyes framed with the blond curls, smiled at him.

"I am glad you are going to be staying with us," she whispered to him.

"I am glad too." He wanted to touch her, to feel the warmth of her kiss. Abruptly he turned away.

"What are you doing, Josef?" he rebuked himself. Tonight he would write to Maria.

After the meal Mr. Kulak and Mr. Braun retired to their rooms, Benjamin found his place in the parlor where his paper was waiting, and the rest of the men started a game of poker.

The women sat in the rocking chairs on the back porch until the sun set. When the card game was over Josef looked for Erzsi. With regret he realized he had missed the opportunity to say good night. "Just as well," he told himself.

"Mr. Sykes, so nice of you to join us today," Ethel said with evident pleasure at seeing her handsome, well-dressed boarder. The women, settled under the oak tree, had already filled one bucket with shoes. "We missed you yesterday."

"Benjamin, I don't think you have been properly introduced to Miss Viarka," Adel was making the introductions before Benjamin was settled in his chair. "She will be staying here and helping Ethel and me with the care of the boarders."

"*Örülök, hogy találkoztunk*, pleased to meet you, Miss Viarka." Benjamin gave Erzsi a small, polite bow.

"*Örülök, hogy találkoztunk*, Mr. Sykes."

"Benjamin," he pointed to himself.

"Erzsi."

"Shall I read to you today?" Benjamin settled into his seat and took out a small brown book with a creased and torn binding.

"Please do," Adel looked up from her work, giving him an appreciative smile.

"I found this in a thrift shop yesterday, a book of poems by Edgar Allen Poe. The poem I would like to read to you is called *Annabel Lee.*" He began to read, his voice gentle and soft.

Erzsi did not understand the words but she could appreciate the haunting rhythm of the poem.

Benjamin, his face reflecting pain and loss, paused for a brief moment while reading the poem. He was thinking of Harry, his forbidden love. "He has lost someone dear to him," Erzsi thought, her heart warming to this man she hardly knew.

When the poem was finished Erzsi could do nothing but continue working as the women discussed the meaning of the poem with Benjamin. "I am missing so much," she thought. "Perhaps, if I asked him, Benjamin would be willing to teach me English."

17 Discovering New Places

Rondout, New York
July, 1882

Benjamin, spectacles sitting on the bridge of his nose, busily writing in a notebook, waited for his student. Mrs. Timko had agreed that Erzsi could spend time with him on Friday afternoons. "It will be a benefit," she had said. "Erzsi will be more efficient if she can talk with the boarders and attend to their requests."

He was sitting on a bench under the oak tree in the backyard. A kitchen chair had been placed directly in front of him so he could see his student. The lesson was to begin promptly at two o'clock. Benjamin was ready to begin.

"Goot-afternoon, Benjamin." He stood as Erzsi greeted him.

"Good-afternoon, Erzsi," he said, beginning the lesson by gently correcting her pronunciation.

"Please sit," he said pointing to the seat directly in front of him.

"*Kezdjük*, we begin." Benjamin took a slice of bread from a basket near his chair. "*Ismételjeutánam*, repeat after me."

"Would you like some bread?" He held the bread toward her. She was confused, uncertain what he meant. He placed the bread in her hand and gently lifted her arm so that she appeared to be offering the bread to him.

"*Ismételjeutánam,* repeat after me," he instructed. "Would you like some bread?" He spoke slowly enunciating each word.

"Vould you like some bread?" She stammered as Benjamin helped her with the words. He nodded with approval, Erzsi smiled in return. The lesson continued, simple phrases she would need as she served the boarders.

That evening at dinner Erzsi was eager to practice what she had learned. Maybe Josef would notice.

"Goot evening, Mr. Sykes," Erzsi spoke slowly, carefully enunciating the words.

"Good evening, Miss Viarka," Benjamin smiled encouragement at his student.

"Vould you like some bread?" she stumbled, trying to remember the word for bread and Josef noticed Benjamin quietly helping her.

"Yes, thank you," Benjamin nodded pleased with her progress.

"You are velcome."

Josef, appearing indifferent to this exchange, continued to eat his soup. Jimmy noticed the way Josef's muscles tightened and saw the disapproval on his face.

"He likes the lass," Jimmy thought.

Saturday afternoon Josef, Jimmy, and Mr. Bartos were on the front steps enjoying their cigars. Mr. Bartos was acting as interpreter, as Josef still struggled with the language.

"Think the girls would like to see Rondout?" Jimmy asked casually waiting for Mr. Bartos to interpret. "Erzsi hasn't left the boarding house since you arrived."

"Doesn't hurt to ask," Josef shrugged, but the thought of spending the afternoon with Erzsi pleased him. He missed being with her, talking with her, touching her. They saw each other every day but he was always careful not to do anything that would cause Mrs. Timko concern.

"Wait here. I'll check with Adel," Jimmy said, finishing his cigar and moving toward the door. He found Adel and Erzsi in the kitchen.

"Adel, my love," he grabbed her by the waist and gave her a kiss on the cheek.

"And what might you want, Jimmy?" She pulled away from him, laughing. They were friends, nothing more, and she wasn't offended by his forwardness.

"Josef wants to see Rondout." Erzsi, who had been sweeping the floor, looked up when she heard Josef's name.

"Come with us, bring Erzsi."

"Sure. Erzsi needs to get out. I'll tell Ethel I need to make some purchases. We will meet you on the porch."

Adel took Erzsi's hand, "Come with me," she ordered, pulling Erzsi into the tiny bedroom behind the kitchen.

"Did I do something wrong?" Erzsi had seen Jimmy talking to Adel but she was unable to understand what they were saying. Worse, she had heard Josef's name. Had something happened?

"You need to change."

"Change into what? It is too hot for my wool dress."

Without giving Erzsi a chance to object Adel went to the trunk in the corner of the room. She was looking for one of Ethel's discarded dresses.

"Ethel only wears black since her husband died. She doesn't need this," Adel said while inspecting an emerald green dress. "It is hopelessly out of date," Adel thought, "but anything is better than the dress Erzsi came in." She held it up for Erzsi to see. "Do you like this one? I think the color would be flattering on you."

"It's beautiful," Erzsi said, admiring the shimmering fabric and color of the dress. The gown had a long bodiced jacket trimmed in lace at the elbows and around the front. The skirt was pulled tight around the front and gathered in voluptuous folds of green silk and white lace and ribbons around a bustle at the back.

"Try it on. It should fit. I can tuck it in further at the back if needed. You are much thinner, but you are about the same height as Ethel." She held the dress in front of Erzsi, scrutinizing the length. "It doesn't matter if it drags a little on the ground at the back."

"Where will I ever wear a dress as elegant as this?"

"You can wear it now, if you like it. Josef and Jimmy are taking us into town."

Erzsi removed her work dress; excitement, anticipation, and nervousness all combined to make her feel light-headed. Adel pulled on the corset strings. Erzsi had never worn a corset, she worried that she might faint and spoil everything. Finally, she was in the dress.

"Perfect," Adel said, admiring the transformation. She returned to the trunk, producing a felt hat with yellow roses and green satin ribbon that matched the dress.

"No need to wear the scarf, this hat will be perfect." Adel carefully placed the hat, securing it with a hat pin.

Erzsi had never worn, or even imagined, wearing a dress that was so elegant. Her posture straightened, her head held high, like a grand lady she admired herself in the mirror. "The finishing touch," Adel said, handing her a pair of gloves and a small satin purse.

Ethel and Benjamin were sitting under the oak tree. Ethel had a small lace fan which she slowly moved in front of her face while Benjamin read to her from the newspaper.

"Ethel, we are going to town with Josef and Jimmy," Adel said as she approached her sister. Her tone was a statement, not a request. Erzsi was behind her, feeling apprehensive. "I have some purchases to make and Erzsi has not had an opportunity to see the shops."

A frown creased Ethel's forehead, her lips clinched tightly together. Erzsi was wearing her dress. "How dare she!" Ethel needed to bite her lip to keep the words from being uttered. Ethel had worn that dress when she had been courted by her husband. The dress held wonderful memories of love and dreams. When her husband had died she had carefully folded the dress and put it in the chest. Not only was Erzsi wearing her dress but she had not been given the afternoon off. "I am still the owner of this boarding house," Ethel thought. "I will speak with Adel later."

Benjamin stood, his eyes focused on Erzsi. "Good afternoon ladies," he said with a courteous bow. "You look lovely, Erzsi," he said in Hungarian, causing her to smile appreciatively. The transformation, from peasant girl with babushka and red calloused hands into an American girl with a saucy hat and gloves was not lost on him. He was familiar with the latest fashions for both men and women and recognized that the dress was outdated. Still, the dress and hat looked charming on Erzsi.

"We will talk later," Ethel said giving her sister a warning look. "Be home by four o'clock."

"Yes, Ethel," Adel said, her voice condescending.

"Enjoy your afternoon," Benjamin said politely. He could see the excitement and anticipation on Erzsi's face. "Be careful, little one," he thought. He had noticed Josef watching her and was not sure he trusted the man.

Josef and Jimmy were sitting on the front porch stairs. Hearing the door open, they turned expectantly. Erzsi was standing in the doorway suddenly self-conscious and awkward in the tight-fitting dress. The men stood quickly, Jimmy uncharacteristically at a loss for words.

Erzsi, embarrassed by their stares, reached for her hat to be sure it was still in place.

"You look beautiful," Josef stammered in Hungarian, his eyes moving from the tight-fitting bodice to the curve of her hips. "Maria had never looked like this," he pushed the thought quickly from his mind.

"You look like an angel," Jimmy, recovering from the awkward moment, walked to Erzsi, giving her a gallant kiss on her hand. "Shall we go then?" He offered Adel his arm. Erzsi, in her elegant dress, felt like a grand lady as she took Josef's arm.

Rondout was a thriving town with uneven, crooked and narrow streets. It was a noisy, dirty place with small buildings closely packed together. Jimmy led the way, Adel on his arm. Josef and Erzsi walked behind them. They walked past stores, restaurants, hotels and numerous newsstands with what seemed like an endless variety of newspapers and magazines. Adel bought a fashion magazine, some lavender soap, and embroidery thread. "I must have something to show Ethel when we get back. I don't want her to think we wasted the afternoon."

"Erzsi, look at the lovely hats," Adel had stopped by a window where hats of the latest style were tastefully displayed. "Let's go look."

"We'll wait here," said Jimmy, lighting his cigar and leaning against the building. His attention was focused on two young women walking arm in arm on the other side of the street.

"Can I help you?" The clerk asked looking warily at Erzsi and Adel as they entered the store. He was doubtful that the woman in the out of date ill-fitting dress could afford anything in his store.

"My friend would like to try on that one," Adel said, pointing to a hat covered with layers of white lace and lavender ribbons.

"Yes, Miss," the clerk removed the hat from the stand and warily handed it to Erzsi.

Josef, leaning against a lamppost, a cigar in his hand, could see them through the shop window. "How lovely she looks," he thought, watching Erzsi admiring herself in a mirror. As Erzsi reluctantly returned the hat Josef repressed a foolish impulse to rush into the store and buy the hat for her.

"We need to get back," Adel said to Jimmy as the women left the store. "I don't want Erzsi to be in trouble with Ethel."

"Next Saturday we should go to Kingston. We can take the trolley," Jimmy suggested. Adel translated, Josef nodded agreement.

Erzsi hesitated, "What about Ethel, she didn't look pleased that I went out today."

"I will talk with Ethel."

"It is agreed then!"

Erzsi smiled, moving a little closer to Josef. They would be spending time together. He wanted to be with her.

An image of Maria, standing in the doorway saying good-bye, intruded into Josef's thoughts. "We are just friends," he justified to himself, although he knew this wasn't true. He pushed the image of Maria away.

When they arrived back at the boarding house Josef and Erzsi lingered outside on the porch. Neither wanted the afternoon to end.

"I had a wonderful time today, Josef." Erzsi was standing very close to Josef, looking at him with adoring eyes that spoke of love and desire. He wanted to take her in his arms, to kiss her lips, to feel her body close to his.

"I did too," he said backing away, lowering his eyes. Jimmy and Adel were standing a short distance away. Mrs. Timko was sure to be watching from a window.

18 Jealousy Changes Everything

East Kingston, New York
July, 1882

It was a Friday, a hot afternoon in July. Josef had been assigned to work in the quarry behind the cement factory. His shirt stuck to the sweat on his back, his clothes were covered with dust and dirt. As he loaded the stone onto the mule drawn cart there was a noise, a rumble, pebbles fell out of the sky, a voice shouted, "Get down!" He looked up as a huge boulder came loose above him; a torrent of smaller rocks hit his arm and ribs, a sharp stone gashed his cheek. The boulder missed him by inches as he ducked behind the cart.

"You okay?" the man who had been working near him asked. Josef nodded yes, but when he moved, there was a sharp pain in his ribs. They sent for the foreman. "You are no use to us today. Go home. Report back tomorrow."

Hobbling home, using his shirt sleeve to wipe the blood dripping down his cheek, he thought of Erzsi. Perhaps she would nurse him, put salve on his ribs and clean the blood from his face. She would look at him with concern. The thought aroused him, distracting him from the pain. He imagined her hands gently touching his body, applying the soothing lotion. He could almost feel the warm cloth she would use to clean his face. His pace quickened in anticipation.

With effort he walked up the stairs and opened the door. The house was quiet. Perhaps she was in the kitchen. He wanted to go to his bed but he needed to find her first.

Glancing out the kitchen window he saw her. She was with Benjamin. They were sitting close together, too close, enjoying a private, perhaps even intimate moment. Erzsi was looking at Benjamin with the look Josef thought she had reserved for him. He clinched his fists. "You arrogant, self-assured, perfectly groomed, donkey's arse," he said, his jealousy apparent in the mumbled words. He gingerly touched his sore ribs, rubbed the bruise on his left arm. "You have no claim on her," he admonished himself and turned away from the window.

No one knew he had come home early. It was Jimmy who told everyone what had happened. "He'll be all right," Jimmy assured the worried women. "It is just his pride that is hurt." When Josef didn't come down to dinner, Erzsi went to check on him but he was asleep. He heard her come in, of course, but he was still angry at the scene he had witnessed in the garden.

Josef spent a restless night. His dreams were tormented with visions of Maria crying, scolding him, pounding his chest, her nails cutting his cheek. Erzsi, seductive, naked, caressing his body, bringing his body to a frenzy of desire, followed by penetration, release.

Benjamin entered the dream. Ignoring Josef he climbed into the bed next to Erzsi. She turned from Josef welcoming Benjamin into her arms. He woke up covered in sweat, his fists clenched. His body ached from the impact of the falling stones, his mind was in turmoil. He wanted this woman, could not live without her. Benjamin could not have her.

The next morning he was up early. He knew Erzsi would be feeding the chickens in the backyard. He wanted to talk with her alone. When Erzsi saw him she stopped, surprised. The men rarely ventured into the backyard, favoring the rocking chairs on the front porch.

Josef had meant only to talk with her. Perhaps ask her to go for a walk with him without Jimmy and Adel as chaperones. He wasn't sure what he wanted to say or what he intended to do. He just needed to be with her, to claim her as his own.

Lost for words he walked up to her and gently touched her face, caressed her shoulders, put his arms around her. "Erzsi," he whispered. She melted into his embrace. The kiss, soft and gentle at first, changed; arousing emotions they had both struggled to control.

"Josef," she whispered as she returned his kiss.

The intimate moment abruptly ended when Adel called from the kitchen window, "Erzsi!"

Adel had been looking for her, she was needed in the kitchen. If Ethel saw them she would tell Josef to leave, or worse, fire Erzsi.

"Erzsi, I need you," she called again. Erzsi ran into the house leaving Josef standing alone.

A week later the four friends were going to spend the afternoon watching the Rondout Base Ball Club play against a Kingston team. Josef and Jimmy were on the porch waiting for the women. Josef, looking awkward, was holding a large round box tied with a blue ribbon.

Adel gave Jimmy a knowing look when she walked through the door and saw the package Josef was holding. Erzsi just stood still eyeing the package, wondering what it was about.

"For you," Josef said, with a bit of awkwardness, as he handed Erzsi the box. He had never given a woman such a fancy present before. Their eyes met as she accepted the gift.

"Erzsi, bring it into the parlor. You can open it there," Adel was already headed for the door.

Ethel was in the parlor arranging the newspapers for Mr. Sykes. He liked them folded neatly and placed on the table next to the lamp. Hearing the commotion in the hall she looked up to see Adel leading Erzsi into the room. Erzsi was holding what was obviously a hat box. "When had the girl had time to shop or the money to buy such a frivolous item?" Ethel was sure Adel had something to do with this.

"Ethel, Josef bought Erzsi a gift." This revelation caused Ethel to raise an eyebrow in disapproval.

Slowly, with anticipation and controlled delight, Erzsi lifted the lid. She inhaled, and with a soft exclamation, reached in the box removing the contents for all to see. The straw hat, in the modern style, had a short, flat crown and a broad brim trimmed with white ribbon and delicate white flowers. It was the most beautiful gift that Erzsi had ever received.

"Oh, it is lovely, Josef. Adel, is this not the most fine-looking hat you have ever seen?"

Erzsi removed the hat she had borrowed from Ethel, turned toward the mirror, and donned the new hat, tying the ribbon under her chin. Holding the brim and smiling demurely like a princess, she turned toward her friends.

"Let me fix the bow. This is how it is tied. You fluff the ribbon like this," Adel worked with the ribbon under Erzsi's chin until it was just right.

Jimmy gave Josef a playful jab in the ribs. "Good-work, ol'boy! You will get your reward," he whispered with a mischievous grin.

Adel fussed over Erzsi using large hat pins to fasten the hat in place.

Ethel did not try to hide her disapproval. It was not proper for a young man to give a young woman such a gift.

"Erzsi, you look radiant! The hat is perfect for you," said Adel. She did not have her sister's concerns about propriety.

"Ethel, doesn't she look lovely? The hat is perfect for her. So very stylish."

"It will do," responded Ethel. "Now you can return my hat to the chest."

The four left for the game. Erzsi held Josef's arm as she proudly flaunted her new hat, accepting the admiring glances of the men they passed.

Jimmy knew that Josef wanted to talk to Erzsi so he guided Adel to the bleachers telling her not to worry when Josef and Erzsi didn't follow them.

"Don't worry, Josef just wants to talk with her."

"There is a village," Josef spoke without looking directly at Erzsi. "It is about three miles from Rondout. There is work there. I'd like to rent a house and take in boarders. It is the only way to get ahead. There is a house available. Would you come with me to see it?"

Erzsi didn't know what to think. There had been that kiss, the hat, the pleasant afternoons exploring Rondout and Kingston. Now he was talking of moving away. Was he asking her to go with him? Was he asking her to marry him? Maybe he just wanted her to see the house.

"Yes, Josef, I would love to go with you."

19 Seduction

East Kingston, New York
August, 1882

The house was quiet, everyone was asleep. Thoughts of Josef and his plans to leave the boarding house prevented her mind from settling. Sleep wouldn't come. Was he leaving her? Agnes had warned her to be careful. Why did he want her to see the house? Was it simply to get a female perspective or did he have plans for their future? She pictured the hat which was carefully stored in the hat box under her bed. There was the kiss in the backyard, the tender way he touched her hair, and the way he looked at her. "Surely he loves me," she told herself, but doubts lingered.

Ethel stood in front of the only mirror in the tiny room adjusting her hat. As usual she wore a somber black dress with just a hint of lace around the collar. Adel was fussing with Erzsi's hat. "It must be placed just like this to best flatter your face," she told her friend as she tilted the hat at a saucy angle. The women were preparing for Sunday Mass at Saint Peter's Church.

"She looks fine, Adel." Ethel walked to the door assuming her sister and Erzsi would follow. "Enough fussing, we are going to church not a ball at the palace," she said as she disappeared into the kitchen.

"Don't forget your gloves." Adel had taken ownership of Erzsi's appearance whenever they left the boarding house. Gloves and hats had not been a part of Erzsi's childhood experience. It was all new to her and she valued Adel's attention. "Now walk tall, wear your hat proudly, like this," Adel demonstrated the way an elegant lady of means would walk. Erzsi giggled giving her friend a little kiss on the cheek. "Let's go then, my sister is already in a sour mood."

Jimmy and Josef were sitting on the front stairs cigars in hand, mugs of coffee within easy reach.

"Morning, Ladies," Jimmy stood and tipped his hat as they walked past. "Seeing such beautiful women in the morning brightens a man's day. And Adel, I would be happier still if you would favor me with a kiss."

"Not this morning, Jimmy," said Adel shaking her head no, but there was a smile on her face. It was a familiar ritual between the friends.

"Good-morning, Mrs. Timko, Miss Viarka, Miss Toth," Josef was always careful to be proper with Ethel.

"Good-morning, Gentlemen," Ethel greeted them with a hint of a reprimand in her voice. The men were obviously not going to join them at mass.

"I will see you after church," Josef said quietly to Erzsi, briefly touching her hand as she walked past.

"They are fine looking women," Jimmy said to Josef as they watched the women walk down the street.

Ethel, dressed in black, looked the part of a proper Victorian widow. Adel and Erzsi, arm in arm, looked striking walking next to each other. Adel's beige and blue plaid dress accented her slender figure while her blue straw hat, adorned with feathers, bobbed playfully on her head. Erzsi's blond curls were no longer hidden under the peasant's scarf but drifted softly from under the hat that Josef had given her.

The women walked down Pierpont Street with Ethel purposely keeping a steady, almost vigorous pace. "We mustn't be late," she scolded Adel who had stopped in front of a shop window.

Everyone in the boarding house, even Ethel, knew that Erzsi was going to East Kingston with Josef that afternoon. As the responsible adult she felt it her duty to warn Erzsi of the perils that awaited her.

"Young women these days need to be very careful," she said this while looking straight ahead. "We were safe back home, you know. Family and friends were there to watch over and protect us." She paused for effect and was pleased to notice that Erzsi was looking uncomfortable. "In America, it is our responsibility to be mindful of our virtue."

"Ethel, please, we will be hearing a sermon in church," Adel interjected, hoping her sister would stop. "There are other things to talk about on this beautiful morning."

"A husband values chastity in the woman he marries," Ethel was determined to finish what she felt needed to be said. "There is a reason God gave us the Ten Commandments."

Ethel's comments were interrupted by a woman waving frantically to her from across the street.

"Ethel! Ethel Timko!"

Ethel pretended not to see the flamboyantly dressed woman who was calling to her in a loud shrill voice.

"Wait, Ethel, I have news for you," the woman yelled while picking up her skirts and making a dash across the muddy street to join her.

"Have you heard about Sally Jenkins and that young man who recently came from New York City?" she whispered while pulling Ethel aside to share the exciting, titillating gossip she had just heard.

With Ethel distracted, Adel took the opportunity to talk with Erzsi who was looking very uncomfortable. "Don't worry about Ethel," Adel said, taking Erzsi's arm. "Ethel doesn't mean to be unkind. Life has been difficult for her since her husband died. They were very much in love. She is concerned about you. I am sure she feels responsible for you since you are far from your family."

"It's all right, Adel. Her words were meant kindly."

"Just have a wonderful day with Josef. I will be waiting to hear the details tonight."

The two friends continued walking arm in arm to the church.

Josef was waiting for them on the porch. Ethel walked past him, her disapproval plainly visible. She did not trust this man. Adel gently squeezed Erzsi's arm in a gesture of reassurance, "Have fun." She smiled at Josef and went into the house. Erzsi thought she saw the curtain in the parlor flutter, a figure standing behind it. She wondered if it was Benjamin.

"Ready to go?" Josef offered Erzsi his arm.

"I'm ready."

Her hand gently rested on Josef's arm as they walked down the well-shaded dirt road. It was a pleasant three mile walk to the small village of East Kingston. Occasional glimpses of the river evoked memories of the *Mary Powell* and the day they had spent on the river. The Catskill Mountains in the distance reminded the young immigrants of the home they had left behind.

For a moment she thought of Robert her first love. "We were so young, this time it will be different. We are in America; I will follow Josef wherever he goes."

Walking beside Josef, her arm in his, feeling the warmth of his body the confidence in his step, Erzsi felt that her life was about to begin. She had found the man she loved.

Josef was quiet. He was trying to settle his mind, organize his thoughts, and understand the confusing and powerful attraction to the woman walking next to him. The Lord knew he had tried to keep his feelings for her under control. He wanted to do the right thing by Erzsi and Maria. But Maria was far away and the desire for the woman walking next to him was becoming too strong to be resisted. God must have some plan for them.

"Renting this house is the right thing to do," he rationalized. "The money from the boarders will pay the rent. I will be able to send money to Maria."

His thoughts were interrupted by Erzsi.

"Josef, tell me about the house."

"I know very little. A widow lived there. She kept boarders. Now that she is old she wants to move in with her daughter."

With that Josef fell silent again. The road turned around a bend; they could see houses that appeared to be welcoming them to the village. The house was on John Street, near the river. Together they walked down the wide dirt road dotted with a haphazard assortment of modest homes. In front of them was the Hudson River with gently rolling hills on the opposite shore.

"I could live here," Erzsi thought. She squeezed Josef's arm giving him a smile to show her approval.

A group of boys, perhaps eight to ten years of age, were running through the yards, frightening the chickens, ignoring the complaints of the pigs and goats.

"Playing tag," said Josef, as though Erzsi had never seen boys playing before. He was picturing his own sons playing tag on the farm he would buy when he went home to Maria. A group of giggling girls were playing hopscotch with braids flying, dust from the dirt road covering their sturdy shoes. Erzsi thought how wonderful it would be to watch her own children playing on this street.

They approached a tired looking frame house with a rigid rectangular shape that looked like a shipping crate with a peaked lid. Josef stopped for a moment to take in the details of the house. The narrow side of the rectangle faced the street. A plain windowless door was on the far left and two windows with dingy curtains were on the right.

Three windows on the upper floor provided light, possibly to one of the two bedrooms Josef knew were on the second floor. Devoid of the elaborate trim found on many of the homes in Kingston, the house was strong and defiant in its simplicity. Josef felt that it would suit his needs. "Just needs a coat of paint," he said more to himself than to Erzsi.

There was a scrawny pine tree next to the front door. Erzsi wondered if she would live in this house, perhaps have the chance to watch the small tree grow tall and strong. "Like my children," she smiled at the thought.

Josef had been told that the house would be empty, the door unlocked. After a quick knock on the door he turned the knob and walked into the house.

They entered a small parlor that contained old dusty furnishings. There was a thread-bare sofa with faded upholstery, two matching armchairs, and a wooden cabinet with the faintly visible images of violins on the doors. A small table with a kerosene lamp was next to the sofa.

"Josef, imagine this room with fresh curtains, a cloth on the table under the lamp, and some lace doilies on the couch. Of course, a good dusting would help as well."

Josef smiled, barely listening to her. He was not interested in the quality of the furnishings.

"I will need at least eight boarders to make a profit. I need to see the rest of the house to be sure there will be enough room." He walked into the kitchen, Erzsi followed.

Erzsi inspected the stove, bending over to open the oven door. Josef watched her, the bustle on her skirt inviting his eye. Why had he brought her here? She moved to the dusty window using her hand to clean off a small opening. "There are fruit trees in the backyard, and a chicken coop."

He barely heard what she was saying; the tight fitting bodice of the dress accented her small waist. A vision of her in bed crept into his thoughts. The possibility that he might wake up in the morning with this woman next to him was causing stirrings in his body. "I want her. I can't be without her. It is fate," he rationalized. "I am just a man."

There was a doorway near the stove. Josef moved past Erzsi, gently touching her arm. She felt a shiver run through her body, wetness between her legs. Although their bodies did not touch, each one knew that if she entered the room there would be a resolution to the passion between them. "Fate," Josef thought, as she followed him into the room.

It was a small room with a bed and table. The curtains had been pulled shut and the room was dark.

"I can sleep in here," Josef said trying to sound casual. "The boarders will sleep upstairs."

When Erzsi entered the room, she knew what she wanted; Josef, a family, to be here in this house with him. She touched his arm and looked into his eyes. He put his arms around her, lifted her and carried her to the bed. It was inevitable. It was meant to be. It was all out of their control.

Book 4

Betrayal

20 Lives Changed Forever

East Kingston, New York
October, 1882

Erzsi was content, happier than she had ever been. Even the mundane chore of plucking feathers from a hapless chicken brought her pleasure. When Josef came home he would be greeted with the welcoming aromas of chicken soup simmering on the stove and an apple pie cooling on the kitchen table.

It was a crisp early fall day. From her vantage point on the stoop she could see the river and the hills beyond. They were aflame with the colors of fall, russet browns, shades of orange and red. In her yard bright red apples clung to the old apple tree and littered the ground. A blue jay settled onto a branch of the pear tree. She paused from her work for a moment to watch him as he moved his head looking for something terribly important. A flock of birds on their long journey to their winter home darkened the cloudless sky. "I wish you a good journey," she spoke to the dark mass of restless creatures as they disappeared on the horizon.

She was sitting on the stoop of the back porch, her porch, she reminded herself whenever she had occasion to sit there. Today she was collecting the down for a pillow she was making for Josef. She would give it to him at Christmas.

The rug from the parlor was folded over a rope clothes line where earlier she had beat it with a broom removing what might have been years of dust. The dingy curtains from the parlor window had been washed and were now hanging on the line to be bleached by the sun.

"We have been in this house for almost two months," she smiled, her thoughts drifting to the day Josef had asked her to live here with him. Her life had changed forever when Josef picked her up and carried her to what she now thought of as her marriage bed. Josef had been gentle at first but as his passion grew he had forcefully thrust himself inside, hurting her just a little. Her body had reacted to him in ways that she could not have imagined. She had been surprised at first, no one had given her the details of a wedding night, but she had been so filled with love and desire that she freely gave in to the waves of passion that coursed through her body. When they finished making love, they rested on the bed holding hands, looking at the peeling paint on the ceiling. Feeling content, occupied with their thoughts, perhaps a little embarrassed, they did not say anything.

"We should get ready to go back to Rondout," he had said, breaking the silence, his tone devoid of any emotion.

She was hurt, desperately disappointed by his abrupt, passionless, statement.

"Yes, Josef," she said softly, trying not to show her feelings. The love making had been fulfilling, but she had thought it would be followed by words of love, perhaps even a proposal of marriage. His dispassionate words about returning to Rondout were not what she had expected to hear.

They dressed, straightened the bed and walked out the front door. Josef stopped, turned, wanting one last look at the house.

"This is a good house, Erzsi. I could have eight boarders." There were still no words of love. "The income would be enough to pay the rent, I could save most of my paycheck," he paused, still looking at the house as if deep in thought. "If you lived here you could help me manage the house."

Was this it then? Was this the proposal of marriage she had anticipated? She was silent, looking at the house. He turned to her realizing how cold his manner had been. "I love you, Erzsi," he said reaching for her hands. "I want you to live here with me." All she heard were the words "I love you." That was all she needed. To be with him was everything. She melted into his embrace. His proposal had not included a mention of marriage but he had said he loved her. In time, when they were settled, when they had enough money, she was sure they would be married. This was enough for now.

She had written to her sisters telling them about Josef. "I will be helping Josef manage his boarding house," she wrote. "When the time is right and we have the money we will be married."

Clara, happily married to Elmer, was relieved to hear that Erzsi had found someone to love. Iren, trapped in an unhappy marriage, worried. "Who is this Josef? Will he be kind to Erzsi? Will he give her the love she deserves?"

When Josef and Erzsi told their friends in Rondout about their plans the reactions were predictable. Adel had reacted with excitement, wanting to know every detail of the romantic afternoon and plans for the future. If she had concerns she didn't express them. It was obvious to her that they were in love. She could see how happy Erzsi was. "You will have a home of your own, Erzsi. You will be with the man you love."

Ethel just frowned while walking out of the room. The impropriety! She did not understand why the others were being not only supportive, but happy for the couple. She chose not to remember the love she had shared with her husband before their wedding night.

Jimmy had slapped Josef on the back, pleased for Josef and Erzsi. "They are perfect for each other," he thought. Josef is a lucky man. Perhaps there would be a marriage in their future, perhaps not. It was not his place to judge.

Benjamin shook Josef's hand, solemnly wishing him well in his new endeavors. "She is a good woman, take care of her," there was a warning in his voice.

"I hope you always consider me your friend," Benjamin said to Erzsi when he could speak to her privately. "Know you can turn to me for support if the need should arise. I wish you well." He worried about her. He didn't trust Josef. Erzsi was a young woman in love. She was too trusting, too innocent.

Now, sitting on the stoop in her backyard, Erzsi smiled, remembering her friends in Rondout. "Mama, she said reaching into her pocket, coming to America has fulfilled all of my hopes. I have good friends but most of all I have Josef." She stroked the prayer book. "Perhaps I will ask Josef to plant a rosebush for me in the spring. It will, of course, be a yellow rosebush," she smiled at the thought.

The chicken was ready for the pot. Reluctantly Erzsi stood and headed for the kitchen. But even here, inside the modest house, there was much to give her pleasure. Fond memories of the day her friends came to visit invaded her thoughts. They had not come empty handed. She glanced into the dining room, which had been transformed by their gifts. "For your new home," Adel had said as Erzsi opened each carefully wrapped package.

Adel had guided the gift purchases. "Ethel, give her the embroidered table cloth that you no longer need. I will embroider linen napkins to match." Ethel did not want to acknowledge this sinful relationship but she had become fond of Erzsi and Adel was persuasive.

Jimmy was instructed to purchase a ceramic bowl that Adel had seen in a store window. It was decorated with swirls of green vines and red roses that coordinated with the table cloth and napkins.

Benjamin brought a matching pair of candlesticks. "They are far too extravagant, Benjamin," Erzsi had admonished him while admiring the shiny silver candlesticks with their elaborate design. "You are so kind to me." She had stood on her toes to give the tall man a gentle kiss on the cheek.

It was difficult keeping the house clean when nine men came home every day covered with dust from the brick yards or the quarry or the cement factory. She tried, in vain, to get them to shake out their jackets and stomp the dirt out of their boots before they entered the house.

The men were pleasant and for the most part she enjoyed their company. The Frenchmen, who worked in the brick yards in the summer and cut ice in the winter, were so charming when they kissed her hand and called her Madame. The German, who worked for the cooper, always enjoyed her cooking and the pitcher of beer she placed on the table in front of him. "It reminds me of home," he frequently told her.

Her favorite was Matthew who was hardly more than a child. With his unruly head of curly black hair, his careless way of dressing caused Erzsi to take a motherly interest in his well-being. She fussed over him at meals, encouraging him to drink milk rather than whiskey, frowning when Josef encouraged him to try a cigar. Matthew worked for the blacksmith and his hands and face were always dirty when he came home. Erzsi insisted that he make an attempt to clean up before sitting at the table.

Caring for all these men was hard work but the reward was being with Josef. When Josef met her in bed each night and held her in his arms she knew she was where she was supposed to be. She was with the man she loved and they were building a life together.

Josef still hadn't mentioned marriage. This caused her some dismay but when she was in his arms it did not matter. He was here with her. He wanted to be with her. The way his body reacted to hers told her everything she needed to know. When the time was right they would be married.

Josef's shift at the cement factory was over; he was troubled and needed time alone. He had been living with Erzsi for almost two months. Erzsi had proven herself to be quite capable managing the affairs of the boarding house. They had eight boarders. Josef enjoyed their company and welcomed their rent payments. After giving Erzsi money to cover expenses he was able to put some money away to send to Maria. Erzsi never questioned him about money, it was not her place.

Today he had received a letter from Maria, she had sounded sad, weary. As always she was supportive. She understood why he needed to spend this time in America. But she missed him terribly. All was well, she had assured him, but her sadness caused him concern. She spoke of her love and her vision of their life together. He missed her. But Maria was far away and it was Erzsi who welcomed him home each night, Erzsi who shared his bed, freely giving her love, her body. The thoughts of Maria and Erzsi were unsettling, confusing. Guilt was mixed with desire and obligations; his vows competed with the passion that enveloped him each night.

He ordered a whiskey and found a place in the corner of the bar. He thought back to the day in August when he asked Erzsi to live with him. He knew he had been wrong to trifle with her emotions, but she was so desirable, his physical need for her unbearable. At night, in Mrs. Timko's boarding house, his body had ached for her, knowing that she was so close, yet out of reach.

And then they were alone in that room, she was looking at him, her eyes warm, inviting, and her body close to his, not offering any resistance. The temptation had been beyond his ability to control. If she had not been so willing he would not be in this impossible situation. When they had finished making love he had felt awkward and guilty. He did not know what to say to her. But later, just looking back at the house and picturing her in that bed every night, without thinking of the consequences, he had asked her to come and live with him.

The last of the sheets were hanging on the line, a few more towels to hang and the task would be done. She had been sick that morning, and the morning before. For days now exhaustion had replaced her endless energy. She would go to bed as soon as the table was cleared and the dishes washed. The men could fend for themselves tonight; she was too tired to care. Often now by the time Josef joined her, she was already comfortably snuggled under the feather blanket, snoring softly. There were changes in her body that were unmistakable. As she finished hanging the last towel her hand came to rest on the small swelling in her belly

"A baby!" she whispered. "Tonight I will tell Josef."

Deep in thought she was momentarily startled when a young child, perhaps three years of age, came running into the yard. Laughing excitedly, he hid himself behind a sheet hanging from the clothesline. A young woman was chasing him, pretending to be angry but obviously enjoying the game. Engrossed in their game they did not notice Erzsi as she hung the last of the towels on the line.

"Willie! Willie, come back here right now or I will tell your father when he gets home!" Although her words were harsh there was laughter in her voice. She saw Erzsi who, with a nod and a smile, motioned to where the boy was hiding. Quietly the woman made her way to the boy, moving around the sheet in such a way that he could not see her. The boy, thinking himself invisible since his face was buried in the sheet, did not suspect that his hiding place had been discovered. The woman grabbed the boy from behind and while he squealed with laughter she lifted him from the ground. The mother held her child close, hugging and kissing him. The little boy squealed with laughter.

"Don't you ever run away from me like that again!" she said, putting him down and once again attempting to demonstrate her authority.

"No, Mama," the little boy hung his head. "I'm sorry, Mama."

"All right then." Holding the boy's hand firmly, the woman turned to Erzsi.

"I am so sorry for the intrusion. He thinks it is fun making me chase him. Allow me to introduce myself. My name is Sarah Drinkle and this is my son Willie."

"Hello, Sarah, pleased to meet you. I'm Erzsi," she hesitated for a moment. "Erzsi Farkas." She had been introducing herself as Mrs. Farkas since they had moved to East Kingston. Josef had done the same. They were living as a married couple, no need to explain the circumstances to strangers.

"What a precious little boy. Seeing the two of you laughing has brightened my day. Would you like to come inside for a few minutes? I was just about to go in for tea. I have malted milk for Willie, if it is all right with you."

Tonight she would tell Josef. She hoped he would be pleased. Perhaps the news, anticipation of having a son, would hasten a proposal of marriage.

She was still reluctant to address the issue of marriage with him. Deep in her heart, in a space she refused to acknowledge, she was not sure what his response would be if she asked him directly. Better to wait for him to ask her. That was the proper way. The man should make the proposal of marriage. For now, she reassured herself, he came home to her every night, they were building a future together, and now they were going to have a child.

It was dark when Josef left the cement factory. Sleet stung his face, he pulled his scarf tighter around his neck and his hat further over his ears. He would not visit the tavern tonight. Hot soup and some whiskey shared with the boarders was what was needed on this icy night.

Erzsi smiled at him as he entered the dining room. She was holding a steaming bowl of pirogues, dripping with browned butter. Baskets of warm bread had been placed at each end of the table. A bowl of preserved pears, to be enjoyed later, waited on a buffet chest in the corner of the room.

Erzsi approached Josef, bending close to him, "Come to the kitchen after dinner, I have something to tell you." Her lips felt warm and soft as she kissed his cold, pink cheek. There was conspiracy in her voice but he didn't notice. He just nodded, assuming there was an issue with the house. There was always a need for a repair, an unexpected bill to be paid, or a concern about a boarder.

After he finished his whiskey, sampled the pears, and enjoyed his evening cigar, he went to the kitchen to find her. She had finished the dishes and was sitting at the kitchen table sipping a cup of tea. He noticed that she had fixed her hair and was wearing a clean apron. There was a glow on her face, a faint smile as she pensively looked at her teacup, stirring it in a slow, mindless motion. "She is beautiful," he thought. "You had something to tell me?" he asked casually while watching her as she slowly stood and moved toward him. He reached for her, one arm around her waist pulling her closer, the other stroking her breast.

"Josef, I have wonderful news." She pulled away from him just a little. He looked into her eyes not really hearing her words, wanting to carry her to their bed.

"Not yet," she whispered, understanding his mood as he stroked her breast and bent to kiss her. Slowly she moved his hands to her belly. She hesitated for just a moment. "We are going to have a baby." The room was suddenly silent, only the rhythmic ticking of the clock could be heard. "You are going to be a father."

His hands were resting where she had placed them. Had he heard correctly? She put her hands on top of his, pushing his hands firmly on the warm place where their child was growing.

"The baby will be here in May." She looked at him, unable to read his expression.

He regained his composure. "A son, I am going to have a son!" he whispered.

"Maybe a daughter," she replied, slightly tilting her head and giving him a playful smile.

Now, accepting the reality that he was going to be a father, he grabbed her around the waist, and while kissing her, twirled her around, her skirts flying, her head on his shoulder. "A son! Yes. I am going to have a son." They were both laughing.

"Enough Josef, enough!" But she was still laughing with relief and joy when he put her down.

He lifted her gently and carried her to their bed. When the love making was finished they lay in the bed, Erzsi's head resting on his shoulder. Content in the arms of the man she loved, Erzsi fell into a gentle slumber. Josef thought of Maria and quickly pushed her image into the deep recesses of his mind. "A son," he thought as he drifted off to sleep.

21 Anticipation

East Kingston, New York
January, 1883

As usual, Erzsi awoke long before dawn. It was warm under the heavy down comforter; the room would be cold. A gust of wind rattled the panes of glass in the window that would be covered with frost. She snuggled closer to Josef, listening to his steady breathing. "I do love you, Josef," she whispered, gently stroking his cheek. The mattress creaked as she stood up; he mumbled something incomprehensible. Wrapping herself in her shawl, ignoring the shoes by her bed, she walked to the kitchen.

The kitchen was cold, the floor like ice beneath her bare feet, her breath was visible in front of her face. "Like winters at home," she thought. With haste she added fresh coals and stoked the fire until she could feel the heat that would warm the room.

Combing her hair, tying it into a tight bun, she listened to the soothing sound of percolating coffee. Sitting close to the stove she savored a cherished moment alone with her coffee and her thoughts. "There are some privileges when you are mistress of the house," she smiled to herself as she wiggled her bare toes, free from the confines of tight shoes.

As the room slowly warmed, the pinkish hues of the first light of dawn began to stream through the frosted window. Slowly rising from the chair, holding her coffee cup in one hand, clutching her shawl in the other, she walked to the kitchen window.

During the night a light dusting of snow had changed the bleak January landscape into a white sparkling wonderland. Glancing in the direction of the apple tree, shrouded in the shadowy morning light, she was able to make out a deer and her fawn looking back at her.

"Good morning my little one," she spoke softly to the child growing inside of her. "Someday you will play in this yard," she smiled, gently stroking her stomach, picturing her son climbing the apple tree, her daughter picking the wild flowers that grew in the spring.

The morning passed quickly. Routine chores kept her busy while her thoughts were pleasantly occupied with the baby she was carrying. She made plans to buy some fabric for a baby dress and maybe some yarn for a sweater and bonnet. She sang to her child, songs she remembered her mother singing.

Pál, Kata, Péter, Jó reggelt,
Márodakünn a nap felkelt.
Szól a kakasunk, az a nagytarajú:
Gyereki a rétre,
Kukuríkú!

Good morning, Paul, Kate, Peter,
The Sun already rose outside.
Our big crested rooster says:

"*Come out to the meadow,*
Cock-a-doodle-doo!"

A soft knock on the front door, a creak as it opened. "Erzsi, it's only me, Sarah. I'm here with Willie. Can we come in?"

The question did not need a response. Sarah had become a frequent visitor. She claimed she needed to get Willie out of the house for a few hours every afternoon or he was impossible to manage. It was a welcome diversion from the monotony of their chores as the women sipped their tea, gossiped, and watched little Willie play with the truck Josef had bought for him.

Today Sarah had another idea. "We should go down to the river to watch the men harvest the ice." It was a big industry in towns up and down the Hudson River Valley, providing work for the men when the brick yards were closed and the farms idle.

The friends, with Willie holding Sarah's hand, walked down the snow covered street heading toward the river. Erzsi, now five months pregnant, walked carefully, cheerfully, thinking of her child and the fun they would have in winters still to come.

Women, many with small children, had gathered near the edge of the river to watch the spectacle of hundreds of men and boys working on the ice. Everyone knew that the work was dangerous. Last year two men had fallen through the ice and were thought to have drowned. Miraculously one of the men was later rescued, returning to work the next day, the other was never found. The little boys, not yet aware of the dangers or the worries of the adults, imagined the day when they would work on the ice.

A few of the older boys, with the restless exuberance of youth, grew tired of simply watching the show on the ice. A game of tag began, with laughter and taunting and rolling bodies in the snow. Willie let go of his mother's hand and ran after the boys, determined to join in the game. Even though he was a year or two younger and much smaller than the others, he was not concerned. Clumsy in his hand-me-down boots, slipping on the snow, and ignored by the older boys, Willie was not deterred.

Sarah, with a look at Erzsi that said, "See what I am up against," ran after him. Despite his brave efforts he was defeated by a slippery patch of ice and fell hard on the ground, scraping his chin. His mother, not far behind, came to his rescue, picking him up as tears of humiliation began to form.

"There, there my big boy, you are all right. Come, let's look at those horses over there. Can you see the plows they are pulling?" With a last sniffle, to be sure his mother understood his distress, Willie wiggled out of his mother's arms. This time, Sarah tightly held his hand as they watched the drama on the frozen river.

Hundreds of men and boys were working with determined precision, cutting the ice into blocks and moving the large blocks to the ice house where it would be stored until needed.

Plows drawn by horses were cutting shallow grooves in the ice, marking out slabs about three feet wide. A man, dressed in warm clothing of a finer make and style than the others, held a paper and appeared to be giving instructions. Three men, a distance away, were huddled against the wind, attempting to light their cigarettes.

Further up the river men using large hand saws were making deeper cuts in ice that had already been marked.

"There's André, your boarder," Sarah was pointing to a young man wearing a beret and a scarf wrapped loosely around his neck. "Handsome, isn't he?"

"And so charming," Erzsi smiled. "Bon jour! Ma Cherie," she mimicked him gently taking Sarah's hand and pretending to give it a long, lingering kiss.

Sarah had no trouble imagining André's long slim body, bent low at the waist, floppy black hair tumbling over his devilishly smiling face as he kissed Erzsi's hand. "And what does Josef think of this behavior?" Sarah asked.

"He turns away, pretending not to notice, but I can see he is annoyed. I find it sweet that he cares but doesn't want to show it."

"I'm cold, Mama," Willie interrupted the women. His cheeks were red and his gloves wet from the snow.

"Time to go back home."

Winter passed, friendship grew. The women gossiped, talked about their concerns, and planned for the birth of Erzsi's baby. On Sunday evenings the men drank their whiskey, smoked their cigars, and played poker.

Erzsi wrote her sisters about her pregnancy. "I am doing well," she wrote. "The usual discomforts of my condition can be a trial but Josef is solicitous and kind. We are both looking forward to the arrival of our little one. Josef, of course, is sure it will be a boy but claims he will welcome a daughter if that is what God gives us."

She was content, very much in love, planning for the birth of her child, their child. Since Josef brought her to this village he referred to her as Mrs. Farkas. He seemed comfortable with their arrangement, never mentioning marriage. "He loves me," she would tell herself. "I can see it in his eyes, feel it in his kiss."

Still, there were times when he was silent, distant, unwilling to share his thoughts with her. He never spoke of his family, always evaded her questions. There was a secret, something in his past that he did not want to discuss with her. They never talked about marriage. She was afraid to confront him, afraid of what his answer would be. "We are so busy, money is so scarce, marriage can wait," she would tell herself.

Josef watched the progress of Erzsi's pregnancy, proudly anticipating the birth of his child. "If it is a boy he will be strong and capable. If it is a girl she will be as beautiful as her mother," he would tell his friends in the tavern. Walking home from work he would imagine teaching his son the skills his father had taught him. "I will be a good father," he told himself. But the image of Maria waiting for him often intruded into his thoughts, taunting him for his betrayal.

"It is hard here without you," she wrote in her frequent letters. "But I am surrounded by my family, you are alone."

He regretted his betrayal of his marriage vows, but what could he do? "I send her money, she is with her family," he mollified himself. "I am going to have a son."

22 An American Citizen

East Kingston, New York
May, 1883

Spring arrived. There were blossoms on the apple tree, chickens and kittens freely roamed the backyard, and Josef had begun to dig out an area for a vegetable garden. Erzsi had completed preparations for the baby.

A white blanket edged in lace was draped lovingly over a wooden bassinet placed close to her bed. The bassinet was a gift from a neighbor who had eleven children of her own. She was sure she would not have any further use for the bassinet, or the children's toys and clothing. She was happy to give them all to the new mother.

Adel and Jimmy came to visit bringing knitted booties, a sweater, and a rattle. Benjamin sent a book of children's rhymes and poems. Ethel, much to Adel's annoyance, did not send a gift. She would not celebrate the birth of a child who was the result of this sinful union.

Erzsi was resting in a rocking chair that Josef had placed in the front yard for her. She was about to fall asleep when she heard a child's voice and looked up to see Willie proudly pushing a baby carriage, Sarah following close behind.

"This is for the new baby, Mrs. Farkas. I don't need it now that I am a big boy."

"Well, thank you so much, Willie. I am sure the baby will enjoy the carriage. Perhaps you and your mama will come with us when we go for walks in the afternoon." Willie nodded his consent and ran off into the house to retrieve the truck Josef had given him.

While the women were talking, Erzsi felt the beginning of her labor. "It is time," she told her friend. "Get Josef."

"I'll get the mid-wife, Josef can stay at my house. You don't want him here," Sarah counseled her friend as she helped her into the house and settled her on the bed.

Josef spent a restless night at the Drinkle's pacing up and down the front yard, a cigar in one hand, a glass of whiskey in the other. Finally, at dawn, Sarah arrived with the news.

"You have a son, Josef. Congratulations."

"A son, I have a son!" His face glowed with excitement as he shook hands with Tim and gave Sarah a hug. "I have a son!" he said again as the magnitude of the event settled in. "How is Erzsi?" he asked, turning to Sarah with a slightly worried expression.

"She is fine. Now go and see your family."

Josef, overflowing with excitement, ran down the street only stopping to shout, "I have a son!" to anyone who was close enough to hear.

Walking quietly through the kitchen he could hear the soft sounds of a mother cooing to her baby.

"Erzsi," he whispered, entering their bedroom.

The mid-wife was in the room arranging blankets and clean towels. "Congratulations, Josef," she said smiling. "Mother and baby are doing fine. I'm going home now. I'll check on them in a few hours."

Josef walked to the bed where Erzsi was propped up on pillows holding a tiny bundle.

"Josef, come closer and meet your son. He is perfect."

Josef bent over and gently lifted the baby. His eyes filled with tears as he cradled the infant in his arms. "My son," he whispered, "I will always take care of you."

"Josef, I would like to name him Janos after my father."

"Janos, in English that is John."

Moving the swaddling blankets away from the infant's face he admired the perfect features and gently touched the soft skin. "John, you are an American citizen." The new world held endless opportunities, and John would have access to them all. In that moment Josef knew he was not returning to Hungary. He placed the infant in Erzsi's arms, she smiled with contentment.

23 Maria

Busica, Hungary
July, 1884

Her son was asleep. "My precious little boy," Maria whispered looking down at his tiny face, so peaceful, so innocent. Gently she stroked his chin, letting her love for the child relieve her for a moment from the melancholy and longing that filled her days. The little boy, just over a year old, had never met his father. "Your father is in America," she would tell him, even though he could not understand what that meant. "He will come back to us soon."

Terèz, Maria's ten-year-old sister and self-appointed guardian of her nephew, was holding Maria's other hand. She watched, captivated, as the child's glistening pink lips started to move and his tiny hand pulled his blanket closer to his face.

"Do you think he is dreaming?" Terèz asked her sister.

"Perhaps," Maria nodded, a smile lighting her face, momentarily erasing the sadness that was often there.

"I want to have lots of children when I am grown," Terèz solemnly informed Maria. "I will have a husband as strong and handsome as Anton." Anton, their oldest brother was six years older than Maria and seventeen years older than Terèz. He had taken responsibility for the family when their father had died. Anton had a special fondness for the little sister who showered him with adoration and brought a child's innocence and unqualified love into their lives.

"I am sure you will have beautiful children," Maria said, giving her a little hug. "Come, let Krisztian sleep. We have much to do to prepare for tonight. You need to help me find the plumpest chicken for dinner. It will be a celebration."

Leaving the house, Terèz let go of Maria's hand. She stealthily approached the chickens, inspecting each one as it busily pecked and scratched the ground, completely ignoring the little girl.

Maria had lived in this house all of her life. She had helped her mother plant the seeds in the vegetable garden. In the summer she had picked cucumbers and beans, eating them right from the garden. Looking out over the yard her eyes rested on an open space where the women of the village gathered to make sauerkraut. It was a social event for them; they laughed and gossiped while cutting the cabbage into slivers and packing it into crocks. Maria imagined she could hear their laughter as they worked, gossiped, and shared stories, often at the expense of their husbands. "When Josef comes home we will have our own home in this village and I will make sauerkraut with my friends in my yard," she thought wistfully.

A noise behind her interrupted her thoughts. She turned as her mother came out of the house. Silently, almost ghostlike, Anna walked to her vegetable garden and began frantically pulling weeds. "There is work to be done, Maria," she said without looking up from her task. Although today was a special day for the family, Anna's face was expressionless, devoid of any emotion as she relentlessly pulled the weeds.

Everyone was worried about Anna. Her son Daneil had died fighting in the Balkans; a year later her husband had died from an infection. Since their deaths Anna had become withdrawn, showing little interest in her home or her family. She spent her time tending to her garden or sitting quietly with her embroidery. She left all other responsibilities to Maria and Anton.

But tonight was to be a night of celebration, Maria's brother Kolos, a private in the Royal Hungarian Army, the Honved, was coming home. He was bringing his bride Alana to meet the family. Kolos had not been home since he enlisted in the Honved four years ago. Today they would be reunited with Kolos and would welcome Alana to the family.

Kolos had met Alana at a coffee shop owned by her family. He had been stationed near Pressburg, lonely and far from home, when he first saw her. She had been serving coffee to customers seated at the counter when the soldiers entered the shop sitting at a table near the window.

"Alana, see what the young men would like," her mother had ordered.

Alana, her thick chestnut colored hair tied playfully with a large blue ribbon, her knee length dress, with its many layers of petticoats swilling above her high black boots, approached their table. Sparkling green eyes with specks of deep gold, rimmed in black, with large black irises and long lush lashes smiled down at Kolos. He felt that he could get lost in them for all eternity. When she asked if he would like some coffee, he could do nothing but stare at her.

"Kolos, the young woman asked you a question. Are you too shy to answer?" teased one of his companions. Everyone at the table had laughed at him.

"I will bring all of you some coffee with cream and sugar. Perhaps when I return you will order a Kolash," Alana had smiled at Kolos turning away from the other soldiers.

That night, Kolos could not sleep thinking of the beautiful girl with the green eyes and inviting smile. He promised himself he would see her again.

Frequenting the coffee shop at every opportunity, he eventually had the courage to ask her if she would honor him with her company at dinner at a local restaurant. She had declined, saying her mother would never allow her to go without a chaperone, especially with a soldier from the Honved.

Nevertheless he had persisted. Alana's parents watched with disapproval as the romance flourished in the restricted environment of the coffee shop. When Alana told them that she loved Kolos and would marry him they saw the futility of preventing the marriage and reluctantly gave their blessing.

Tonight, Maria's family would meet Alana for the first time. Maria was determined to make her brother and his bride feel welcome. From his letters she knew that Alana made her brother happy and that was all that was important. She would see to it that the dinner was perfectly prepared and she would admonish her siblings to be polite. No one could predict or control how Anna would receive the new member of the family.

Preparations for the meal began while Krisztian was taking his nap. Terèz had watched with admiration as Maria prepared the chicken she had selected. From the perspective of a ten-year-old the process had not been without drama. Maria's skill and lack of emotion as she removed the head of the hapless creature earned respect. The spectacle continued as the headless chicken was held by its feet and quickly dipped into a large pan of boiling hot water and pulled out, only to be further subjected to having its feathers removed and its feet cut off.

"Terèz, go and find some flowers for the table," Maria said, handing Terèz a pail. "When you come back it will be time for Krisztian to wake up. You can feed him and take him outside to play."

As Terèz was leaving, Anna, looking tired and pale, came into the kitchen.

"Here are some cucumbers, Maria." There was no emotion Anna's voice. "Kolos always liked my cucumber salad."

"Thank you, Mama," Maria said with a smile, hiding her concern for her mother.

"I need to take a little rest," said Anna as she walked slowly out of the kitchen. Sleep allowed her to escape her sorrow.

"Maria, I see them. I can see the wagon!" shouted Terèz, poking her head inside the door, forgetting about the flowers. "Come, Maria, hurry. There are four people in the wagon." Terèz darted out of the house not waiting for a reply.

The shouting had awakened Krisztian who toddled into the kitchen dragging his well-worn blanket, his cheeks still pink from sleep, his thumb securely tucked in his mouth. Maria smiled, looking at her little boy with his dark brown wavy hair. "Just like yours," family and friends had told her. But, to Maria, there was no doubt that he had Josef's brown eyes and stocky build.

"Come, my precious little boy, Uncle Kolos and Alana are here," Maria said, picking up her son.

"Look, Maria, I think it is Jakob! Jakob is in the wagon with Anton and Kolos," Terèz said while pointing to the wagon still a distance down the dirt road. "Did you know he was coming?"

Jakob, Maria's favorite younger brother, shared Maria's deep religious faith. Jakob had spent many hours with the priest in their village, who encouraged the religious fervor of the boy. They prayed together for the fulfillment of Jakob's desire to become a priest. When he was eighteen Father Stefan facilitated Jakob's admission into the prestigious seminary at SpišskáKapitula. The day Jakob left for the seminary his mother cried tears of joy, his father's heart was filled with pride. Maria felt sorrow as she watched her friend and brother leave for the distant seminary. But that night when she prayed for him, she was comforted knowing that he had been called to serve the Lord. "We are surely blessed," she had thought as she finished her nightly prayers.

Maria had been two years old when Jakob was born. She loved him from the moment Papa had carefully placed the tiny bundle into her arms while admonishing her to be very gentle. As children they were inseparable, their devotion to each other obvious to everyone. But it was their religious faith that bound them together. Their beautiful young voices brought joy to everyone who heard them as they sang hymns of praise to the Blessed Mary. Maria, being older by two years, took it as her responsibility to teach him his catechism. When he misbehaved she reminded him that the Lord Jesus was always watching. At eighteen, he was admitted to the seminary and she had cried tears of joy. When he celebrated his first mass she would be there to share the holy sacrament with him.

Now Jakob was coming home for the first time since he had left for the seminary. Anton had written telling him that Kolos was bringing Alana home to meet the family. The young seminarian, unknown to Maria, had requested, and was granted, leave to return home for a visit. Jakob wanted to surprise the family and Anton had kept the secret. Now the sisters watched with growing excitement as they saw that Jakob was in the wagon with Kolos and Alana.

"Mama should be here to greet them," Maria thought as the wagon drew closer. "Kolos will be disappointed and hurt."

"I can see her. I can see Alana!" said Terèz, clapping. "Jakob! Kolos!" Terèz said running to greet the wagon. Jakob, with the agility of youth, jumped out of the wagon not waiting for it to completely stop.

"My little Terèz, I have missed you," he said as she jumped into his arms. Hand in hand brother and sister followed the wagon until it stopped in front of the house.

Maria watched smiling as Kolos helped Alana out of the wagon. They looked so happy. Krisztian, suddenly shy, pulled his blanket to his face and nestled his head into Maria's shoulder. Only one little eye peeked out to watch all the activity.

When Kolos lifted Alana from the wagon her petticoats swirled under her short full skirt, her long shapely legs visible above her calf-high black boots. A white blouse with puffed up sleeves was topped with a tightly fitting pale blue vest. The vest, the color of the summer sky on a cloudless day, was embroidered with swirls of gold thread and maroon flowers. The sleeves of the blouse were embroidered with a twisted vine of maroon thread matching the vest. Her deep blue apron, contrasting with the vest, was trimmed with a delicate white lace that her mother had given her as a wedding present.

When he introduced Alana to Maria she was greeted with a warm smile and a welcoming hug. It had been a long time since the family had been together. So much had changed since the last time he was home. Anton was now in charge since their father died, Maria looked older, her little boy shy, sweet, nestling his head against her shoulder. Sweet little Terèz still holding Jakob's hand had grown taller and would soon show signs of becoming a woman. Jakob was wearing the clerical garb of a seminarian.

"Where is Mama?" asked Kolos, with concern.

"She is resting."

"How is she doing?" asked Jakob, he knew is mother was not well.

"She is always tired, always sad. She works in her garden and sits for hours in her chair, her knitting needles just resting in her lap. But we will talk about all this later. Alana, you must be tired from your trip." Maria was now ready to take charge of her siblings, making sure that everyone knew what needed to be done. "Kolos and Jakob go and help Anton, Terèz take Krisztian outside. Alana, I will show you where to put your things," Maria spoke with authority and everyone obeyed without question.

Anton put one arm around each brother. "It is so good to have both of you home. It has been too long."

"Everyone is home except for Papa and Daneil," said Jakob. "So much has changed."

When Daneil was sent to Bosnia in 1880 his father was proud, sure that his son would fight bravely for his country. "We have a right and a need to be there. We must protect our border." Their father had told his family. "Conditions there are deplorable. We will reform their society and their economy. They will be grateful to us."

"What about Daneil?" Anna was worried about her son.

"He will do his duty. We should be proud of our son."

"I will pray for him, Mama. I will pray to the Blessed Virgin to keep him safe," Maria had reassured her mother.

"I will also pray for him, Mama," added Jakob.

But the Habsburg regime had failed to reform Bosnia's economy or society and political turmoil had increased. The army had a sustained counterinsurgency campaign to put down lingering resistance. In 1882, shortly after Josef and Maria were married, Daneil's military patrol was attacked on the orders of a local Serbian chieftain. The rebels eventually surrendered, but Daneil had been badly wounded and was sent home.

His mother would not leave his bedside. Despite her efforts, a mother's love could not heal his wounds. She watched helplessly as her once strong son no longer had the will to live. Two months after he returned home, the village mourned the death of the young soldier.

Now, as Maria finished the preparations for the meal, she stood by the chair where Daneil had once sat. Tonight Alana would sit there. Anton would sit in his father's chair at the head of the table.

Father had died in 1883 shortly after the birth of Krisztian. At first, the injury had seemed to be a minor inconvenience, not worthy of special attention. While working with Anton in the barn Istvàn had stepped on a rusty nail. He was a strong healthy man, he chose to continue with his task, planning to attend to the wound after the evening meal. He had smiled to himself thinking of Anna. While cleaning and dressing the injury she would surely chastise him for not coming to her sooner.

Days passed, the tissue around the wound became red, swollen, and inflamed. Walking became painful but he was careful to hide this from his wife. "I will not worry her. The wound will heal in its own time," he told himself. But it did not. When the fever developed, he could not get out of bed. Anna, frantic with worry, sent for the midwife. There was no doctor in the village.

As she had done with her son the year before, Anna stayed by her husband's bedside, nursing him, praying for him. When he died, she was physically and emotionally exhausted. Anton had picked her up and carried her to her bed. She did not cry. She simply withdrew into herself. Her grief for her husband and her son was impossible for her to endure.

Maria, standing by her father's chair, smiled, remembering the almost imperceptible tender glances which had often been exchanged between husband and wife during the course of a meal. Now, Anton, as head of the family, would sit in his father's place.

After the evening meal and the children were asleep, Maria, her brothers, and Alana sat together on benches next to the vegetable garden. Their mother Anna had gone to her bed. It was a cloudless summer evening and they sat quietly watching the stars, enjoying the gentle breeze that gave some relief from the oppressive heat of the day.

Kolos had not been home since Maria's wedding. So much had changed. But it was the changes in his mother and Maria that caused him concern.

Although still a young woman of twenty-three, Maria had lost the glow of youth. Her beautiful, thick, dark brown hair was now pulled back in a tight bun. The hazel eyes that had shone with love and desire were now filled with sadness, the light only returning when she was with her son. Her dress was the dark, simple muslin of a matron. Her only vanity was a richly embroidered scarf that she wore all day, even in the house.

"How is Josef?" asked Kolos, turning to his sister.

"He works hard, sends home money, but he does not write as often," the pain in her voice was obvious to her brothers.

"Does he say when he is coming home?" asked Kolos.

"He talks about America, the opportunities for work. It has been a long time since he has talked of coming home."

"Surely he wants to meet his son!" Jakob exclaimed, bewildered.

"He does not know about Krisztian," Maria's voice was soft, sad, filled with regret.

"Maria! Why? What is that about?" Kolos could not believe what he had just heard.

"I did not want to worry him. I thought he would be home soon after the baby was born," Maria paused; she could not bear the look of concern in her brothers' eyes. "I kept waiting for him to come home. I was always sure it would just be a little longer. The time never seemed right. First Daneil was killed and then Papa died. I have been so worried about Mama," Maria's voice faltered, tears rolling down her cheeks.

"You must write him, Maria. He has a right to know he is a father," Anton's tone was authoritative.

"I am afraid to. What if he wants me to bring Krisztian to America? I cannot leave Mama and Terèz. They need me. I have a duty to my family."

"God has commanded that a wife belongs with her husband," Jakob, now the spiritual leader, admonished his sister.

Maria put her hands over her eyes and lowered her head, the tears slowly rolling down her cheeks.

"This is my home. I cannot leave," she whispered, the agony of her dilemma obvious in her voice. "I have a duty to my husband and to my family, my heart is breaking. Why must I choose?"

"Krisztian must be with his father and you must be with your husband." Kolos could not understand his sister's deception. "Anton will take care of the family, you mustn't worry," Kolos tried to reassure her.

"Mama will recover over time. She has her faith and her family. Come pray with me." Jacob took Maria's hand, they knelt on the hard floor, the others did the same. Jakob led them in prayer.

When the prayer was over, Anton made the decision. "I am responsible for you and for this household. You must go to Josef. You must go to your husband," he commanded.

Maria prayed long into the night, seeking guidance from the Lord. By the morning she had made her decision. She would tell Josef about their son and if he did not want to come back home then she would go to him.

With tears falling, she wrote a letter to Josef, unsure what his response would be. If he wanted her to, she would join him in America. She enclosed a picture of Krisztian, with his child's smile and thick, dark, wavy hair, sitting on her lap.

24 Facing Consequences

East Kingston, New York
July, 1884

It was a pleasant Sunday afternoon in July, a breeze from the river offered respite from the summer heat. Josef, cigar in his hand, a glass of whiskey at his side, was sitting on a weathered wooden bench under the apple tree. He watched, his expression relaxed but pensive, as Erzsi gently rolled a ball to their son John. The little boy had Erzsi's blond hair and blue eyes. His stocky body, round arms, and strong legs reminded Josef of his brother Markas.

"Catch it, Janos. Catch the ball," Erzsi smiled encouragement, pointing to the ball slowly moving through the grass to her son.

Giggling, John, now fourteen months old, moved with unsteady but determined steps towards the moving object. To his surprise, when he reached for the ball he suddenly found himself sitting on the ground. Startled, he looked at his mother, his tiny mouth beginning to quiver and his eyes filling with tears.

"Good boy, Janos. You caught the ball. You are all right. Bring the ball to Mama," his mother said, reassuring him. Seeing his mother's smile the little boy forgot to cry. Carefully, he wrapped his arms around the ball, stood up, and looked at his mother for approval.

"That's right, Janos, bring it here," Erzsi said while clapping her hands. With a self-satisfied grin, he swayed, almost fell, but managed to make the few steps required to meet the welcoming arms of his mother.

"My clever little boy," Erzsi said reaching for him and giving him a hug and kissing his neck, making the child squeal with delight.

"Did you see that, Josef? Our son caught the ball and brought it to me," beamed Erzsi.

"He will be a baseball player for sure!" Josef said. "Bring him to me, Erzsi. I want to reward my son."

"Really, Josef, we will be eating soon. You spoil the child," she said carrying John to his father. To the child's delight a candy mysteriously appeared in Josef's hand.

"Play with him for a while, Josef. I will call you when he needs to come in." Erzsi walked back to the house leaving father and son to enjoy their precious time together.

Watching Erzsi, Josef tried to remember his own mother. He had vague memories of a woman who held him and comforted him when he would fall. That was all. His mother had died when he was three, leaving his father with four young sons.

Three months after the death of his wife Josef's father had married a widow with a young daughter. It had been a marriage of convenience, but his new wife found she was ill-suited for raising boys. Unlike her daughter, the boys were rough, dirty, and disobedient.

When she attempted to discipline them, their father always intervened, undermining her authority.

Her world was the kitchen and the vegetable garden, while her husband tended the fields and livestock with his sons. She served them their meals, cleaned their clothes, and left them alone when they sat around the table after dinner talking about the day.

It was a lonely life, but her husband did not notice or care. He rarely talked with his wife except for household concerns and he dismissed her daughter as an insignificant burden on the family.

Josef didn't realize that he had never witnessed the love that should exist between a husband and a wife. He barely remembered the special bond that existed between a mother and her son. Now, memories of his father and brothers invaded his thoughts.

Josef's father had been a stern man who did not hesitate to discipline his boys. The brothers often had large welts where their father had beaten them. The welts from one particularly vicious beating had left permanent scars. When Erzsi's hand paused over one of the scars he had pushed her hand away. He had been embarrassed and evasive when she had asked about them.

Despite the punishments, Josef respected his father. His father worked hard for his family, never favored one brother over the other, and offered praise when it was deserved.

Hard work was valued, unproductive activities were considered a waste of the precious time given to them by God. When Josef spent time with friends after school or on Sunday afternoons, he would return home to a father who would sternly voice his disapproval.

Growing up Josef had experienced the love that was shared by brothers. Without a mother to offer solace the brothers had turned to each other causing the bond between them to become unshakable. Imre, the oldest, would often come to Josef's rescue, taking the blame and the punishment when Josef had made an error in judgment. Imre was their hero. He was tough and strong, never hesitating to fight with anyone who posed a threat to his brothers. When he was sixteen Imre had lost an eye in a fight defending Josef. He would wear the injury as a badge of honor the rest of his life. No one bothered the Farkas boys.

Jenci was the gentle one. He liked to read and to study. Regretting his own limited education, their father had encouraged Jenci to be diligent in school, thinking perhaps Jenci would eventually find a job in the city and send money home.

Josef smiled to himself, "Jenci, Papa would be proud of you." Jenci had gone on to develop an interest in government and now worked as a clerk in the Hungarian parliament. He had married well and had two daughters. "Jenci, perhaps next time you will have sons," Josef smiled picturing Jenci with his daughters. Perhaps that was the way it should be.

Markas was closest in age to Josef. They had been best friends, sharing the same bed, confiding secrets, and on occasion complaining about their father or one of the other brothers. When Josef began to notice that girls had certain desirable attributes, it was Markas who had shown him the pictures of young women that Imre had hidden under his mattress.

Now, sitting in the garden, playing with his son, Josef made his decision. He knew that his responsibility and his duty was to his son.

For the last two years Josef had been content. His son John was growing strong and healthy. Erzsi was an attentive mother as well as an efficient mistress of the boarding house. On occasion he had thought of Maria. He was remorseful thinking of the deception, but what could he do now that he had a son? He wrote to Maria when there was an opportunity, but he was not worried about her. She was safe and content in Hungary with her family. He sent her money whenever it was possible. Maria wrote telling him about the events in her family, the marriage of her brother Kolos, the tragic death of her brother followed closely by that of her father. Anna's poor health concerned him. She had always been kind to him. Josef knew that Maria with her kind heart and efficient manner would manage. It was her responsibility to care for her family. She was safe, loved and needed.

His duty was clearly here in America with his son. He loved John and was proud that he was an American. On occasion, Josef and Erzsi had experienced the resentment towards newly arrived immigrants. Josef had been harassed at work, the best jobs and possibilities for promotion were not given to foreigners. Erzsi was especially embarrassed by her accent and spent most of her time with a few close friends, avoiding lengthy conversations with strangers and shopkeepers.

Things would be better for John. He was born in America. He was an American citizen. When the weather was nice, and John was asleep, Erzsi and Josef would sit under the apple tree and talk about their son. They talked about how fast he was growing, the friends he had played with, a scrape he got on his knee while trying to catch a rabbit, but talking about John's future, the endless possibilities, gave them the greatest pleasure. He would go to an American school, learn to play American games, and someday vote for the President of the United States of America.

Josef smiled at the thought. Perhaps he would become a citizen as well, he would talk politics with John and they would argue over which party deserved to win the election. Josef was no longer planning to return to Hungary. His future was here with John.

Josef's thoughts were interrupted when John, finished with the candy, became restless and attempted to climb down from his father's lap.

"Let's run, John," said Josef, gently placing his son on the ground and taking his hand. "Come, let's run and catch the chickens." Father and son, hand in hand, laughing, sharing a special moment together, ran across the lawn.

The next day everything changed. On his way home from work he had not been surprised to find a letter from Maria waiting for him at the post office. Maria wrote frequently and he looked forward to receiving news from home. As usual, he went to the tavern where he would find a quiet corner, order some whiskey, and read the letter away from prying eyes.

Opening the carefully sealed envelope, removing the neatly folded pages with Maria's unmistakable handwriting, he was surprised when a photograph fell to the table. He frowned as he picked up the picture and a tightness gripped his stomach. Maria was sitting in a chair holding a little boy. The child, about the same age as John, looked like Maria, but his eyes reminded Josef of his own.

With trembling hands he read her letter.

Buzica, Hungary
July 3, 1884

"My dear Josef,

It is with a heavy heart that I must confess to a deception. I did not want to worry you and always expected you to be home soon. But time has passed and I can no longer withhold news which I hope will fill you with joy. Please forgive me for not telling you sooner. You have a son. His name is Krisztian. Krisztian is a strong, healthy little boy, and as you can see from the picture he has your eyes. A son needs his father. If you cannot come home, I will bring Krisztian to you."

Josef let the letter fall to the table. He was unable to finish reading Maria's lengthy explanation for her dishonesty. He had a son in America and a son in Hungary. Maria must have been with child when he left her. His sons would only be a few months apart in age. Maria's deception filled him with anger. She had deprived him of his right to know of the birth of a son. Holding the photograph he looked into the eyes of his son and he knew what he must do. Krisztian and John were brothers and he was their father. "My sons will live with me in America," he said, his clenched fist landing hard on the table. "Maria is my wife," his voice was defiant and angry. "She will bring my son to me." He had made up his mind, there would be no argument.

"Time to go home, Josef," someone said. "You have had enough. Erzsi is waiting."

He picked up the whiskey bottle which was now almost empty, and walked, with unsteady legs, out of the tavern. On the way home he solidified his self-righteous plan. "Maria will be mother to both of my boys. Erzsi will see what is best for Janos. She will be hurt, of course, but she will recover. She will find a good man to marry. Maria will forgive me."

He stumbled as he entered the house, knocking over a table. "Shush," he said putting a finger to his lips.

The evening meal had been over hours ago and the house was quiet. Erzsi, unwilling to confront Josef for being late, pretended she was asleep. Janos was in bed and she did not want him awakened. She did not suspect this would be the last night they would be together as a family.

Josef was evasive and distant at breakfast and dinner. Erzsi assumed it was just a result of too much whiskey. "Best to leave him alone," she thought, it was not the first time he had come home like this.

After Janos was asleep and the evening chores complete, Erzsi sat on the bench under the apple tree. It was a warm, humid mid-summer night, a layer of thin clouds covered the sky that glowed red on the horizon as the sun set. Dogs barked in the distance and a baby's cry could be heard. They were familiar and comforting sounds.

Reaching into her pocket she took out the little prayer book with the yellow rose. She thought of her mother. "I wish you could see Janos," she said looking at the heavens. Holding the prayer book in her hand she said a little prayer for her family. "Sweet Jesus, look after my Josef, he looks troubled."

Josef was watching her from the kitchen window. "There is nothing to do but tell her the truth," he spoke to the bottle of whiskey in his clenched fist. There would be tears, he was sure, but Erzsi would see what must be done. She would understand that his place was with his wife and Janos must stay with him.

Erzsi watched him coming to join her. She was pleased that he wanted to spend time with her, but was concerned by the look of worry on his face. He sat on the bench next to her, his head lowered, his hands clasped together. He did not look at her.

"What is it, Josef?"

There was a long pause. Josef shifted in his seat, suddenly reluctant to say the words that would cause so much pain. He did not want to hurt Erzsi, but it was time to face the consequences of his deception.

"Erzsi, I have a wife in Hungary," he struggled to keep his voice steady; he still could not look at her.

Erzsi grasped her stomach in pain, her eyes welled with tears. She had always suspected that Josef had a secret. She had refused to acknowledge the doubts in her heart or listen to the warnings from her friends. All she had wanted was for Josef to love her as she had loved him.

"There was a letter today. I have a son in Hungary, his name is Krisztian."

"Janos, Janos is your son," confusion filled her thoughts but her voice was defiant and angry. She thought of her beautiful little boy sleeping in his bed, so innocent. What was to become of Janos?

Josef had not been prepared for the depth of the pain on Erzsi's face. Surely she knew that he would not abandon Janos.

"Yes, Janos, too, is my son. Erzsi, you do not need to worry about Janos."

For a moment, Erzsi's fear subsided. Of course Josef would stay with her and with Janos. Nothing had really changed. His wife was in Hungary. Josef was here with her.

"You will stay here then. You will stay with us?"

"Erzsi, please, listen. I need to make this right. I need to think of Krisztian and his mother."

Again fear gripped at her heart. She stood, agitated, grasping her skirt with her fists. She could no longer sit next to this man she did not know. She could not look at him. This was not her Josef. This was not the Josef she loved.

"You will leave us then? How will I care for Janos on my own? I will not have a husband and he will not have a father." Tears filled her eyes, she spoke softly, almost to herself, "My baby, my poor little boy."

Josef stood and started to reach for her, but she pulled back, repulsed.

"Erzsi, Janos has a father. I am his father. I will raise him as an American. That is what we have always wanted. He will continue to live here with me and with his brother. They will be educated here and will have the future we talked about." Josef felt confident now, surely she would understand. She would see what was best for Janos.

"You would take my son from me?" her voice quivered as she fought back the tears. She would not let him see her cry.

"It is best, Erzsi. I can provide for Janos. A boy needs his father."

"No, I will not abandon my son!" Too shaken to say anything more, she turned her back to him and ran into the house.

Josef stood there watching her. Knowing she would be leaving him forever, he felt a sadness he had not expected. "I loved you, Erzsi," he whispered. "I did not mean to hurt you."

Now defiant, he looked up at the sky and shouted to the stars. "I am a sinful man but my duty is clear. My sons will be with me," and he started to walk in the direction of the tavern.

25 A Mother's Sorrow

July, August 1884

Erzsi nestled her face into the rumpled curls of the sleeping child in her arms. Her warm tears dampened his hair, joining mother and son in grief. John, nestled in his mother's arms, lulled by the rhythmic rocking of the chair, slept peacefully. He was unaware of the turmoil in the lives of the adults who loved him.

"My little one, my precious little boy, what is to become of us?" she whispered, clutching the prayer book she held in her hand.

"I have sinned. I did not listen to the warnings."

She pictured Josef on the ship when they first met. She had smiled at him, teased him, and invited him. Filled with desire, her own needs, she had not listened to the warnings in her heart. He kept secrets from her but she did not question him. When he was evasive she made excuses for him. She had gone into his bed driven by her love, her desires, not heeding the possible consequences.

Mrs. Timko had warned her, "Young women these days need to be very careful. We were safe back home, family and friends were there to watch over and protect us. A husband values chastity in the woman he marries. There is a reason God gave us the Ten Commandments."

Erzsi had ignored her. "Josef is a good man," she had rationalized. "When the time is right we will be married."

Benjamin had warned her although she had not recognized it at the time. "I hope you will always consider me your friend," he had said. "Know you can turn to me for support if the need should arise. I wish you well." Now she understood the warning in his voice. Even Josef tried to warn her. He never spoke of marriage, he never made a promise. She knew very little about him, he was always evasive when she asked him about his home and his family. But she had not cared. She loved him and wanted to believe that he loved her.

When Josef had not mentioned marriage she had made excuses for him. Perhaps he needed to get settled first, they would get married when there was time. She had told herself they would get married when they had enough money, when they were settled, when life was easier.

Sleep came, unaware and unwelcome. The child was still held tightly in her arms but rational thought was replaced by restless, fearful images. She was running, lost, a baby was crying in the distance. Her mother was there, near the horizon, beckoning her to follow, but she could not. It was raining, she was stuck in the mud, her wet skirts dragging her down.

A clap of thunder, the unsettling images were gone. John started to cry; she stroked his hair and whispered softly to him until he fell back asleep.

Putting the prayer book deep in her pocket, she made a decision. Today she would leave this house.

Gently, she placed John in their bed, hoping the child would stay asleep while she made preparations to leave. She was alone, the house was quiet. Josef was gone. He had not come into the house after she left him in the garden. It was too early for the boarders to be awake.

In the pre-dawn light, with a rooster crowing in the distance, she made her way to the kitchen. There was money in the tin on the shelf above the stove. "It is my money. I am the one who fed and looked after the boarders," she spoke defiantly to herself as she tied the coins in a napkin and placed them in her skirt pocket next to the prayer book.

"John will need to eat," her voice was softer as she hastily placed cheese, bread, and preserves in the basket Iren had given her years ago.

"The rest is yours, Josef. I do not want anything from you."

Returning to the bedroom she put on her best dress and shoes she had recently bought. She reached for the box that contained the hat that Josef had given her just two years ago. She fingered the flowers on the rim and remembered how happy she had been. After a moment's hesitation she placed the hat on the bed. Instead, she covered her head with an old bonnet that Adel had given her when she had first arrived in Rondout.

"All right my precious, it is time to leave." She wrapped the sleepy little boy in her shawl and secured it around her neck. Without looking back she opened the front door and began the long walk to Rondout.

The village was quiet, peaceful, its occupants still asleep. She shivered as the morning mist dampened her face, thankful for the warm shawl that protected John. Walking was difficult. The muddy street pulled at her shoes making each step a challenge. The sleeping child was heavy and the wooden handle of the basket cut into her arm. "Keep moving," she whispered to herself as they left the village behind. "Soon we will rest."

With the morning sun now above the horizon, John opened his eyes and smiled up at his mother. His cheeks were flushed from sleep but his blue eyes sparkled with playfulness and his blond curls were a tangled mass of flaxen gold.

"Good morning, my precious," she said while pulling him closer.

He began to move in her arms, no longer content to stay confined in the shawl. It was time to play.

"All right, my big boy. We will stop here."

Sitting on a stone wall, she released the restless child, placing him gently on the ground. With an ache in her heart, she watched as her son began to explore his unfamiliar surroundings.

"Josef, what have you done?" she turned away from the boy so he would not see the tears that were filling her eyes.

Benjamin was the first to see her. He was sitting on the porch of the boarding house, feet resting comfortably on the railing, his notebook neglected on his lap. A woman, head bent, firmly holding the hand of a small child, was walking down the street. Despite the warm afternoon and the bright summer sun, a heavy shawl was incongruously draped around her shoulders.

"Erzsi?" He frowned, hesitant, unsure.

As they came closer to the house, he stood and looked over the porch railing. There was no doubt that the child was John. He recognized the cap the boy was wearing. It had been a birthday present from Adel.

"Adel! Come quickly," he shouted through the open window behind him. "Adel! Ethel! It is Erzsi and John."

Dropping the notebook, he ran into the street.

"Erzsi?" he called as he approached the woman. The face that looked up at him was pale, the eyes swollen and red.

"Erzsi! What happened? Where is Josef?"

Recognizing her friend, Erzsi started to sway, all her strength suddenly drained away. She let go of John; the basket she had been clutching fell from her hand. Benjamin caught her as she collapsed, exhausted, trembling, and unable to control her tears.

"Mama!" John pulled at his mother's skirts.

"Benjamin! What is it? What happened?" Adel and Ethel hurried down the rickety stairs.

"What happened, Erzsi, are you hurt? Where is Josef?" Adel wrapped her arms around her friend.

John began to cry, clinging tighter to his mother's skirt.

Ethel knelt close to the little boy. "John," she spoke softly, her tone reassuring as she reached for him. Still holding his mother's skirt, he tilted his head toward the familiar voice. Ethel's disapproval of Erzsi had disappeared when she had first met John. Holding the innocent baby, her heart had softened and she had developed a fondness for the child.

"We have kittens in the shed behind the barn. Would you like to see them?" He nodded, slowly relinquishing his grip on his mother's skirt. With a gentle reassuring embrace, Ethel picked him up and walked back to the house.

"Thank you, Ethel," Adel whispered.

Benjamin gently lifted Erzsi, she did not speak or resist.

They placed her on Adel's bed, removed her bonnet and shoes.

"John, where is John?" her eyes still closed but her voice was terrified.

"He is with Ethel. Rest, we will talk later."

"My baby, my precious little boy," the words were spoken softly into the pillow beneath her head.

"I will go tomorrow to find Josef," Benjamin whispered to Adel as he left the room.

Adel closed the curtains and sat by her friend, stroking her hair until Erzsi had fallen asleep.

Erzsi opened her eyes, the room was dark. Her body ached and the sheet that covered her was wet. She could hear the gentle breathing of someone in the bed next to hers.

"Adel?" Erzsi tried to sit up but was overcome with nausea and exhaustion.

Adel, worried about her friend, had not been able to sleep. Silently she moved across the room and reached for Erzsi.

"I am here," she said, feeling Erzsi's burning face and damp hair.

"You have a fever, Erzsi, try and sleep," she spoke quietly so as not to wake up Ethel or John.

"Janos? Where is Janos? Where is my son?"

"He is here, asleep. We made a bed for him on the floor next to the window."

"John, asleep," the words were barely audible as she closed her eyes and drifted back to a fitful sleep.

Erzsi slept the next day, too exhausted and ill to leave her bed or care for John.

Adel was sitting next to the window in the parlor, mending socks for the boarders, when she heard the carriage. Parting the lace curtains she saw Benjamin walking toward the house. The news could not be good. He looked worried, eyes cast down, a slight frown around his mouth. Filled with apprehension, she put her mending aside, took a deep breath to bolster her courage, and walked to the door.

"Benjamin!" she opened the door for him, he met her gaze and tried to smile. "Come in the kitchen, we can talk there," she moved aside making room for him to enter the hallway. "We are alone. Ethel has taken John to the cobbler and Erzsi is asleep."

"How are they doing?"

"Ethel has been taking care of John. I have never seen her so happy. The boy is quite taken with her and follows her around all day. Erzsi is exhausted; she has been sick and has not left her bed. We are worried about her." She paused for a moment trying to find answers in Benjamin's worried face. "What about Josef?"

"I found him in the tavern, sitting alone, angry, tired, worried about his son," he paused for a moment as he pictured the man in the tavern, so different from the Josef he had known. "He has a wife in Hungary, they have a son." How could he explain to Adel what Josef had told him, or describe the torment he had seen in his eyes?

Josef, his sadness and guilt evident on his face, had showed him the picture Maria had sent of their son. "His name is Krisztian," Josef's hand gently touched the face of the boy in the picture. "I did not know Maria had a child, our child. He looks like me, don't you think?"

Benjamin had nodded, perplexed, trying to understand. "How could Josef not have known he had a son?"

"I have brothers," Josef continued, a melancholy smile for a moment lighting his eyes. He was remembering, but not sharing with Benjamin, how Markas had shown him pictures of young women hidden under Imre's mattress. "Krisztian and John are brothers, they must be together." Josef's voice was strong now, defiant. "Brothers need each other, family is everything." He paused, hoping to see understanding on Benjamin's face but all he saw was anger. "Maria will bring Krisztian to America." Josef said, his face red with defiance, his breath rancid with the smell of whiskey. He pounded his fist on the table. "She is my wife. Krisztian and John are my sons. We will be a family." Benjamin had heard enough. This man was not worthy of Erzsi. He got up from the table and left the tavern with Josef's self-righteous eyes boring into his back.

Now Benjamin looked at Adel and could see the concern on her face. "He wants to bring his wife and son to America. He wants to help Erzsi but he will not let her take his son."

"His son! He does not deserve his son."

"Adel, sadly, I have come to the conclusion that John just might be better off with Josef," Benjamin paused, wondering how to say what needed to be said. "Erzsi is a woman without a husband, without prospects. How will she care for the child? How will she protect him from the circumstances of his birth? The law will side with Josef if he takes her to court."

"Erzsi loves the boy. Her heart would break if she lost him."

Erzsi, pale, her hair matted and uncombed, a shawl wrapped tightly around her shoulders, appeared in the doorway. She had heard!

"No! He will not have my son!" her voice was angry, her fists tightly grasping the shawl. She tried to stand straight but her legs grew weak, her head began to spin. She leaned against the door for support.

Benjamin, shocked by her appearance, hesitated for a moment, then stood, and with two swift strides was at the doorway. He reached out for her, hoping to offer her comfort, but she pulled away from him.

"Erzsi, think what is best for John."

"My son belongs with me. I am his mother," her voice was shaking, if not for the support of the wall she would have collapsed.

"Erzsi, you are not well, you need to rest." Adel was now at her side with her arms around her friend.

"My son! He is my son," she said, putting her hand to her mouth, trying to control her tears.

"Yes, Erzsi, he is your son," Benjamin tried to console her.

Her heart filled with sorrow and regret, she turned away from her friends, lowered her face into her hands, and staggered out of the room.

Later, Adel found her asleep. Her pillow was wet from her tears, her prayer book clutched in her fist. "Your family needs to know what has happened," she spoke, knowing her friend could not hear her. "They love you, Erzsi, we all love you." Adel quietly left the room, she would write to Iren.

Long empty days turned into weeks, her pain worn on her face, the tormented mother moved quietly around the house, avoiding conversations, only smiling when she saw her son. Hours were spent rocking John, singing to him, watching his sweet face as he slept in her arms.

"What do I have to offer you, my precious? I love you more than my life but you cannot live on love. You need a father and a mother." She stroked her son's hair and he smiled up at her, not understanding. "If you stay in America you will go to school, learn a profession. Perhaps you will become a lawyer or a doctor. Maybe even President of the United States of America. I will be so very proud of you."

She was filled with guilt and shame. She had committed adultery, had lived with a married man, and had born him a child. Would God forgive her? Would John forgive her when he was old enough to understand? What could she do? How could she care for her son?

"My precious little boy, I have nothing to offer you," her voice was shaking, her eyes red from crying.

Adel entered the room. "There is a telegram for you." With trembling hands Erzsi reached for the paper.

Erzsi

Come home-stop-Our hearts share your pain-stop-will wire money

Love Iren and Clara

Book 5

They Dared To Dream

26 Love Lost, Love Found

Kosice, Hungary
September, 1890

Mihaly carefully picked up the infant, only hours old. In his eyes she was perfect. His wife lay exhausted, asleep, under the fresh blankets brought by the neighbor women.

The birth had been difficult. There had been some damage to the infant's leg; the doctor predicted the child would have a slight limp. It didn't matter. Mihaly knew he would love the child as much as he loved her mother.

He remembered when he had first seen her, the woman who was to become his wife. They were just children. He had been delivering a rosebush to her father, she was sitting on a horse, eyes sparkling, laughing at him. He had never seen a girl like her and was surprised, and a little embarrassed, by the unexpected stirrings in his body. That was so long ago and life had changed them both.

It had been six years since he had driven Iren and Clara to the train station. Their sister Erzsi was coming home from America. He knew that Iren and Clara were worried about her but he had not expected the depth of pain he saw on her pale face, her eyes red from crying. She was clinging to her sisters for support as though her legs could not, on their own, manage the task of walking. The magnitude of her sorrow had touched Mihaly's heart. He wanted to embrace her, to draw her close, to let her know he understood her sorrow. It was not his place; he was just a friend.

Mihaly had helped the sisters into the wagon. Iren barely noticed as Mihaly reached for her arm. Erzsi gave him a weak smile, for the moment the tears had stopped. Clara had touched Mihaly's sleeve, smiled and whispered, "Thank you."

Clara and her husband had been very kind to him. Since the death of his wife Veronica, he had become a frequent guest in their home. He would bring flowers for Clara, brandy or a cigar for Elmer, candy for the children. There was always interesting conversation; the men would talk politics, concerned about alliances being formed and the prospects of war. There were modern marvels to be discussed, particularly the automobiles powered by engines being made by the German, Karl Benz, and *The Flocken Elektrowagen*, the world's first electric car.

Clara, who preferred to talk about the latest fashions, would stand and position herself a few paces away from the table. With an authoritative expression on her face, everyone understood that she required respectful silence and attention.

"Gentlemen and children, there is a matter of great import that needs your consideration. Allow me to instruct you on the latest fashion for women," she would begin, pausing to look at each member of her audience. She would raise one eyebrow, attempting to look stern while suppressing a giggle.

"It is of utmost importance that you are aware of these developments." Everyone would look at her expectantly knowing there would be some drama to follow the stern expression.

Her gaze focused on her husband, a flirtatious gleam in her eye. "The skirt must fit snug and smooth over the hips," she spoke softly as her hands moved seductively from her waist to her thighs. Elmer smiled with appreciation. Clara's hips were no longer those of a young girl but full and in Elmer's opinion, perfect. Mihaly accustomed to Clara's coquettishness managed to maintain a serious and attentive expression.

"From there, the skirt should flare dramatically to a wide hem," slowly turning, her arms and hands moving down the phantom skirt in the shape of a tulip. Elmer smiled as he pictured the beautiful legs that appeared from under her full skirts when they were in the privacy of their bedroom.

"The bodice and collars must have contrasting fabric, lace, braids, puffs, frills, gathers, tucks, and," she paused for effect, "pleats." Her husband blushed as she seductively brought her hands across her ample breasts to illustrate where the puffs and frills should be placed.

"The hat should be tilted just like this," she said tilting her head and dramatizing the placement of the hat. The children giggled and clapped as they watched their mother assume the expression of a fashionable lady who knew she was being admired.

"Mauve," she informed her audience, "is the preferred color for the ensemble."

"Of course," Elmer responded, looking serious and attentive, although he had no idea what the color mauve looked like.

After the meal, Clara cleaned up the dishes, and Elmer settled down with the newspaper. Mihaly would sit with the children, telling them stories, stories that his mother had told to him, stories that he had hoped to share with his own children. With the little one asleep, her tiny head resting on his shoulder, and the others listening intently, he was able, for a little while, to forget his loneliness and sorrow.

When he was eighteen, Mihaly had left his village looking for work in the city of Kosice. Work was hard to find, the pay meager, he was often hungry. He shared a room with five other young men, most sleeping on mattresses on the floor, their meager possessions hung from hooks on the wall. At night he would think of home, his bed, his family, and most of all the smell of the bread baking in the oven and the cabbage soup cooking on the stove.

The room had one dingy window providing a view of a dirt courtyard. It was a Sunday afternoon when Mihaly stopped to look out the window. The view was not pleasant, only a dirt courtyard, surrounded by wooden tenements with rickety stairs leading to balconies that seemed to defy gravity.

A door from a neighboring tenement opened and a puppy, tail wagging, scampered into the courtyard, closely followed by a young girl, her hair wrapped in a towel. He watched with mild interest as she lifted the puppy, snuggling him to her face. Putting down the puppy the girl removed the towel from her head, allowing black shimmering waves of hair to cascade down her back, almost reaching her waist. Mihaly caught his breath, "Beautiful," he spoke out loud, surprising himself at the intensity of his reaction. She shook her head; her hair glistened in the afternoon sunshine. Still watching the puppy, calling to him, she tilted her head first to one side then to the other, the shimmering black tresses moving like waves under a strong wind. Mihaly watched, imagining droplets of water evaporating into the air. He felt his heart stop as she drew her hair across her chest and stroked it with her towel. He knew he should turn away, it was not proper that he should watch her like this but he was unable to move until she walked back into the tenement building and the door closed behind her.

"She is beautiful, it will be a lucky man who earns her love," he thought as he walked to the door to meet his friends.

In the days that followed he often found himself drawn to the window hoping he would see her again. In his dreams he could feel his hands lost in the silky softness of her hair as it draped loosely over milky white breasts. But when he looked out the window she was never there.

After work on Saturdays he liked to stroll through the market in the center of the city. Joining the swarming masses of people, his loneliness would be abated for a while. He would listen to the street musicians with their bagpipes and dulcimers, the calls of vendors, the laughter of children. Selecting an apple or a pear, he would eat while he walked remembering the fruit trees that were abundant in his village.

Sometimes women from his home village would be there with their chickens, flowers, or preserves and he would ask for news from home. Marta, a crippled old woman who sold sausages and sauerkraut, was a favorite; she had known his mother since she was a young girl. She would laugh with Mihaly, pat him on the cheek, share gossip from home, and tell stories of the old days when his father was courting his mother.

"And when are you going to find a wife?" she would ask. "A young man should not be without a wife," she said shaking her withered finger at him.

On this day, he was working his way through the crowd, looking to buy sausages from Marta, when he saw a girl with long waves of shimmering black hair flowing from under her scarf. She carried a basket on her arm, a loaf of bread extended from under the towel that protected her purchases. His heart stopped and for a moment he could not breathe. He was sure it was the girl he had seen in the courtyard.

She was about to disappear in the crowd. His legs began to move, he pushed past a woman blocking his path, tipped his hat in hasty apology, but kept moving in the direction the girl was going. He had one thought; he could not lose her, he must find out who she was.

There she was, standing in front of a flower cart holding a bundle of lavender flowers. As he stood there working on his courage to approach her, he watched her hesitate for a moment, her eyes drifting to a bucket overflowing with purple lilacs.

Somehow his legs carried him to the cart where he stood a polite distance from her.

"Lavender is my mother's favorite. She says it symbolizes serenity, grace, and calmness," his voice was soft, but authoritative.

She turned to the voice, startled at first by the forwardness of the man next to her.

"And what would your mother say about purple lilacs?" she said, recognizing the young man, boy really, who had moved into the tenement next to hers. Her friend Emma, who did not waste any time investigating newcomers to their street, pronounced him to be "very handsome, suitably employed, and eligible."

"Lilacs speak of first love," he blushed at his forwardness but quickly recovered. "I am Mihaly."

"I am Veronica. I believe we are neighbors."

They smiled at each other, it was an awkward moment, and neither knew what to say.

"It was nice meeting you, Mihaly." Veronica completed her purchase of purple lilacs, smiled at Mihaly, and disappeared in the crowd.

The vision of her, of Veronica, would not leave his thoughts. Her smile, her hair, the soft, sensual voice saying his name, he wanted and needed to see her again. Food was no longer important; he was quiet and distant when he was with his friends. They began to notice.

"Are you in love, Mihaly?" they teased. "Tell us, who is the girl?"

"No one," he had responded evasively. "Just a girl I met at the market."

"Does she have a name?" one friend enquired.

"Veronica."

"My mother considers herself a match maker," volunteered another. "She knows everyone."

"Could she help me?"

"Consider it arranged, my friend."

They were married six months later. The young couple found a one room apartment in a congested working class neighborhood. With care and attention to detail, Veronica set about the task of making a home for her family. Crocheted doilies made by her mother were placed on the table and draped over the back of the chairs while a richly embroidered cover, made by Mihaly's mother, adorned their bed. Sacred icons lovingly placed in a corner, curtains on the windows, and an old Grandfather clock turned the small living space into a comfortable home.

In time, the birth of a healthy baby girl, who announced her arrival with a hearty cry, added to their joy. They named her Matilda after Veronica's mother. When Mihaly's mother came to visit, the grandmothers nodded and congratulated each other, as they discussed Matilda's every accomplishment. The match maker, who had arranged the wedding, took credit for the birth of the new member of their community. Mihaly could not believe his happiness and good fortune. Providing for his small family and protecting them from harm became his greatest joy. But the love of a husband and a father could not protect them from the sickness that ravaged the city that summer.

In the sweltering heat of July, an epidemic swept through the crowded neighborhood. The cries of infants echoed through the dark hallways. Fear was unmistakable on the faces of fathers as they walked the streets, frantically searching for a doctor. Church bells rang daily, calling families to the burial service of yet another innocent child.

Veronica stayed in their hot, airless room, hoping she could protect her child from the devastating sickness. Mihaly, feeling helpless, hurried home each night, bringing fresh produce, medicinal herbs, and potions sold by vendors claiming they had health giving properties.

Despite the efforts of her parents the illness found its way into their home and Matilda, not even a year old, became ill with the fever.

Veronica, refusing to eat or sleep, had rocked the child in her arms through the night, hoping her love would somehow make the child well. Mihaly paced back and forth, watching, helpless, as the child grew weaker. The doctor was little help, the medicine he left did nothing to reduce the fever or ease Matilda's distress. When the long night finally ended, the child's cry grew softer and then stopped, she lay lifeless in her mother's arms.

Veronica never recovered from the loss of her baby. Her own sickness started with a cough. "It is nothing, Mihaly," she said trying to reassure her worried husband.

She ate little, her clothes, which had once flattered her figure, were loose and hung limp on her withering body. At night, she was drenched with cold sweat; the cloth she used when she coughed was streaked with blood. When she developed chest pain and had difficulty breathing the doctor suggested sending her to a sanatorium. She would not go. Leaving Mihaly and her home was not an option.

Women in the tenement in which they lived tried to help. They brought food, washed the soiled bedding, and straightened the apartment. Mihaly barely noticed. He went to work and hurried home to sit by her bedside, stroking her hand, reading to her, feeding her.

One morning she did not wake up. He was alone without a purpose. There was no future, only memories and pain.

It was Clara's and Elmer's kindness and friendship that had helped him to find peace. When Clara told him Erzsi was coming home, that she had been terribly hurt and was forced to give up her little boy, he had understood her suffering. He wanted to help but all he could do was offer to take them to the station in a wagon he borrowed from a friend.

Clara and Iren had put Erzsi into bed that night, bringing her tea laced with brandy. They sat next to her holding her hands while Erzsi slowly told them everything that had happened. She described the love she had felt for Josef, the depth of the pain caused by his betrayal. Her eyes brightened as she told them about her beautiful son. "He can walk now, and catch a ball," she said with pride. "His hair is soft, like an angel, his eyes the clearest blue." Finally she had fallen asleep in Clara's arms. They were together as they had been as children.

Slowly a routine was established. Erzsi busied herself helping Clara with her children and her home. When Mihaly joined them for dinner she entertained them with stories of her journey to America. She told them of the daring adventure she had shared with her friend Agnes as they evaded the night watchman and made their way to the upper decks. "They might have thrown us overboard if we were caught, you know," she said to the children, who were impressed by her daring.

When she was alone with Mihaly she was comforted by his strength and his compassion. He understood her loss, her pain. Clara watched with satisfaction as their friendship developed. This time Erzsi was not in a hurry, she needed time to heal her pain. But the night when Mihaly took her in his arms and said that he loved her, she felt like she had finally found the man she had been looking for. They were married in a quiet church ceremony with her sisters in attendance.

Now, six years later, Mihaly, humming softly while cradling the infant, walked to the window. The early morning mist had left droplets of water on the petals of the yellow roses in the garden. He had planted the rosebush in the courtyard behind their tenement on their wedding day. She had picked one perfect rose. "For me the roses represent continuity," she had said placing the rose next to the one in her prayer book. "The first one is a memory of childhood and my mother, this one is a memory of the day we were married."

Now, Erzsi slowly opened her eyes, her body ached, she was exhausted. A contented smile appeared as she watched her husband, standing by the window, humming slightly out of tune, rocking their daughter.

For a brief moment her thoughts drifted to another time, a man cradling another infant in his arms. She remembered the first time she held her son, the love she had felt as she looked into his beautiful blue eyes. As she always did, she buried the memory deep in her heart.

"Mihaly," she spoke softly, watching her husband. It was an effort to speak. "I love you."

27 John

Bridgeport, CT
June, 1902

Comfortable in the overstuffed chair, his face hidden behind the newspaper, John did not hear the door open.

"John, I am glad you are here," Aunt Terèz, proclaimed loudly, entering the house as if it were her own. "Is your father home?" She looked around the room knowing full well Josef would not be there. Josef would be at the tavern with his son Krisztian. It was a ritual that started when Krisztian had left school, choosing to work with his father at the foundry.

John, unlike his father and twin brother, had no interest in going to the tavern or working in the foundry. He had found work as a bookkeeper; his free time spent playing baseball, reading the sports page, or courting Margaret.

Terèz, a frequent visitor to the home of her sister Maria, knew when Josef would not be home. She had no wish to encounter Maria's husband. Years before John had heard them arguing. "Your other woman," his aunt's voice had trailed off. "None of your damn business." He heard his father bellow.

Later, in his innocence, John asked his father if he had another family. "You, your brothers, and your mother are my family," he said, walking out of the room, the conversation over.

On holidays, when Josef and Terèz could not avoid each other, the friction between them was obvious to everyone, even the children. "Why is Aunt Terèz so angry with Papa?" John had asked his mother. Maria's expression had abruptly changed; a frown furrowed her thick brows. "Hush," she had responded, an unusual harshness in her voice. "It is not your concern." She had turned away from him, the discussion over, as she resumed scrubbing the pan in the sink.

It seemed that adults had secrets not to be shared with children. But sometimes, when he was noticing how different he was from his brothers, he wondered if he was part of the secret.

Terèz, feeling confident that only John was home, closed the front door. With a disapproving look her eyes scanned the airless parlor, the ash trays filled with remnants of cigars, newspapers scattered around the room, and tables that had not seen a feather duster in weeks.

John stood, putting his newspaper aside. "Aunt Terèz, come in! What an unexpected surprise."

"John, I have a small favor to ask," she said while kissing his cheek.

"Anything, come in, sit down. No one else is home. Can I get you some tea?"

"No, no. I will just sit for a few minutes, then I must leave." She settled her very round figure into an overstuffed chair, carefully arranging her skirts. John watched her brown, boat-shaped hat hover on top of hair that was piled impossibly high. "A marvel of modern engineering," he thought, smiling.

With his aunt, comfortably settled, John took a seat next to her. With effort, he moved his gaze from her hat to her eyes. He did not want to be disrespectful.

"I miss your mother terribly," she said, her eyes filling with tears, a lace bordered handkerchief clutched in her hand. Maria's heart attack, unexpected and unthinkable, had been devastating for everyone, especially her sister.

"We all miss her. Papa is particularly saddened by the loss." John reached for her hand in a comforting gesture. He was not surprised when Terèz ignored his comment.

"Your mother had a locket. It contained pictures of our parents," she paused for a moment, dabbing at tears. "I would very much like to have that locket."

"Of course, Aunt Terèz, do you have any idea where she might have kept it?" Rummaging through his mother's belongings was not a task he relished.

"She once showed me a cigar box where she kept pictures and letters from home. If you could find the box, the locket might be in there."

"I'll look for it. I am sure Mama would have wanted you to have it."

"No need to mention this to your father. I am sure he is not interested in an old locket."

"Of course."

"That's my good boy. Now I must leave, your uncle will fuss if dinner is not ready when he gets home."

John moved quickly to her chair, offering his arm. She held him close as he escorted her to the door. "You must remember to give my love to your brothers," she said, as usual not including Josef.

"Of course, Aunt Terèz."

Kissing her on the cheek he opened the door and watched her walk down the sidewalk to the street. With her thick brown hair and determined stride he was reminded of his mother. He remembered the locket, his mother always wore it. It was too precious to be hidden in a drawer; Terèz should have it. "Now, with no one home, it is a good time to look for it," he thought.

He had not entered his parents' bedroom since his mother had died. His father slept there, dressed there, and nothing more. The door was always closed, maybe it was locked.

Reaching the door of the bedroom, John hesitated. Would his father be angry? It didn't matter, he turned the knob and with an almost ghostlike creak the door opened.

There was a brown cast iron bed, with a dingy pillow and blanket crumpled in the center. John pictured his mother in that bed. When he was little she had been a haven of safety, her arms welcoming him when he was frightened by a storm. He missed her. The white chenille bedspread, a gift from

Terèz that should be covering the bed, was thrown unwanted in a corner.

John walked to the small square table next to the bed. It was covered with a white lace doily, a wedding gift from a friend in Hungary. An oil lamp with red roses painted on the base and a family photograph were still where his mother had left them.

Picking up the photograph, his fingers caressed the image of his mother. Julius, his younger brother, just a baby was on her lap, tiny shoes peaking from under his long white gown. Krisztian, with his playful smile, stood on one side of her, John, looking self-conscious, on the other. Josef, one hand in his pocket the other holding his watch, stood proudly behind his family. "I look like a girl with all those blond curls," John thought, frowning. "Where did they come from?" His parents and his brothers had thick brown, wavy hair. As always he pushed away the confusing questions, shutting down the little alarms that there was something different about him. Whispers among the adults, followed by furtive glances his way, had often made him uncomfortable. "Your other woman." The words would come back unbidden, unwanted, but there were no answers to his questions.

He returned the picture to its delegated place on the table and moved to the bureau. A hairbrush and comb, placed in front of the mirror, awaited their owner. John felt Maria's presence close to him. "Mama, do you want me to find the box?"

His mother's drawer was a forbidden place. "Give me permission, Mama." His hands gripped the knob and with a firm tug the drawer creaked open. Maria's drawer, the handkerchiefs carefully washed and folded, the broken rosary beads, the small black missal that she carried to Sunday Mass were all arranged as she had left them.

Moving aside a carefully folded infant's baptismal gown he saw the cigar box with the familiar white owl on the lid. He hesitated briefly as his hands touched the box. "Mother, I am doing this for Terèz," he whispered the words as he lifted the box out of the drawer, placed it on the bureau, and opened it. The locket was there. "Good, Aunt Terèz will be pleased," he thought, casually placing it in his pocket. Beneath the locket were photographs, probably sent from relatives in Hungary, tied together with a white ribbon. Mildly interested, he pulled at the ribbon with the intent of quickly viewing the pictures. Perhaps he would see a family resemblance, someone else with blond curls.

Two soldiers, standing proudly, rifles at their side, looked out at him. "My uncles," he guessed. His mother had spoken proudly and lovingly about her brothers. "Daneil was killed in a heroic battle defending the Empire," she had told him. "Kolos had married the beautiful Alana when he was stationed in Bratislava."

A few other pictures, perhaps friends or relatives of his mother, were quickly glanced over. The last picture was of a woman holding a little boy. It looked like his mother, her smile, her hair. Puzzled he turned it over and read "Krisztian, SzletettFebruár 5, 1883." With his limited knowledge of Hungarian he translated, "Krisztian, born Február 5, 1883." The markings on the back were in Hungarian. The photographer's address, Kosice, Hungary.

A tightness gripped John's stomach, a restless, unsettled thought that was not new, struggled to be recognized. The picture had been taken in Hungary. Why was his mother in Hungary with Krisztian? There were questions, mysteries, secrets that had been hidden and he was somehow part of it. Did his mother take them to Hungary when they were little? Why is she only holding Krisztian? "Your other woman," the words echoed, haunting him. He searched the box, removed a pile of letters, hoping another picture would be there, a picture of his mother holding a little boy with blond curls. Nothing.

In bed that night he could not sleep. Krisztian, who shared the bed with him, had begged him to be still. "Go to sleep! A man needs his sleep." John tried to lie motionless in the bed but his mind would not stop. "Your other woman," the words echoed in his ears. Who was his father's other woman? Questions, distant memories, that unspecific feeling that he was somehow different.

"Aunt Terèz knows the answers. I will go to see her." Finally sleep, dreams of a woman holding him, singing to him. Sadness, an unbearable sadness, surrounded them.

When he awoke, his father and brother had already left for work. Even though it was Saturday they would work half day at the foundry. The office where John worked was closed. He would go to see his Aunt Terèz. He needed answers.

John walked up the familiar dirt road that led to the home of his mother's sister. The picture of his mother holding Krisztian was tightly clutched in his hand. Terèz was sitting in the rocking chair on the porch gently stroking a white cat that was nestled in her lap.

"It is so early," he thought. "She must have known I would come." Again he felt the tightness in his stomach. He had questions, but did he want the answers? When he reached the porch stairs, he stopped, his eyes reflecting his inner torment.

"Good morning, John," her voice was soft, her expression compassionate. "I have been expecting you."

"Good morning, Aunt Terèz," he said kissing her cheek. "I found the locket."

With a smile she took the locket from his outstretched hand. He watched her as she opened the locket. There was a faint smile, a look of longing, as she gently touched the images of her parents. "Thank you, John. Won't you sit with me for a while? You look troubled."

John could not sit. Leaning against the railing for support, working to control his voice, he held out the picture. "I have questions."

"Yes, I thought you would," she watched him with concern. "Please sit down."

"Aunt Terèz, did my father have another wife? A child?" his voice faltered. "When I was little I heard you arguing with him."

"Your father did have another child but the woman was not his wife."

John's grip on the railing tightened. "Aunt Terèz, please. Am I that child? I need to know!"

She was quiet for a moment, studying his face, searching for the right words. "Will I make things worse by telling him the truth?" She had struggled with this question but did not have an answer. "He deserves to know, no matter what the consequences."

"When I asked you for the locket I knew you would find the picture. I knew you would have questions. I needed to be sure you wanted answers." Again she paused watching for his reaction. "I have a letter for you. It is from a woman who loved you very much." Reaching into her apron pocket she retrieved a letter. "Maria gave this to me to keep it safe, away from your father."

With a frown John reached for the letter. It was fragile, slightly aged with time. The envelope was addressed to Janos Farkas care of Maria Farkas, the postage date, October 30, 1890.

"I was seven years old."

"Yes, when it arrived we felt you were too young to understand. Your mother gave it to me to hold until the time was right."

Terèz rocked slowly while John studied the envelope. His expression was thoughtful, wary; this letter would change his life. She knew she could not help him as he struggled to control the confusing emotions he was experiencing.

They sat there in silence, both understanding the import of the letter. Finally, John put the letter in his pocket. "I will read it when I am alone."

With concern, Terèz watched her nephew. "John, remember that we all love you."

"Thank you, Aunt Terèz. I love you too." He kissed her cheek and turned to leave. She watched him slowly walking down the sidewalk, his shoulders slightly bent, hands in his pockets.

"Maria, I hope I have done the right thing." With a heavy heart she continued to rock in her chair, quietly saying a prayer for her family.

He walked along Black Rock Harbor, not hearing the waves crashing on the rocks, or feeling the sea breeze in his face. Eventually, he sat on a bench, looking across the expanse of Long Island Sound the grey shadow of Long Island barely visible. When they were small Maria had brought them here for picnics. She had watched her sons play on the rocks and chase the gulls. When they bruised their knees she would nurse their wounds and offer comfort cradling them in her arms.

Now he was trying to remember another woman. He was trying to remember the woman who wrote the letter he was holding. "Why can't I remember you?" Slowly he opened the letter.

"My dearest Janos, my precious little boy," the letter began.

"Janos," he could almost hear her voice calling to him. She was laughing, playing with him. "Am I remembering, or just imagining?"

He looked back at the letter, the words were written in a neat, flowing handwriting that seemed to drift along the page. The words were of love, of longing, filled with the hope that he would understand. Despite the broken English, and occasional Hungarian word or phrase, the meaning and intent was clear. It told of her love for him. How, with his father, she had envisioned a life for him in America. Her heart had been broken when she needed to leave him but she knew she had nothing to offer him. He deserved the life in America that only his father could provide.

"Time has passed, my dear Janos," the letter continued. "I have married a good man. His name is Mihaly Vasko. You have a sister, Gisela. She was born just a few months ago. When I hold her in my arms I can close my eyes and remember holding you. When I sing to her I remember how you loved to hear me sing. Do you remember the song about the big crested rooster?"

John put down the letter and closed his eyes. He could imagine he heard her voice, playful, happy, a young mother singing to her son.

Good morning, Paul, Kate, Peter,
The Sun already rose outside.

Our big crested rooster says:
"Come out to the meadow,
Cock-a-doodle-doo!"

He read the letter again. "Janos, you are always in my heart. You will forever be my precious little boy."

Putting the letter in his pocket he started to walk. His mother, Erzsi, had left him. He tried to picture her. "Is this where my blond hair comes from? Do I look like her?" Walking along the sidewalk, his body moved down familiar streets past homes of friends he had known since he was a child. He didn't notice them. He was trying to process what he read in the letter.

His steps led him to Margaret, his sweetheart since high school, the one person he could talk to. He needed to see her, to tell her his story, to hear her voice.

Her mother opened the door, surprised to see him. "John, come in. How nice to see you."

He took off his hat as he entered the house. "I am very sorry to intrude. If it isn't too much trouble I would very much like to talk with Margaret."

"Margaret is upstairs, I will get her. Please sit down," she said pointing to a chair in the parlor.

He stood when Margaret entered the room; his right hand held his hat, his left was in his pocket.

"John, what is it? Mama said you looked pale. She was concerned."

"I went to see my Aunt Terèz this morning, she gave me a letter." There was sadness in John's eyes as he pulled the now crumpled letter from his pocket.

"Who is it from? It seems to have upset you."

"My mother."

"Your mother?" Margaret was puzzled. Why would a letter from his mother cause the pain she saw in his face? "Come outside. We can sit together on the swing; no one will bother us there."

They sat close together on the front porch swing; John, quiet, looking down at the letter, Margaret waiting patiently.

"Margaret, I don't know where to begin. I don't know what to do."

"John, you know I love you. Let me help," her voice was warm and gentle, her eyes filled with love. "What was in the letter? What could be so terrible?"

His voice wavered as he handed her the letter. "Something I have always suspected. Something I think I always knew."

Margaret slowly read the letter, trying to imagine the woman who wrote it. How could she leave her child? What mother would abandon her little boy? The thought was beyond anything she could imagine. She read the letter again.

She tried to picture Erzsi, a mother and her child; tenderness and love pervaded the words on the page. The letter spoke of regret, of longing, a pain that would not heal. But it also spoke of hope. There was the hope that her son would find a better life in America.

"John, there is only one thing to do. You must go to her, find her and talk with her."

They sat there for a long time, talking about the letter. They tried to form an image of a woman with blond hair holding her little boy. The happiness she must have known playing with him, caring for him, loving him. And then the difficult, painful choice she made.

"You need to go to her and tell her that you have the life she wanted for you."

He looked at Margaret thinking how wise she was, how much he loved her. "Perhaps in time Erzsi might be willing to come back to America. She will know her grandchildren." He looked at Margaret with a mischievous smile.

"She will have beautiful grandchildren," Margaret countered, giving John a gentle, lingering kiss.

28 The Fulfillment of a Dream

Crossing the Atlantic
May, 1913

Gizela was standing at the railing of the steamship. The dark waves of the Atlantic Ocean beckoned her forward to America; she was leaving the old world with its wars and poverty behind. Europe was in turmoil, endless alliances being formed, men from her village conscripted into the Austrian army in greater numbers than ever before. She was seventeen years old, her future before her. It was time to follow her mother's example and search for a new beginning.

Gizela, like her mother Erszi, was making this journey alone. But the America that would welcome her was different. Her brother John and his wife Margaret would be there to help her. Gizela had family waiting for her.

John, the little boy Erszi had left in America, was now a grown man. He had come to find his mother. There had been tears of regret but also joyous celebration as mother and son were reunited. Erszi told her son of her love for Josef, John's father, the pain of the betrayal, the hopelessness of her situation. Her face in her hands, her shoulders shaking with sobs, she relived the agony of leaving him all those years ago. John had taken his mother in his arms, holding her close the way she had done for him when he was little.

"It is all right, Mother," he had whispered, his lips feeling the moisture on her cheeks. "We have found each other again."

He told her of his life in America, his experiences in school, his job as a bookkeeper, and about Margaret, the love of his life. Erzsi was pleased as she listened to her son, her tears slowly vanished and a smile of pride formed on her lips. "My son, my precious little boy, I do love you." She put her hands on his shoulders, feeling the strength of the man he had become. She stroked his clothes and admired the quality of the fabric, the perfect knot on his tie. He had become everything she had hoped for.

"Have you had a good life, Mother?" he asked, moving slightly away from her so he could look into her eyes. She told him of the years spent mourning her loss, missing him. "But then I met Mihaly," she said, remembering the man who had brought joy back into her life. He had died a few years earlier. "We were friends, John, lovers, companions, as well as husband and wife. Mihaly understood my loss as I had understood his. We comforted each other in the beginning. We would sit together in the park on Sunday afternoons, just holding hands, silent in our grief. When the pain finally ebbed we built a life filled with love. We were always honest with each other, happiest when we were together. There was trust, John, trust and love and compassion."

"Come to America with me, Mother. I will take care of you and Gisela." She had refused. "My life is here, John, with my family and my memories. Do you see the yellow rosebush in the garden?" The rosebush had grown tall and its branches scraped against the window. "Mihaly planted it for me when we were married. It is a reminder of our love." Erzsi told him the story of the yellow rosebush Mihaly had delivered to her home when they were children. "It was a symbol of my father's love for my mother. I keep pressed roses in my prayer book, a reminder of my parents and my husband. But seeing the rosebush Mihaly planted for me gives me the greatest comfort."

Now, years later, Gisela carried the prayer book deep in her pocket as her mother had done so many years before. She thought of the yellow roses pressed within its pages a reminder of her mother's love.

Epilogue

Bridgeport, Connecticut
August, 1965

"Tell me again, why is this our job?" Elizabeth, annoyed with the task before her, brushed a misbehaving strand of hair away from her face. She was sitting on a wobbly wooden chair, looking at a jumble of old clothes, outdated hats, and worn shoes. "Surely we could just pay someone to take everything."

Dorothy, her shoes cast carelessly aside, was no more pleased to be here than her sister. Their mother, Edith, had called them from her retirement home in Florida where she and their grandmother Margaret lived. Their great aunt Gisela whom they had met only a few times when they were very young had passed away. The landlord was in a hurry to have her apartment vacated. There was no one else. Gisela had never married, never had children of her own.

"We just need to sort everything, throw out what cannot be used, and donate the rest. I'll call tomorrow." Dorothy added a bundle of yellowed newspapers to the pile of items growing near the door. They were all in Hungarian, of no use to anyone.

A cheaply made trunk sat in the corner of the room, its musty odor attesting to its age. "Lizzie, do you think Gisela brought this trunk from Hungary?" Lizzie just shrugged. The sisters knew nothing of the story, never thought to ask. Opening the trunk,

Dorothy removed the clothes, letters written in Hungarian, a scarf, and an old hat wrapped in tissue paper.

All that was left was a black cloth-bound book lying forlornly in a corner of the trunk. Something about the book made Dorothy hesitate. It must have been in the trunk for a very long time, buried, and forgotten. The broken binding no longer held the cover in place, only a few worn threads kept the yellowed pages together. She lifted it carefully from the trunk. It fit perfectly in her hands.

The book was small, her thumbs met in the center of the cover, her fingers gently touched in the back. The deep black color of the frayed fabric focused her vision on the ghostlike image of a cross imbedded in a corner. The book felt solid, conveying a feeling of strength, but was not heavy. The perfect symmetry of the book brought a feeling of peace and comfort.

Carefully Dorothy turned the fragile pages. The words, Imprimatur, Coloczae die 17. Oct. 1876, gave a clue to its age. The prayers were in Hungarian. A small card, the image of a saint kneeling before an angel, left no doubt as to the purpose of the book.

"I wonder if this book belonged to Gizela or maybe to her mother, our great grandmother. Lizzie, do you know her name?" Elizabeth, absorbed in her own work, shook her head no. "I think it was Essie or Erzsi or something like that."

Dorothy continued to turn the pages of the little prayer book. In the center of the book two yellow roses, dried and crumbling, were pressed between its pages. As Dorothy lifted them they crumbled into dust, revealing a picture of a young woman holding a little boy.

"Lizzie, look at this. Do you think this is our grandfather with his mother? Her hair looks just like yours."

A young woman with light colored hair and a straw hat posed for the picture, a small child in her lap. On the back of the photograph, in neat, almost childish script was the notation:

John Farkas, an American citizen, son of Erzsi and Josef Farkas, born May 5, 1883

Author's Notes: "The Other Woman"

My grandfather was born in Kingston, New York, in 1884. His father's name was Josef. My mother said she met her grandfather when she was very little. "He had a large tobacco-stained beard," she told us. Her description reminded me of pictures I had seen of men in the late 1800's with long unkempt beards and dark clothing. That was all my mother remembered about him except that her mother, my grandmother, would not speak to Josef. As a child and young adult I didn't pay much attention to this. If my grandmother was angry with her husband's father it was because of something that happened over one hundred years ago. It had nothing to do with me.

There were no stories about my grandfather's mother, my great grandmother, no one mentioned her name. Her existence, her loves, her dreams all faded into the distant past.

When I retired I had the interest and the time to reflect on the past. What was the name of my great grandmother, the woman no one mentioned? I could almost feel her presence asking to be remembered.

The search started with the 1910 census. There was my great grandfather's name, the names of his wife Maria and their youngest children. Josef came from Hungary in 1882 was employed in a foundry, and he owned a boarding house, all this was vaguely interesting. Then I read the information given by his wife Maria.

According to the census Maria came to America in 1889, five years after my grandfather was born. Maria could not have been my grandfather's mother. Further, the census stated that Josef and Maria had been married for twenty-eight years. Josef was married to Maria before he came to America but she did not come with him. I later learned this was not uncommon. Many men from Eastern Europe came to America to work with the expectation they would return to their families in one year. Josef was in America for seven years before his wife joined him.

The evidence was clear. Josef had a son, my grandfather, born in America, with a woman who was not his wife. Suddenly the quest for my great grandmother became very interesting. Who was this other woman in Josef's life? There was a mystery here, a long kept secret. I wanted to know who this woman was. What was her name? What happened to her? She was my great grandmother and her life, her existence was a secret no one wished to talk about.

The mystery deepened when an obituary for my mother's uncle revealed my grandfather had a half-sister, Gizela. I knew the names of my grandfather's siblings and Gizela was not one of them. How then was Gizela related to my grandfather?

I asked my mother about Gizela. "Yes," my mother said, "my Aunt Gizela. My father, would take me to visit her on Sundays." But she offered no more information. I asked my mother's sister about Gizela and my aunt said, "I made a promise not to talk about it and I will keep that promise," Even after one hundred years had passed the circumstances of my grandfather's birth were to remain a family secret hidden in the shadows of time.

Josef had seven children that I knew of and he took care of all of them. Yet Gizela never lived with him. Why? My mother never mentioned her when she listed Josef's children. Eventually I realized Gizela and my grandfather had the same mother. Using records from a funeral home I learned my great grandmother's name was Elizabeth, Erzsi in Hungarian.

Evidence suggests that Erzsi returned to Hungary leaving her son with his father, Josef. There is no record of why she left. She eventually married and had a daughter, Gizela. Erzsi returned to America in 1913 with Gizela. She lived in Bridgeport, Connecticut, not far from her son. There is no evidence that she reunited with Josef even though his wife Maria had died some years earlier.

This novel is my attempt to understand the events in the lives of my great grandparents, Erzsi and Josef. I do not know what was in their hearts or what circumstances led to the family secret. I know that my grandfather did reunite with his mother. My mother said her father would take her to visit Gizela. There was a piano in my grandfather's house given to him by his half-sister. Perhaps it had belonged to Erzsi. I found a photograph in my grandfather's belongings of an elderly woman. On the back it says "Mother, 1920." Was this Erzsi, my great grandmother, my great grandfather's "other woman?"

Cast of Characters

Reiste, Hungary
Erzsi's family
Iren- Erzsi's older sister
Erzsi
Clara- Erzsi's younger sister
Viktor- Iren's husband
Bianka- Erzsi's childhood friend

Ujak, Hungary
Robert's family
Robert- Erzsi's first love
Dominik- Robert's abusive father

Kosice, Hungary 1882
Clara's family
Elmer- Clara's husband
Her children
Stefan
Matilda
The baby

Buzica, Hungary
Maria's family
Maria- Josef's wife
Krisztian- Maria's son
Josef- Maria's husband
Anna – Maria's mother

Anton- Maria's brother. Anton takes care of the family
when their father dies.
Terèz- Maria's younger sister
Daneil- Maria's brother who died in the Balkans
Kolos- Maria's brother closest to her in age, a private
in the Royal Hungarian Army the Honved
Alana- The wife of Kolos
Jakob-Maria's youngest brother who was studying at
the seminary in SpišskáKapitula

Budapest, Hungary
Peter's family
Peter- Erzsi's cousin
Yolanda- Peter's wife
Their daughters
Bernadette
Jolàn
Dora

The *Closinda*
FrauMueller-amatronwhosupervisesunaccompanied
women
Ludwig- a steward
Agnes- a friend on the ship
Rosa- Passenger
Franceska- Passenger
Ilona- a young girl befriended by Agnes and Erzsi
Rudi- Ilona's lost love

Rondout, New York
Ethel Timko- Owner of the boarding house

Adel Toth- Ethel's s sister
Boarders
Jimmy Chase
Benjamin Sykes
Mr. Braun
Mr. Kulak
Mr. Bartos

East Kingston, New York
Sarah Drinkle- Erzsi's friend
Tim Drinkle- Sarah's husband
Willi- The son of Sarah and Tim Drinkle

Josef's family in Hungary
Imre- Josef's oldest brother
Markos- Josef's brother closest to him in age and his best friend
Jenci- Josef's gentle quiet brother who prefers to read and study

Kosice, Hungary 1890
Mihaly- marries Veronica. When she dies he marries Erszi
Veronica- Mihaly's first wife
Gizela- The daughter of Mihaly and Erszi

Bridgeport, CT 1902
John- Josef's and Erzsi's son
Margaret- John's high school sweetheart, later his wife
Krisztian and Julius- Josef's and Maria's sons
Aunt Terèz- Maria's younger sister

Bridgeport, CT 1965

Edith- The daughter of John and Margaret
Dorothy- Edith's daughter
Elizabeth- Edith's daughter

Appendix

Babushka
As used in this story the term refers to a triangularly folded head scarf often worn by Eastern European women.

Buda and Pest
In 1873 the cities of Buda and Pest along with Óbuda were united into the city of Budapest.

Buzica and Reste
Small villages in the Kosice region of Eastern Slovakia. At the time of the story they were part of Hungary.

Castle Garden
Over eight-million immigrants passed through Castle Garden between 1855 and 1890. Currently named Castle Clinton it is located in Battery Park, in Manhattan, New York City.

Chain Bridge
The chain bridge spans the River Danube connecting Buda and Pest. It was opened in 1849 and was the first permanent bridge in the Hungarian capital.

Czárdás
A traditional Hungarian folk dance characterized by a variation in tempo: it starts out slowly and ends in a very fast tempo.

Emigrant
A person who leaves their own country to settle permanently in another country.

Erzsi
Elizabeth in English.

Erzsinéne
Néne is the Hungarian word for aunt. Aunt Erzsinéne.
Frau
A German married woman.
German Mark
German currency from 1873-1948. It was known as the Goldmark.
Hamburg-Amerika Linie (Hamburg America Line)
A transatlantic shipping line established in 1847. The Hamburg-Amerika Linie was one of the major steamship companies to handle the immigrant trade.
Honved
The Royal Hungarian Honved was one of four armed forces of Austria Hungary from 1867-1918.
Humenne
A town in the Presov region of Slovakia.
Imprimatur
An official license by the Roman Catholic Church to print a religious book.
Kolash
A sweet pastry filled with jam, fruit, or cheese.
Kosice
The biggest city in Eastern Slovakia. At the time of the story it was a part of Hungary.
Magyar
Hungarians, also known as Magyars, are a nation and ethnic group who speak Hungarian.
Pista
Pronounced Peesh-ta it is a nickname for Stefan.

Port of Hamburg
In 1882, 1,606 Hungarian emigrants passed through the Port of Hamburg in Germany.
Pressburg
Modern day Bratislava the capital of Slovakia.
Puszta
A grassland biome on the Great Hungarian Plain in eastern Hungary.

Acknowledgements

I would like to thank my friend Neva Weisskopf for her limitless patience and encouragement. This book would not have been possible without her. A special thank you to my sisters Stephanie Grossman, Gloria Freel, and Dr. Diane Dusick for sharing their talents, suggestions, and boundless love.

In addition I would like to thank my readers and friends especially Janice Milne, Mary Strine, Shirley Hendrick, Mary Milliken and so many others.

Cover design by Neva Weisskopf

About the author

Virginia Rafferty earned a Bachelor of Arts Degree from Merrimack College and a Master's Degree from Antioch New England Graduate School. She was a middle school science teacher for thirty-two years and has a daughter, son-in-law, and two granddaughters.

She began her quest for her ancestors in 2008 when she retired. Using family stories, census records, and obituaries, she soon learned that there was a long hidden family secret.

Her novel, *Family Secrets... Hidden in the Shadows of Time,* is an attempt to understand the events in 1882 that led to a family scandal and was hidden in the shadows of time for over one hundred years.

Made in the USA
Charleston, SC
05 February 2016